ROUTES OF ALEXANDER

ALEXANDER THE GREAT

Nikos Kazantzakis

ALEXANDER

THE GREAT

A Novel

translated by Theodora Vasils
illustrated by Virgil Burnett

Ohio University Press
Athens, Ohio
London
Riverside Community College
Library
4800 Magnolia Avenue
Riverside, CA 92506

Library of Congress Cataloging in Publication Data

Kazantzakis, Nikos, 1883–1957
    Alexander the Great.

    1. Alexander, the Great, 353–323 B.C.—Fiction.
I. Title.
PA5610.K39M413   889'.332   81-11307
ISBN 0-8214-0654-X   AACR2
ISBN 0-8214-0663-9 pbk.

English translation copyright © 1982 by Theodora Vasils
Greek language edition copyright © 1978 by Helen N. Kazantzakis

Printed in the United States of America.
All rights reserved.

This translation is dedicated to my father, Peter Vasils, at whose knee I first discovered the ancient world of Greek heroes.

TRANSLATOR'S PREFACE

Alexander the Great has stirred the imagination of posterity as few heroes have. In this historical novel based on his life, Nikos Kazantzakis recreates the historical reality of one of the most brilliant periods the world has ever known. Written for the young reader, it is intended for the adult mind as well, and like the legends of old, is entertaining as well as instructive for readers of all ages.

Kazantzakis, sometimes referred to as the Homer of modern Greece, is no stranger to heroes of Greek antiquity. His stories are filled with modern characters grafted on the heroes of the ancient world. Zorba, the most popular of his creations, was fashioned in the image of the crafty Odysseus, and his own *Odyssey—A Modern Sequel* picks up where ancient Homer left off and continues the adventures of this resurrected hero into the twentieth century.

In his portrayal of Alexander the Great, Kazantzakis has drawn on the rich tradition of Greek legend to present us with an Alexander in the image of the two ancestral heroes with whom his name has been most commonly linked. There have been many myths surrounding the origin of Alexander. From his mother, Olympias, who was the daughter of Neoptolemus I, he inherited his lineage to Achilles. From his father, King Philip II of Macedonia, he claimed an ancestry that descended from the legendary Heracles himself.

As if this were not enough, Olympias his mother, was said to have confided to Alexander that he was the son of the god Zeus

Ammon, who had visited her in her sleep one night and begot Alexander. Add to this the myriad titles he amassed in his short lifetime—Pharoah of Egypt, Lord of Asia, King of Macedonia, Suzerain of Indian rajahs, god of Greece and Egypt—and we can see how Alexander might well have viewed himself as part god, as others viewed him, destined to carry out a divine mission.

In physical appearance the handsome fair-haired prince is believed to have borne a strong resemblance to the Achilles he was purported to descend from, giving rise to the myth that the Homeric hero had returned to Greece again, in the reincarnated image of Alexander. We can imagine the challenge such illustrious ancestors presented to the young Alexander to equal, if not surpass, their glorious exploits. He bemoaned, it is said, the lack of a Homer in his lifetime to hymn his own labors for posterity. In balance, his name has dominated posterity as few others have.

Anecdotes about him abound, and while no doubt none of the stories that have survived the centuries occurred exactly as they have been retold, they nonetheless contain a grain of truth. "Truth," the philosopher Callisthenes tells us in this novel, "is to believe in what you see; Myth is to believe in what you do not see; and History is the daughter of Truth and Myth."

In the ancient world there was no sharp distinction between myth and history. Even in our modern age of scientific exactitude, the most discriminating historian finds it impossible to draw a precise line between myth and history and is compelled to blend the two.

Despite the mystery and romance that surround and cloud much of Alexander's personality, certain historical realities are clear. At the time of his birth in 356 B.C., Greece was in her decline. The Greek states were all but destroying one another with their petty rivalries and fierce insistence on independence. Macedonia, under his father's rule, was in her ascendancy, and as the strongest among them, became the protectorate of Greece, eventually succeeding in unifying most of the fragmented Greek states into one nation.

Although from backwoods mountaineer stock himself, King Philip cultivated the friendship of cultured men. His court in Pella was open to visitors from all over Greece and parts of the East, and young Alexander grew up in an atmosphere of intellectual and political vigor. With these beginnings, his own natural aptitudes—a keen mind, a burning curiosity about the world, an appreciation of the artistic—had ample stimulus for growth.

In the heated discussions that were part of the royal household gatherings in Pella, the Persian threat of conquest that constantly hung over Greece was the dominant topic of conversation, and Alexander was introduced at an early age to the ideological and political conflict that existed between East and West. Indeed, that conflict still exists between the modern Persians of Iran and the West.

When Alexander was thirteen years old, his father summoned the great Greek philosopher Aristotle to undertake his education. Aristotle, it was said, found him an astute pupil, a youth with an adult and grasping mind far beyond his age. Years later, when Alexander had become king himself, he was reported to have commented that while Philip was the man who gave him life, Aristotle was the man who taught him how to live.

Both Alexander and his father Philip shared a fierce pride in their native Macedonia, but it was Athens that commanded their admiration as the symbol of the Greek nation. Though in her decline, Athens continued to reflect the brilliance of a century earlier when, under the reign of Pericles, she had reached a summit of civilization never before achieved by the human race.

The history of Alexander, and indeed of Western man, is inseparable from the Hellenic world that he inherited. It was this world, this culture, that Alexander wanted to spread to the non-Greek races of the globe. Like his father, who envisioned unifying the fragmented Greek states into one nation, Alexander envisioned unifying the nations of man into one world, governed by the Hellenic ideal. What he succeeded in doing, and what the succeeding ages owe to his brief life, is astounding. In the short span of a dozen years he carved out the direction that an entire world was to follow for the next two thousand years. Had he not carried the Hellenic ideal, which forms the basis of our Western civilization, into the vast regions beyond Greece, Hellenism would most likely in time have died and history would have taken a different course.

In his depiction of Alexander in his novel, Nikos Kazantzakis has drawn on both the vast storehouse of myth, and the documented manuscripts from the archives of history to recreate an Alexander in all his many-faceted images—Alexander the god; Alexander the descendent of Heracles performing his own twelve labors: Alexander the mystic, the daring visionary destined to carry out a divine mission; Alexander the flesh-and-blood mortal who, on occasion, was not above the common soldier's brawling and drinking.

The novel, which resists the temptation to portray Alexander in the mantle of purely romantic legend, was written primarily as an educational adjunct for young readers and was originally published in Greece in serial form in early 1940. It was republished in a complete volume in 1979, coinciding with the recent discovery in northern Greece of the intact royal Macedonian tomb at Vergina, believed to be that of Alexander's father King Philip II. In all likelihood, were Kazantzakis alive, he would have edited the second printing and condensed the serialized novel to adapt it to its new book format. The translated work in this volume is unabridged, and remains faithful to the original text.

Oak Park, Illinois
February 1981

I

"Stephan! Stephan!"

Little Alka was standing at her threshold poking her sprightly head through the half-opened door. Her curly black hair was tied back with a bit of red ribbon and her enormous eyes brimmed with precocious spirits.

She was calling Stephan, a boy in the doorway across the alley. Stephan was dressed in his best clothes today, a blue chiton with a silver buckle that held up the robe at the right shoulder. He had black curly hair like hers and was tall and slender, with skin bronzed by the sun. At the moment he was bending over his right foot which he had steadied against a rock and was fastening his sandal. You could see from the boy's strong arms and sturdy legs that he had exercised his body well and was at the top of his class in wrestling and running.

"Stephan! Stephan! Can't you hear me?" the girl was calling with impatience.

Stephan turned. At sight of her, his face brightened. "Good morning, Alka!" he shouted. "How are you?"

"Where are you going? Why are you dressed in your good clothes today?"

"It's a holiday," Stephan called back, finishing with his sandal and brushing back the long hair that had tumbled over his handsome, sunburned face.

"What holiday? My father went out early this morning with old General Antipatros and your father came, too, with his box of medicines. Where are they going? Off to war again?"

Stephan laughed. "How curious you are," he said. "You want to know everything."

"Of course I want to know everything!" bristled Alka. "Do you think because I'm a girl I should sit in the house and play with dolls all day? I'm the daughter of Captain Nearchos—or have you forgotten!"

"Ho, ho! Captain's-little-daughter!"

"Don't laugh! I'm grown up now and I go to the gym along with the boys. I can run and throw the discus and spear, and the other day, don't forget, I beat you in running."

Stephan reddened. He lowered his head, embarrassed. It was true; the other day she had beaten him, and his friends had been

1

laughing at him ever since. "Alka beat you!" they taunted, "a girl beat you!" And Stephan swore to himself that quickly he would race her again, and beat her, to wipe away the shame.

He fastened his other sandal hastily and made ready to go. "I have to go," he said. "I'm in a hurry."

"Oh, no, you don't, not until you tell me where you're going!" Alka came out of the door and stood in the middle of the path, determined. Her cheeks had flushed and her enormous eyes sparkled.

"Okay, okay," laughed Stephan. "Don't get mad."

"Then tell me!"

"Okay, I'll tell you. They brought a new horse in from Thessaly yesterday and the generals are all coming out to the stadium today to see who'll be able to mount it. It's wild, with a huge head. They've named it Bucephalas because it's head is as big as an ox's. The King's coming, too."

"And Alexander?" asked Alka eagerly.

"He'll be the first." A tone of pride was in Stephan's voice.

"Is he going to try, too?"

"I don't think so. They won't let him. He's still young, how could he compete against the generals?"

"What do you mean, young?" cried Alka. "He's fifteen, five years older than you. A grown man! Just let them give him a chance and you'll see."

"See what?"

"That he'll win—he's the one who'll mount the horse!"

"I hope so," doubted Stephan. "I hope so."

"You don't believe it? You'll see. But promise me one thing."

"What?"

"That you'll come back and tell me. You hear?"

"Don't worry, Alka, I'll be back to tell you everything. So long now."

"So long."

Stephan took off. Alka followed him with her eyes, admiring his ease and grace as he ran.

"Hey, Stephan!" she called, "Stephan!"

The boy turned. Alka laughed.

"If you had been running that fast the other day," she taunted, "I would never have beaten you!"

2   Stephan bit his lip and didn't answer. He broke into a run again and soon disappeared from Alka's sight.

2

The sun was high in the sky now, the narrow streets of the city thronged with people. The workshops buzzed with craftsmen forging out spears, helmets, shields, swords; soldiers were coming out of the barracks armed for battle. The whole city resembled an army camp.

For a moment Stephan paused at the huge circular agora to catch his breath. He looked around him, at the theater with its white columns, at the huge temple which was dedicated to Ares, the god of war, at the statues all about of the great heroes of Macedonia who had fallen in battle to glorify their country.

"How beautiful Pella is," he thought. "How beautiful this Macedonian capital of ours!" And indeed, what beauty, what energy, what wealth in this small city which only a few years ago had been nothing more than a big village.

The former capital was located up in the wild forests to the north, nestled among the cataracts and streams. It was called Edessa. It had fallen into ruin now but was still looked upon as a sacred city where the Kings of Macedonia went to be married, and where former Kings were buried.

Now Pella was in her glory. The city was built on a beautiful elevation overlooking a deep lake with the bluest of waters at her feet where the Lydian River joins the lake with the sea. Myriad ships, large and small, filled the harbor, anchoring or spreading their sails to set out with their cargoes.

Stephan gazed out at the ships and his heart raced.

"When will I be able to travel!" he thought to himself. "When will I, too, be able to sail away in those ships to faraway places!"

Stephan had never travelled and knew no other city. He had heard many things about famed Athens and Thebes and Sparta. His father Philip, who was the physician to the Royal Court, often talked to him about these legendary cities and Stephan longed to see them. "You're young yet," his father would say smiling. "There's time. You'll see them. You'll see other cities even bigger. Don't be in a hurry."

Last year, though, his father had taken him to distant Acarnia, to the tiny village where he had been born. "First you must pay your respects to the graves of your ancestors," he told him, and

3

took him to this little village. It was made up of no more than fifty tiny houses, squatty like huts, perched on the side of a fir-covered mountain. Stephan saw his grandfather's humble house and afterwards went to the cemetery where he knelt at the graves of his ancestors and kissed the ground that covered them.

When he returned to Pella, the city seemed enormous to him, without end. What campsites, what ships, what stadiums, what temples, what theaters! And how wealthy and gigantic the Palace where Philip the King lived with his wife Olympias and his generals!

Taking in one more quick glance he set out on the run again. "I'm late," he murmured as he ran. Suddenly, as he was racing through a narrow alley, he felt an arm reach out and grasp him by the shoulder.

"Where are you off to in such a rush, my young lad?" called a mocking voice.

Stephan stopped. He looked up, panting for breath, and there peering down at him through two small cunning eyes was a fat old man in a tattered old tunic.

"Callisthenes[1] the philosopher," he murmured with dread. How he feared this fat old man! Whenever he would spot him from a distance, he'd always cross to another street to avoid him. The old man was forever harping about the stadium and the games and the wars, and forever wanting to take Stephan under his wing and teach him philosophy. "Philosophy," he'd say to him, "means liberty. Become a liberated man!"

"Where are you off to?" he was saying. "Back to the stadium again?"

"Yes," mumbled Stephan.

"For shame!" jeered Callisthenes. "Aren't you ashamed to be wasting your time running and jumping like a goat and wrestling like a peasant? Come with me and become a philosopher—a liberated man. Liberated, do you understand?"

"I don't want to become a philosopher," declared Stephan, his voice growing bolder.

"Why?" sneered the old sage. "Isn't it to your liking? Take a look at your father, a dignified, honorable physician, respected by all. Have you ever seen him running like a lunatic, and wrestling? Become like him, and even better! He serves Kings, but you should become free! Come with me!"

"My father wants me to become a general some day," said

Stephan lifting his head high, "to follow Alexander to war when he is elevated to the throne."

"Alexander! Alexander!" snorted the philosopher. "He's insane! Yes, insane. He walks around with his head in the clouds and wants to conquer the world, he says. What nerve! To conquer the world!" and darting a furtive glance about him lest someone overhear, he continued in a lowered voice: "... but he's not to blame. It's his mother—that crazy Olympias. She's the one who spurs him on and inflates his head. She won't leave him alone, keeps at him night and day. 'Macedonia is too small for you ... Greece is small ... Conquer the world!'"

As the old man was talking, Stephan began to slip from his grasp, slowly, like an eel, he slipped away and fled.

"Stephan! Stephan!" shouted the philosopher waving his staff.

But there was no turning back for Stephan. Off he flew like a bird breaking free of the snare. "I'm late," he muttered. "They'll all be there by now and I'll be too late to see who will have mounted Bucephalas."

3

The stadium stood on a broad stretch of field at the outskirts of the city, surrounded by poplars and cypresses. The section at the rear was made up of stone steps where the spectators sat to watch the games. The front was the long, narrow arena where the young men competed in wrestling, discus and javelin-throwing, and running.

Stephan arrived out of breath. He took one look around and his face lit up. They hadn't brought out the wild horse Bucephalas yet. The Royal Court had assembled at the right. He could see the King in the center, well-fleshed, jovial, restless, in elegant purple with a golden diadem crowning his thick hair. He had only one eye, the other he had lost in the war. His faithful friends, the Companions, were gathered about him. Stephan knew them well as they frequently came to his house to see his father. All of them had, at some time or other, been wounded in the wars and had needed the physician's services. His father would bind their wounds and apply ointments and they all loved him.

5

Stephan paused in his steps now to admire the gallant men

hovering around the King. How they all held their heads high with pride; how their bodies glistened, sunburned and strong! They were girded with their swords and wore heavy bronze helmets.

There was old General Antipatros, always the first in battle, and first in the King's council. How often Stephan had heard his father praise him. No one could match him in courage and cleverness. "I pity the man who crosses him," he'd say.

And there was Nearchos, Alka's father! He was one of Philip's younger Companions, a bit short-statured, but all power and suppleness. Nearchos was famous for his valor at sea. "He's my best captain," the King would say. "I sleep easy when he's in command of my fleet."

And Antigonos, the *Cyclops,* with his one eye! He, too, had lost an eye in the war.

Back at the far end of the stadium were two men with long, carefully groomed beards. They were standing apart from all the others, talking in low voices, and unlike the Greeks in their simple dress were decked out in heavy, luxurious clothing made of costly multicolored fabrics exotically embroidered and adorned with jewels. Their fingers were covered with rings and their arms entwined with heavy gold bracelets.

Stephan knew these two perfumed, splendidly clad men well. They had come from Asia Minor last year and taken residence in the Royal Court. They were Persians, claiming their King had banished them, and had come here asking for refuge. The one was called Arsites; the other, the older one, was called Artabazos.

They must have been very rich because they scattered gold around lavishly and people liked them. Stephan didn't like them at all, though he didn't know why. They had tried to give him gifts, once a small gold sword and another time a fine bow, but he would never accept anything from them. "No, no," he'd say, "I don't want it. I have one."

He noted them now, standing apart from everyone else, talking in whispers and looking about furtively as if they were afraid someone would hear them.

Opposite them at the other end of the stadium Stephan made out a tired-looking old general who was leaning on his staff. "Parmenion!" he murmured with awe. He knew how brave this man was and what vision and wisdom he possessed. He was the King's wisest and most trusted friend. When Parmenion spoke, King Philip listened.

"He doesn't look well," Stephan observed, recalling the previous day when his father had gone to Parmenion's house to check on the old general's wounds that had opened again. "He's in pain... there's Father now, walking up to him to steady his arm," and Stephan made a dash to cross over to him.

But just then a company of youths was approaching at a smart clip from the other end of the stadium and Stephan stopped short. They were about fifteen to twenty years old, dressed in brief chitons and breezy multicolored mantles.

"The young!" scowled King Philip, "The young who are in a hurry for us to move on so they can take our place."

At their head strode a proud tall youth with golden hair, brash gait, his head inclining slightly toward the left. His eyes were blue and shone like stars.

Stephan's heart bounded. Alexander! It was Alexander! How he loved him! How ready he was to give his life for him. "Oh, when will I grow up and go off to war with him and do brave deeds to glorify my country!" he thought, edging his way forward and shyly approaching Alexander's group. All the friends of the golden-haired prince were there: the solemn Ptolemy,[2] the devoted Perdiccas, faithful Crateros, and the fierce Cleitos whom they called "the Black" because he was so dark. Parmenion's two sons were there, too, Philotas the arrogant, and brave Nicanor.

They were all handsome, but handsomest of all was a slender youth with fair skin and black eyes like a deer's. He, too, inclined his head a bit to the left as if to share in Alexander's looks. He wore a wide silver belt from which hung a beautiful sword with a carved golden hilt, and walked alongside Alexander holding him lovingly by the arm.

"Hephaistion!" guessed Stephan with awe. "Alexander's best friend. How handsome he is! And how Alexander loves him!"

Just then Alexander turned and looked about him. "How long must we wait for that famous horse?" he shouted. Then catching sight of Stephan, "Welcome, little brother," he laughed. "You've come to compete in the games with us?"

Stephan blushed. He tried to answer something but was so choked with excitement that he couldn't talk. Alexander called him his "brother" because they had both suckled the same milk. Stephan's mother, the good Elpinice, had been Olympias' midwife the night she gave birth and she had nursed Alexander and loved him as she did her own son. "They suckled the same milk," she would say with pride, "I pray that my son will grow up to be like him!"

7

4

The King looked angry. It was already approaching the hour of noon and he rose now abruptly from the throne upon which he had been sitting.

"We don't have time to waste," he said. "We have other duties, too. I must receive the ambassadors from Persia today, and the day after tomorrow I must leave for war. I cannot sit here all this time waiting for a wretched horse! Send someone to bring it at once!"

The words were barely out of his mouth when a loud neighing was heard and three men appeared holding a fierce horse by the reins. Everyone started with astonishment. Never had they seen such a magnificent, proud horse. It was gigantic, jet black, with a white birthmark like a star on its forehead. Its nostrils, one would think, were snorting flames. It trotted slowly, with an arrogant strut, and as soon as it entered the stadium and saw the crowds, it neighed with anger and quickened its gait.

"I like it," murmured Alexander eyeing the proud animal eagerly.

"Who will mount it first?" asked Philip with a mocking look at his generals.

The Companions were silent. Brave as they were, they held back for an instant. "This is no horse," they thought to themselves. "This is a monster."

"No one?" queried Philip jeeringly.

Old Antipatros stepped forward.

"I am old," he said, "and I cannot compete with the younger men, but with your permission, my King, I will try."

"No, my General," broke in Nearchos then, "we cannot let you do it. We're younger. Don't shame us. I ask permission to be the first to mount this wild beast."

"Let me!" called Antigonos the *Cyclops*.

"I'll do it!" shouted the formidable javelin-thrower, Sitalces. He was the tall Thracian commander with the red beard and long curved mustache. No one could stand up to him in wrestling; indeed he was so powerful that once he stood on a rock that he had smeared with oil and, try as they would, no one could knock him off.

"I'll try!" yelled Calas, the famed horseman from Thessaly. Philip had appointed him commander of the Macedonian cavalry, and so well did he ride a horse that they called him *Centaur*. The Centaurs, as you know, were those mythological monsters that were men from the waist up and horses from the waist down.

"Stop arguing!" laughed Philip. "We'll draw lots!"

The horse, the fierce Bucephalas, meanwhile was standing in front of the generals, thumping the ground furiously with his hoof as though daring them.

Philip dropped the lots into a helmet and turning around saw Stephan, who was standing beside his father now.

"Stephan," he called, "come here."

Stephan hurried to him.

"Put your hand in and draw a lot."

Stephan plunged his hand into the helmet and pulled out a lot.

"Read it," said the King.

Stephan opened the lot and read: "Nearchos!" he said in a loud voice.

Nearchos leaped to his feet and threw off his mantle. In a single stride he was at the horse's side and grasped it by the bridle. 9 Bucephalas reared angrily on his hind legs.

"Careful, Nearchos!" cautioned Philip.

But Nearchos wasn't listening. Pulling at the bridle with his formidable strength, he leaped over the horse and grabbed its mane, clinging to it by the neck. But Bucephalas reared straight up again and with a violent jerk of his neck tossed Nearchos to the ground.

The generals ran to him anxiously.

"I'm not hurt," he said, shamed that he couldn't mount it. "That's no horse, I tell you. It's a monster!"

The two Persians smiled slyly, pleased. "They don't even know how to mount a horse," whispered Arsites.

"Stephan, the second lot!" ordered Philip.

"Sitalces!" called Stephan, opening the second lot.

"Go to it!" said the King.

Sitalces was at Bucephalas in a bound. He grabbed him by the mouth in a powerful grip, his hands clamping tightly like iron pincers. The horse, hurting, tried to rear and break away again but Sitalces' arm pressed on Bucephalas' sweating neck and wouldn't let him budge. And now the horse's eyes were turning red.

"Don't torment the horse!" shouted Philip. "Mount it and ride!"

The barbaric commander leaped, and all held their breath. For a second he sat on the horse's back, but the frenzied Bucephalas bolted straight up and Sitalces crashed to the ground, thudding like a wineskin.

Blood was trickling from his mouth, and Philip the physician rushed to where he lay and knelt at his side to examine him.

"It's nothing," he said, "just a few front teeth broken."

"That cursed beast!" growled the furious commander. "I won't let it get away with this, I..." and leaping to his feet he lunged at Bucephalas. But the King grew angry.

"Enough!" he shouted. "Go, now! Let someone else try."

"Stephan, the lots!"

Antigonos the *Cyclops* was called next, and after him Calas the *Centaur*. Both struggled valiantly with the horse, but both were beaten.

"No one will ever be able to mount it," said Calas, mortified with shame. "No one, not even you, great King." He said this deliberately, to challenge Philip to wrestle with Bucephalas himself so that he, too, would be beaten and not be able to taunt them anymore. But wily Philip laughed.

"No," he said, "I'm not going to try. I don't want to shame you," and turning to the three men who had brought the horse: "Take your horse and go," he said. "Leave immediately! I don't ever want to see it again. It defeated all my generals!"

The three men took the horse by the bridle and made ready to leave.

"It's a pity to lose such a horse!" a strong voice rang out. "*I'll* mount it!"

Everyone turned. Alexander had left his companions and was striding forward proudly, his head held high.

"Better men than you have failed," said Philip sternly. "How dare you utter such words!"

"I'm not uttering words," said Alexander, his cheeks flushing. "I don't utter words, I do deeds."

"On with it then!" said Philip. "We'll see."

Alexander's friends rushed up and were crowding about him now. "Don't do it!" whispered Hephaistion putting his arm around him. "Don't do it. He'll kill you!"

Alexander flung his mantle off and stood stark naked. His slender body, strong and fair, gleamed in the sunlight. Grasping the bridle he turned the horse toward the sun so that its shadow would fall behind it, out of the horse's vision. He had cleverly observed that when the animal saw its shadow, it grew frightened.

Bucephalas tore off like a streak and Alexander followed, racing alongside him, reaching out now and then with his hand to pat the wild animal's neck. Suddenly, without warning, the young prince hurtled himself over Bucephalas and straddled his back. The animal reared to shake him off but Alexander had grasped its mane and welded his body to the horse, becoming one with it. Enraged, Bucephalas broke into a frenzied gallop. Alexander kept glued to him, whispering soothing words, never lashing him, holding the bridle tightly. The maddened horse galloped on and on, out of the stadium into the open fields. All were watching anxiously, Philip on the one side with the old generals, and Alexander's young friends on the other. No one was saying a word. King Philip, his mouth clamped tight, was watching in dread. "If Alexander is killed," he was thinking, "who will sit on the Macedonian throne? Who will continue the grand design?"

Hephaistion, too, was looking at the distant green fields where the daring rider had disappeared, tears welling in his velvety eyes. "If my beloved friend is hurt," he was thinking, "if anything happens to him, I'll die!"

And the two Persians were smiling slyly again. "Let's hope he's killed," they were thinking.

How much time passed no one knows. Each minute seemed a year. All eyes were riveted on the spot where Bucephalas and his rider had disappeared.

Stephan was trembling. The impetuous Cleitos, unable to hold still any longer, turned and rushed with his enormous strides up the amphitheater steps, taking them two at a time. The friends, too, clambered up behind him, all except Hephaistion whose knees were trembling so from concern that he was unable to run, and he stayed below.

Scrambling to the uppermost steps of the stadium, they stood along the frieze and stared out into the distance. No one! The plain stretched before them all green. It was spring. The poplars had sprouted their downy new leaves, and some fields were brilliant blotches of red from the poppies. A flock of stark white doves soared over their heads. "No one!" murmured Perdiccas.

"Have no fear, brothers," said Cleitos in his deep, hoarse voice. "Nothing's going to happen to Alexander."

Five minutes passed, enormous heavy minutes, like five years.

Suddenly, jubilant cheers burst from the young throats. "He's coming! He's coming!"

The old generals below lifted their heads.

"What are they saying? What are they saying?" demanded Philip in anguish.

"He's coming!" answered Stephan who had heard the cry clearly.

"He's coming?" shouted Hephaistion, beside himself, and broke into a run toward the entrance of the stadium to welcome his friend.

They had spotted him beneath the poplars, his naked body glistening in the sun astride the coal-black Bucephalas. He was riding erect now, holding the bridle in a tight grip with one hand, and reaching down with the other to occasionally caress the horse's neck. One could sense that animal and man had become friends, that the wild animal, recognizing the superiority of Alexander, had submitted.

The two Persians looked at one another. They didn't speak, but a glint of dread was in their eyes.

12 The friends were racing down the amphitheater steps just as Alexander was galloping into the stadium. For an instant Alexander

turned, looked at Hephaistion and smiled. Then with a sharp tug at the bridle he reined in the horse and pulled up before his father and the generals. In a bound he dismounted, and standing before his father now he looked at him without speaking. His breathing was easy and joyful. A misty layer of perspiration covered his body like hoarfrost, and Hephaistion, who had sped to his side, hastened to throw his mantle over him.

"Hurray for Alexander!" shouted his friends, breaking into cheers.

But solemn and silent, Alexander kept his gaze on his father. Then, with a brusque wipe at a happy tear, Philip opened his arms. "My son," he said, "seek a larger kingdom. Macedonia can never hold you."

5

Stephan hurried off in search of Alka to tell her of the royal prince's wonderful achievement. And Alexander, surrounded by his friends, returned to the Palace and went into the bath to wash away the sweat and rub his body with oil. Then, having bathed, he tied his hair back with a blue thong and hastened out to the room where his teacher, Aristotle, the most renowned Greek philosopher of the time, was waiting for him.

When Alexander was born, his father Philip had written to Aristotle, who was still living in his native Stagira, a small Macedonian city then:

"Learn, O Aristotle, that I have begotten a son; I am greatly indebted to the gods, not so much because I sired a son but because he was born in your time. When he is grown, you will educate him to be worthy of succeeding me on the throne!"

And Aristotle had replied:

"O King Philip, when he grows a little older, give your son over to a master of gymnastics to harden his body; and later I will come to undertake his soul."

Alexander suckled the milk of Elpinice, the mother of Stephan; he grew, and when he was five years old, his father gave him over to a stern teacher from Epiros, Leonidas.

"Take him," Philip told Leonidas, "and turn him into iron. I want his body to be able to endure hunger, thirst, fatigue and illness. Who knows what Fate has in store for him?"

13

"Rest easy, O King," said Leonidas. "He will become strong as iron."

Leonidas trained him every day for hours. He taught him to wrestle, to throw the javelin, to climb mountains. When he was hungry, he would not allow him to eat so that he could endure periods of hunger. When he was thirsty, he would not allow him to drink so that he could endure periods of thirst. He would not allow him to sleep, except for short intervals; he would not allow him to eat rich foods or wear luxurious clothes.

"You must be ascetic," he told him, "you must conquer your body the way we conquer a wild horse. Don't spare it!"

He taught him to be simple and frugal. Once when Alexander threw too much frankincense into the incense burner, Leonidas scolded him. "Don't squander your father's wealth!" he told him. "It's not yours, nor his; it's the people's." This was the kind of breeding Leonidas gave him. And when at last he became thirteen years old and Aristotle came to take him over, he found a lithe body, hard and strong, and was pleased. "If such a body had a great soul," he reflected, "what could it not accomplish. Miracles!"

Aristotle took him on long walks and talked to him.

How eagerly Alexander listened to him talk about the ancient wise men of Greece, especially about Aristotle's own teacher, the great Plato. And how he loved studying the great tragic poets—Aeschylos, Sophocles, Euripides, and most of all, Homer, the colossal poet of the ages. And of all Homer's heroes he liked Achilles best.

Well, wasn't he, Alexander, a descendant of Achilles, too? His mother Olympias was from Epiros, the daughter of Neoptolemy who descended from the famous Achilles. Then, too, how this pair of magnificent royal princes resembled one another! Both were handsome, like gods, with their golden hair, their fair skin, their lithe build. Both were valiant, both feared no one, their flaming hearts beat fearlessly within their broad chests.

When Aristotle would begin reciting the first verses of the *Iliad* to him, Alexander could never hold still. He would spring to his feet, his eyes shooting sparks:

Muse, sing the anger of renowned Achilles...

Aristotle was waiting with impatience for his royal pupil today. The prince's accomplishment had been heralded all over the city, and the sage teacher, deeply moved, was reflecting how the fate, not only of Macedonia, but of all Greece, now hung upon this youth.

14

He was pondering the fallen state of Greece, the discord and rebellions. The old glory was gone. Any minute now the barbarians could descend upon them and take away their liberty. Who was there to rescue their great country? Who? Only this youth who had already begun at this early age to show such valor and sense of honor.

"I will give him my entire soul," reflected the great philosopher, "I will enlighten his brain, I will make his heart gentle, I will make him an ideal Greek and human being. Who knows, some day this youth may spread the light of Greece throughout barbarian Asia."

These were the reflections that were going through his bowed head, and so deep was he plunged in his thoughts that he didn't hear the door open nor see Alexander who had quietly come in and was standing before him now.

"O Aristotle," said he, "what are you thinking of?"

The teacher raised his head. He smiled. "Sit down. I will tell you."

"You know it isn't easy for me to sit," said Alexander. "Talk, and I will listen standing up."

"I am thinking of Greece," said the philosopher softly in a saddened voice. "How she has ended up! Where is the Athens of Pericles?[3] Where has the great glory gone? What have become of the famed warriors of Marathon[4] and Salamis?"[5]

"They've taken refuge here," murmured Alexander to himself, "here in northern Greece, in Macedonia," but he kept his thoughts to himself and did not respond to the teacher's question.

"Greece has grown decadent," continued the sage. "Why? Because Greeks no longer have harmony among themselves. City is fighting against city, as if they aren't all brothers from the same great race, as if they didn't all share in the same predestination—to enlighten the world!" He fell silent for a minute. Then he shook his head and continued slowly.

"Look at what has been happening in Greece, Alexander. Just take a look. Athens lost her allies; the Spartan army razed her walls and the city filled with demagogues who serve their own desires and petty interests. Then Sparta began expanding and thriving on the ruins of Athens but along came a new rival, Thebes, who pounced on Sparta. The city of Thebes had given birth to two great men, Epaminondas and Pelopidas. They organized an army, lit a flame in the soldiers' hearts, marched into the Peloponnesos, and

15

the invincible-until-now Sparta lowered her head in defeat. Then Epaminondas and Pelopidas died and at once Thebes, too, began falling into decadence. And now look how they've ended up. One city is rising against the other; anarchy and chaos reign..."

Aristotle paused and leveled his gaze at Alexander. The young prince met the teacher's eyes evenly. "What then is to be done?" he asked, his voice tense.

"You are the one who is going to tell me. I'm waiting for the answer from you."

Alexander reddened. His breast inside was boiling. He knew very well what had to be done but kept his secret hidden deep. He hesitated, and was silent.

"Well?" asked Aristotle. "Can't you answer?"

"I can," said Alexander quietly.

"Tell me then, let me hear it."

Still silence. The neighing of a horse from the royal stables down below broke through the open window. Alexander recognized the neighing of Bucephalas and his heart leaped. The decision came quickly.

"I'll tell you," he said.

"I'm listening."

"A great leader is needed to impose order on the anarchy, to unite all Greek souls together, to muster an army from all the city-states, to train it well, and to set out."

"To set out where?"

Alexander was silent again. Where? He knew very well where. Day and night that's all he thought about.

"To go where?" Aristotle demanded again, his voice urgent and sharp like a command.

"To Asia!" answered Alexander.

Aristotle got up. He walked slowly across the room to the window where his student was standing; he put out his hand and placed it lightly on Alexander's shoulder. "And who is that leader?" he asked quietly, his voice gentler now.

Alexander did not turn, nor did he answer. He gazed out toward the southeast in silence. In his imagination he was envisioning the sea out there, and beyond the sea the shores of Asia Minor where he lingered for a moment on the ruins of Troy, at the grave of his great ancestor Achilles. Suddenly his mind was in the depths of Asia, cutting through the desert, crossing the Euphrates River, marching into Persia, breaking down the palace gates of the Persian

16

King in Babylonia, in Susa, in Persepolis, in Ecbatana, and then on into mysterious India....

"Aren't you going to answer?" asked Aristotle again. "What are you thinking of?"

"Nothing," answered Alexander. "Nothing," and he turned toward the door, his face lighting up with recognition at the sound of the light step he had heard approaching. The door opened and there stood Hephaistion, aglow with revived high spirits.

"Alexander," he shouted, "the ambassadors from Persia are here."

"Excuse me, O Aristotle, my learned teacher," said Alexander as he hastened toward the door. "The lesson is over for today."

6

The sun had begun its decline toward the west, and the huge waiting room was in shadows. The last of the rays were filtering in through two large windows illuminating a marble pedestalled statue of the great Macedonian King Archelaos. Of all his predecessors, Philip loved this one best, and he would often point him out to Alexander saying:

"There was a true king. He imposed order on anarchy and compelled all the lesser princes of Macedonia to recognize him as supreme commander. He increased the army, imbued it with an iron discipline, built fortifications, opened roads and subdued the barbarians. At the same time he promoted the arts and learning. He brought in the most renowned poets from Athens, even the great tragedian Euripides, whom he treated like a king. He established Olympian games in honor of Olympian Dia[6] and the Muses.[7] Thus, his Court was filled not only with brave soldiers, but with learned men, poets, and artists as well. That is what a true king should be—powerful and civilized. That is the kind I want to be. And that is the kind I want you to become."

On this particular afternoon the statue of Archelaos which was positioned across from the windows gleamed in the sunlight in such a way that it appeared to be smiling. The two Persian ambassadors were sitting next to it on two low stools. They were talking in muted voices. One of the Persians was a prince named Spithridates. The other was from Rhodes, a Greek named Memnon who nonetheless served the Persian King. He was the Great King's best general (this is what they called the Persian King, "Great King").

"Spithridates," Memnon was saying in a low voice to his companion, "don't forget that Philip is cunning and never says what he thinks. He'll listen to us closely, he'll say a few words, then he'll try his best not to promise anything specific. He wants to gain time. You heard what our friends Arsites and Artabazos who've been here since last year told us—he's preparing; he's building up an army, training and arming it, and waiting for the right moment to attack us. Keep that well in mind when you talk with him. Be careful, control your temper, don't say anything that will give us away. He's a sly one, so let's be just as sly. When you're dealing with a fox, you must fight like a fox."

"And really, what are we asking of him?" answered Spithridates. "Nothing. The Great King has merely sent us to talk with him, simply and honestly. What does he want of us? Why is he preparing to wage war against us? What interests divide us? None! Let's share the world then. Let him have Europe, and we'll keep Asia. Why shouldn't he accept?"

"Because he's ambitious and wants it all," Memnon answered softly.

"See, then I'm right!" said Spithridates raising his tone in anger. "We must bribe some people to kill him."

"Lower your voice," cautioned Memnon looking around. "I'm afraid even the walls have ears here. I'll bet their spies are hiding behind the doors and curtains listening. Lower your voice."

"Let's hire men to kill him," said Spithridates again in an undertone. "Once he's out of the way, we have nothing to fear. His son is a mere boy—harmless."

Memnon shook his head. "Harmless? Let's hope so. I saw him last year..."

"Shh! Someone's coming!"

The door had opened and Alexander was coming toward them with his rapid stride.

"The crown prince," whispered Memnon.

Alexander was standing before them now. "Welcome," he addressed them, smiling. The two ambassadors made silent obeisance.

"You will permit me to speak with you for a while, before my father receives you," said Alexander. "I have heard so many marvelous things about Persia that I'm eager to learn more."

"We are at your command, our prince," said Memnon as Alexander seated himself across from them. His face was in the shadows and the two envoys could not see it; all they could hear was his voice which was deep and solemn.

"Is the Persian kingdom truly as vast as they tell us?" asked Alexander. "How many days must one travel to cross it?"

"Months and months, my prince," answered Memnon. "It stretches from the Hellespont and the seacoasts of Asia Minor to the Indus River. One can travel on horseback for three months and not come to the end…"

Such an enormous kingdom, thought Alexander, has no great value unless it is well organized. "Is Persia well organized?" he asked. "And primarily, does she have good roads?"

"Better than Macedonia's!" snapped Spithridates, unable to resist. "We broke two carriages coming here."

"I'm asking Memnon," said Alexander curtly. He turned to Memnon. "Aren't you the Memnon who came to our Court last year?"

"Yes, you still remember me?" asked Memnon marvelling.

"I never forget," said Alexander looking at him with a slight flicker of scorn. He knew the man was a Greek and yet he condescended to serve the barbarians. Out of courtesy, though, Alexander said nothing. Memnon was a wise man and an excellent general. Besides, he was a guest in his house and he must say nothing that would embarrass him. "Does Persia have roads?" he asked again.

"She has, my prince, big roads, and wide, too, for military transport so that the army can be moved with ease wherever it is needed."

"And is the army well organized? What kind of arms does it carry? How much cavalry? How much infantry? How is it deployed in battle? What generals…" Alexander plied them with questions, impatient to learn, listening intently to what they told him, noting it all carefully in his mind, comparing what they said with other things he had heard, trying to figure out the truth.

Memnon stared at the young Macedonian prince with astonishment and admiration. "This youth," he thought, "is the formidable danger facing Persia. His soul is brimming with grand designs. Who will be able to stand up under the force of such a spirit?"

"We have great wealth, too," broke in Spithridates. "Our Great King has underground vaults filled with gold and precious stones. There is no richer King in the world."

"Riches are worthless," answered Alexander, "if there is no spirit. Spirit is man's only wealth." 19

"Our King has a great spirit, too," retorted Spithridates, raising his voice proudly. Memnon signalled him to lower it.

"We'll see," thought Alexander smiling. He rose now and began to take his leave of them politely.

"Thank you for the information," he said. "I hope some day I will be able to admire with my own eyes all these wonders that you have described to me. I look forward to meeting you again," and extending his hand to the two ambassadors, he departed with his usual rapid stride.

7

The two ambassadors were left to themselves again.

"If this youth grows up," whispered Spithridates, looking at Memnon uneasily, "we're done for."

"Yes," replied Memnon in a hollow voice, "he's a lion all right."

"He mustn't grow up," growled Spithridates clenching his fist. "Let's not lose time. Tonight, when we meet in secret with Arsites and Artabazos, we must come to a decision."

"What decision?"

"We have money, all the gold we want; we'll find the right man, pay him and have him kill the prince."

"That will be difficult," said Memnon, "difficult and cowardly. We mustn't fight our enemies in such a manner."

"How, then?" shot back Spithridates angrily.

"By organizing ourselves the way they do, by building a strong army and navy. Then we don't have to fear anyone. If we're disorganized and weak, even should this Alexander disappear, someone else will come along and scatter us to the winds."

"I don't agree," said Spithridates testily. "You're a Greek; you see things differently. I'm going to confer with my people and we'll decide."

"And I'm going to go back, the minute our meeting with Philip is over, and start mobilizing the troops that the Great King has entrusted in my care. I know now what a formidable adversary we're dealing with."

"King Philip of Macedonia is awaiting you in the Throne Room!" The door had opened and an officer with drawn unsheathed sword was announcing the summons in a loud voice. The ambassadors rose to their feet quickly and followed him.

They passed through a long, dark corridor illumined at intervals by huge flaming torches. To right and left they could make out arms hanging from the walls: shields, spears, swords.

"This is no palace," sneered Spithridates in a whisper to his comrade. "This is an armory!"

"Would that the palace of the Great King were like this!" thought Memnon, but said nothing.

8

Philip was waiting, seated on the lion skins that covered his throne. To his right was General Parmenion; to his left, Antipatros. No one else. Darkness had fallen and huge brass lamps were burning in the corners and along the front of the throne. In the glow of the lamplight Philip's face was discernible smiling slyly.

"They've come to offer us peace," Parmenion was saying. "What should we answer them?"

"What's to our advantage?" replied the crafty Philip, "what's to our advantage? That will be our guide."

"Our advantage is to stall for time," said Antipatros. "We're not ready yet; Greece hasn't settled down yet; the barbarians are causing trouble in Thrace and the Danube. We have to gain time."

"We'll gain it," said Philip. "Don't worry." He was silent for a while. Then, pointing to the lion's skin on which he sat, "I'm going to order some fox skins, too," he said, "so that I can sit more comfortably. I like the powerful lion, but sometimes the sly fox is more useful."

The heavy curtain at the far end of the room moved. It opened and the officer with the unsheathed sword entered. Behind him came the two ambassadors. They approached the King and fell prostrate before him, faces to the ground in Asian fashion.

"Rise," said Philip in a honeyed voice. "You're in Greece and we don't observe the custom of prostration here."

The two ambassadors got to their feet.

"Welcome," continued Philip with a great show of courtesy. "How is the health of my beloved Great King?"

"He greets your kingdom," answered Memnon, "and he sends us..."

"We have time, we have time to talk at leisure," said Philip, interrupting the ambassador. "You must be weary from your long journey. I don't want to tire you anymore..."

"With your permission, my King," persisted Memnon, "it's urgent..."

"Hospitality," interrupted Philip again, "hospitality has always been one of the most sacred laws of Greece. Don't ask me to break it. My dear guests I have given orders. Your bath is ready; your sumptuous table is set—bathe, dine, rest. We have time..."

"Tomorrow?" queried Memnon.

"Perhaps," answered Philip, "perhaps. I very much want to, but as you probably know, I am preparing for war. I must set out for the mouth of the Danube among barbarian tribes to strengthen my borders. I can guess what you've come to suggest to me: that we divide the world between us, that I take Europe, and you take Asia. So give me time to strengthen my country in Europe; don't rush...We have a proverb here: 'When the bitch is in a hurry, her pups come out blind.' Let's not be hasty, then..."

Spithridates glowered. He was ready to blurt something out in anger, but Memnon signalled and he restrained himself.

"My King," he said, "give me permission..."

"When I return, when I return, my dear Memnon," Philip cut him short again. "When I return from the war, we'll talk, you'll see, like good friends. Don't fret; I beg you don't worry yourselves. I'll do all I can to finish quickly just for your sakes. Tomorrow, or the day after, I'll be setting out with my army. In a few days, a week perhaps, or two or three at the most, or four, I'll be back. And then, at our leisure, we'll talk about the serious matters that concern both our countries," and so saying, he beckoned to the officer with the unsheathed sword who was standing at the great door.

"Captain Amyntas," he called, "escort our beloved guests to their apartments, and give orders that they are to be treated like kings." With that he raised his hand and bade them goodbye. And like it or not, they made their obeisances again and left the Throne Room.

"Sly fox...sly fox!" muttered Memnon, angered at being thwarted by Philip.

When the ambassadors were out of sight, Philip began to laugh quietly, well pleased. He turned to his two generals.

"Well?"

"Splendid!" said Antipatros. "We're gaining time, we're gaining time."

9

Night fell over the Palace. It fell over the whole city, the doors closed, the lights went out, and the people gave themselves up to sleep, to rest.

Our friend Stephan lay on his hard soldier-like cot and waited for dawn to come. "When will it come...when will morning come?" he kept murmuring, impatient for the day to dawn. Tomorrow was a holiday and he and Alka had made plans to attend the festival that was going to be held outside the city. They had gone last year, too, and he remembered how much fun it had been. The small temple of Athena had been decorated with olive branches, and all along the square the merchants had set out their wares—toys, sweets, small bows, toy swords, dolls. There had been wines and roasted meats, and fish from the lake, and farther down, splendid chitons and mantles and red sandals...

Stephan fell asleep and dreamed he was at the festival with Alka and his two best friends, Hermolaos and Leonidas. Alexander was there, too, with his friends and all were riding tall red horses. They were singing...

When he wakened, dawn had not yet broken. Bounding out of bed he ran to the window. The morning star was glittering in the east in a cloudless sky; the birds were chirping; it would be a fine day.

His parents were already up. His father was out in the garden and his mother was putting the mint herbs on to boil for their breakfast, to warm them.

"Mother," said Stephan in the kitchen, "is it all right if I go to the festival today with Alka?"

"Of course, my child, of course," answered his kindly mother. "But wait for the sun to rise a bit, or you'll catch cold. I'll come along later, too, with a gift for Her Grace."

His father came in with the handful of herbs he had been gathering in the garden. "Don't you have school today?" he asked Stephan.

"Tomorrow, father, when we'll be having competitions—in running."

"Take care that the girls don't beat you again!"

Stephan blushed. "They won't!" he said, his tone emphatic.

They sat at the simple table and breakfasted on the fragrant herb tea and a bit of wheat bread and olives. Philip the physician was poor. He had many rich patients who paid him well. The King himself gave him gold coins every month, but Philip was kind and generous and not only would he refuse to accept payment from the sick who were poor but would give them money as well so they could buy a little meat for nourishment and clothing to keep themselves warm. Whatever he had he spent on charity. Sometimes his wife, good as she was, would scold. "When your garden is thirsty," she'd chide, "don't go spilling your water outside."

But the doctor would laugh. "O come now, don't nag, Elpinice!" he'd say. "If I eat while my neighbor goes hungry, the food only turns to venom and poisons me. It's better that we all eat bread and olives than for one of us to eat chicken while the others starve."

"You're right; you're right, Philip," the good Elpinice would reply then. "Do whatever God enlightens you to do."

At that hour in the house across the alley, Captain Nearchos was still asleep. It was a fitful sleep. He kept dreaming the same bad dream: he was galloping on his horse and kept falling off. He'd mount it and fall off...mount it and fall off. Then he'd wake up with a jolt and remember what had happened at the stadium when Bucephalas threw him and shamed him before his friends.

He wakened with a start and sat up in bed. "I'm not any good on land," he muttered. "I'm a seafaring man. My horse is the ship. I dare any ship to throw me!" He thought of his distant country, Crete, from where he had come while still young, a barefoot cabin boy. What a perilous crossing! What storms in the Black Sea! Waves towering like mountains tossed the poor creaking ship up and down, breaking its masts and tearing its sails, but the ship never sank. It fought valiantly. That, he would tell himself, was the way man's heart ought to be.

"When will that expedition to Asia begin?" he sighed. "...when will we ever build that huge fleet so that I, too, can show what I'm worth!"

"Eh, Captain!" His wife Melpo had entered the room. She was from Crete, too, and was very beautiful, an austere woman who wasted no words. "The King's waiting for you."

Nearchos sprang out of bed, his heart pounding. "Did he send for me?"

"This very minute. He wants you right away," and she turned and went back to the kitchen to prepare her husband's breakfast. It wouldn't do to let him go out without his morning meal.

Alka, too, was up and had come into the kitchen to help. "Mother," she said, "may I go to the festival with Stephan today?"

"Of course," said Kyra Melpo.

"I've been ready since dawn," complained Alka, "he said he would come early and it's..." but before she could finish there was a knock at the door.

"There he is!" she cried running to open, and there indeed stood Stephan, in his blue chiton again, with his big smile. "Come on," he said, "let's go!"

Alka ran back into the house, snatched up a small basket to fill with flowers on the way, kissed her mother, and raced out the door. "We're late," she said. "The sun was up an hour ago. Let's hurry."

They set out at a brisk pace and in no time were at the outskirts of the city.

The sun was dazzling, the earth redolent, the crops burgeoning, the olive trees brimming with blossoms.

"How beautiful! How beautiful!" Alka kept exclaiming, skipping with delight.

The road was teeming with worshippers this morning. It was the feast day of Athena, the great goddess of wisdom, and everyone was bringing her gifts—a loaf of consecrated bread, a little oil in a beautiful jar, a chicken, a dove—whatever each could afford.

"We're not bringing anything," noted Alka with dismay. "How shameful!"

"What can we do?" said Stephan looking about him. "We don't have anything."

"I know!" Alka cried clapping her hands.

"What?"

"We can pick flowers and weave two beautiful wreaths for her. I'll pick anemones!"

"I'll pick daisies!"

Over the hedges and into the fields they ran, to pick their flowers. They picked and picked and wouldn't stop, except to chase a butterfly that kept fluttering past them or to loiter at a

25

stone where they held their breath and watched a delightful green lizard sunning itself.

"I'm thirsty," said Alka after a while.

"I know where there's a spring around here," said Stephan. "Come on let's get some water."

Over the hedges they raced again, on toward a ravine, Stephan running ahead opening the way, and Alka following behind with the basket of anemones.

10

At the edge of the ravine they came in view of an enormous plane tree.

"See that plane tree?" said Stephan. "That's where the water is. Hold your ear out and you'll hear it."

The two children stood still and held their breath to listen. "I hear voices," said Alka. "There are men out there talking." Then clutching Stephan's hand, "let's creep up on them and scare them," she whispered. "I think I hear my Uncle Menaloas's voice. C'mon, we'll have some fun!"

"Okay," said Stephan, leaping at the prospect of a game. "Let's go! But don't make any noise . . ."

They crept forward cautiously. The earth was soft, covered with grass, muffling their footsteps.

Stephan walked ahead, crouching low, Alka following on tip-toe behind him. Up ahead the voices were growing clearer.

Suddenly Stephan stopped. His face turned white. He crouched lower and hid behind a large rush, looking back at Alka with a warning finger at his mouth.

"What *is it?*" whispered Alka uneasily. "You've turned white as a ghost. . ."

"Shh!" motioned Stephan. He moved a step and took her hand. "Hide here and don't talk. . .don't say a word!"

"What's wrong?"

"Shh! I'll tell you later. . .wait for me here!"

"Where are you going?"

"Don't talk, I tell you. This is serious! I'm on to something. . ."

26 "What?"

"Something terrible."

"Tell me!"

"No, I can't now...don't get in my way...I have to get closer. I want to hear better."

"I'm coming with you."

"No! It's dangerous."

"Well if it's dangerous, then I'm certainly not letting you go alone. We'll go together."

"I don't want you to..."

"But I do!"

Stephan could see it was going to be impossible to dissuade Alka. Knowing how spirited and proud she was, he knew she'd never agree to abandoning her companion in the face of danger.

"All right," he said, "come with me, but be careful. No matter what you hear, no matter how terrible, you can't let out a sound."

"I won't," Alka said quietly.

"Follow me."

Stephan led the way toward the lower part of the ravine that was covered with thick growth. Crouching on all fours he began to crawl on his stomach, Alka crawling behind.

Finally they reached the area near the foot of the giant plane tree. The conversation ahead could be heard clearly now. Stephan stopped, straining his ears. There was the sound of a heavy, low voice, then another in reply.

"It's difficult," the one voice was saying.

"I'll load you down with gold," the other was answering.

"But he's always surrounded by his friends; how will I ever get near him?"

"I told you. His father's going off to war in a day or so. He'll be alone, receiving the nobles and the people in the great Palace courtyard. You'll approach him, pretending that you want to report some injustice. You'll call out, 'Alexander, justice!' and then..."

Alka gasped, barely keeping back a cry as Stephan clamped his hand over her mouth. "Shh!" he warned, straining to hear.

"They'll kill me, too!" the deep voice was saying.

"We'll have a fast horse ready at the Palace gate for your escape. Our Great King will make you a governor in some rich province, you hear? He'll make you a satrap. Now open your hands; take this!"

Gold coins clanged. Stephan cautiously crawled closer, ever so slightly parting the grass that kept him from seeing the men who were talking just a few feet ahead of him. He looked, and clenched his fist. Sitting at the foot of the plane tree like an owl was the Persian Artabazos who pretended to be King Philip's friend. Sprawled out in front of him lay a giant of a man with a reddish blond beard and mustache and hair that came down over his shoulders, who looked like a barbarian from the wild tribes of Thrace. He had both fists open and Artabazos was filling them with gold coins.

Suddenly the giant clamped his fists closed and looked about him in alarm. He thought he saw the grass moving. Stephan froze with fear. If they should catch him spying on them here in the ferns and rushes, they'd kill him for sure, knowing full well that if they let him live, he'd go straight to the King and betray them.

"Didn't you hear the grass move?" whispered the giant to his companion.

Artabazos laughed.

"It was probably some rabbit," he said slapping him jovially on the back. "Don't be so jumpy. Who do you think would be spying on us out here in this god-forsaken gully?"

"I thought..." mumbled the barbarian turning to look at the spot where Stephan was hiding.

Our small friend lay motionless, leaving the grass half-parted just as it was, and now as the barbarian turned to look, he could see the giant's face. It had a deep scar between the eyebrows.

"Come on, relax, there's nothing to be afraid of," Artabazos was saying patronizingly. "Good god! man, what will you do tomorrow when you pull out the knife?"

"Let's go," said the blond giant quietly. "Whatever we had to say, we've said. We'll separate now. You head back to the city. I'll go in front, so they don't see us together."

"So long, then, and good luck!" said Artabazos. "And don't forget..."

"Don't worry."

"...your hair and your beard, don't forget..."

"Don't worry, don't worry," the barbarian cut him off curtly, "I'll do everything I said I'd do."

And easing himself up stealthily, he took one more furtive look around and disappeared in the ravine.

Alka had crawled up to Stephan now and was holding his hand.

"Did they leave?" she asked softly.

"Shh!" He clamped his hand over her mouth. "Down!" he whispered in her ear. "Lie down..."

They both lay down, burrowing in the grass. Heavy footsteps thudded on the narrow path just above them. Artabazos was heading back toward the city. Motionless the two small friends listened to his steps fade away in the distance and when they could hear them no longer, Stephan raised himself slightly and sat up. He was breathing hard, exhausted, as if he had been running for hours. His face was pale, and he had broken into a cold sweat.

Alka sat up beside him. "Now what?" she whispered, taking his hand in a soothing gesture. "What should we do?"

"Need you ask?" said Stephan. "I'm going straight to Alexander to report what I heard and saw. His life is in danger."

A shiver ran through him. "Come, let's not waste time!" and he sprang to his feet.

They hurried back to the city, their minds no longer on the festival or games. As they were about to part, Stephan took Alka's hand. "I trust you," he said. "Give me your word that you won't say anything about this to anyone."

"I give you my word!" she said, and raised her right hand high to punctuate her vow.

I I

An hour later Stephan was coming out of the Palace, somber and pleased. He felt he had performed his duty. He had discovered a terrible secret, his beloved prince was in danger, and maybe he would be the means by which the prince would be saved. "Stephan," Alexander had said to him when he was taking his leave, "be careful! Don't say a word to anyone. Not a word. What kind of girl is your little friend Alka? Can you trust her?"

"I have complete trust in her!" Stephan had answered proudly.

"Then I'll rest easy. No one will learn our secret."

Two days went by. The army assembled in marching order outside the capital and Philip, mounted on his steed, went out to inspect it. Alexander rode beside him, glowing like the sun astride the fierce Bucephalas, his blond hair flowing loose.

Huge crowds of men and women had gathered and were applauding. For a fleeting second Alexander spotted his young friend Stephan in the throngs, watching him with awe, and the prince lifted his hand to him in a casual greeting.

Stephan flushed with joy. "Now he's not only my prince," he murmured to himself with pride, "he's also my friend...my friend..."

He was standing with Alka and both were watching the soldiers with wide-eyed admiration. What heroic bearing, what discipline! Philip and Alexander halted as the army passed in review before them. First the heavy cavalry, all picked horsemen: Macedonians, Thessalians, Greek allies. Then the light cavalry, the so-called *Sarissophori* (lancers) because they carried *sarissas,* extremely long javelins that were over six feet long.

Then came the foot soldiers who made up the famous phalanx. Each phalangite carried an even longer *sarissa,* as long as twelve to fourteen feet. Around their waists they wore short swords and in their left hands they carried round shields. They each wore a breastplate, gaiters and a white leather head-dress, broad-brimmed to screen the sun. All were picked Macedonians and were called the *Pezhetaeri,* or Foot Companions, the friends of the King.

Behind the Foot Companions came the light infantry, the peltasts (missile troops). Then came the Cretan archers, the most famous archers in antiquity.

It was very hot. The dust was rising in clouds, blocking out the sun. King Philip moved forward now, lifted his hand, and began to speak to the soldiers. Stephan was too far away to hear; but suddenly all the shields clanged, the javelins went straight up in the air, and a great roar rose from the foot soldiers and cavalry, a tremendous roar:

"Long live King Philip!"

The two Persian ambassadors were seated on a high platform alongside the Macedonian generals, watching the brilliant spectacle. For a minute Spithridates inclined his head toward his companion.

"How many are there?" he whispered. "Five, ten thousand? We can muster millions! We'll make table scraps of this mouthful!"

"What good are quantities?" said Memnon sharply.

"What do you consider good then, O Greek?" retorted Spithridates angrily.

"Quality," replied Memnon softly. And he stared at these men and marvelled. What spirit and discipline in their step, what menacing new weapons in their hands.

Philip, he reflected, had made some stunning innovations in his army. When he was young and living in exile in Thebes, he had met the great Theban generals Epaminondas and Pelopidas and it was from them he had learned his first lessons. And he had improved on them, he noted. Those long javelins would be formidable in battle! And that wedge-shaped battle formation! What a novel way of attacking and dispersing the enemy. Epaminondas had made this ingenious discovery—and how well Philip had perfected it!

"Take note, Memnon," he said to himself. "Take careful note and learn from this. Who knows, the time will soon come when you will have to do battle with these trained monsters, the Macedonians!"

Such were the thoughts that were going through the prudent Memnon's mind, and he opened his eyes wide and let not a thing escape him.

That same afternoon Alexander gathered his friends at the stadium. All his select companions were present: Hephaistion, Crateros, Perdiccas, Philotas, Nicanor, Cleitos, Coinos, Ptolemy, and Clearhos.

Alexander looked solemn. He was only fifteen, yet he had the appearance of a grown man.

"My friends," he said, "tonight my father leaves for war. He will be going far into the Black Sea up to the mouth of the great River Danube to attack the barbarian Scythians and Triballians. I'm sure he will return victorious again and we'll be standing there on the sidelines like women, cheering and showering him with flowers. For how long? He's winning all the victories and leaving none for us."

"We still have Asia!" shouted the fiery Cleitos.

"He'll conquer Asia, too!" said Alexander in a grieved tone. "He won't leave anything for us younger men."

"What's to be done, then?" asked Philotas.

"That's what I'm here to tell you," replied the prince. "That's why I've called you here. Now that my father is going away, he is leaving me behind as his substitute on the throne. He has turned over the great seal of the kingdom to me so I can do whatever I want as King. How long will he be gone? A month? Two months? Well, then, let's quickly find ourselves a war that we can throw

31

ourselves into and win a victory of our own, so that when he returns victorious from the Danube, we'll be returning as victors, too. Let's show that we're men too!"

"Hear! Hear!" they all shouted, fired up. "Let's show we're men too!"

"And who will we fight?" asked the brave and prudent Perdiccas. "Any ideas?"

"Yes, I've had word that the barbarian Maedi along the northern border of Macedonia have revolted. They've slaughtered our frontier guards and have put up a king of their own. So let's go after them and bring them back in line. Let's raze their towns and establish a new city of our own."

"And call it Alexandropolis!" shouted Hephaistion in a fervor of enthusiasm for his friend.

"The King built a new city in Thrace and named it Philippi three months ago," broke in Crateros. "Now it's our turn. It's time for us younger men to build a new city and name it Alexandropolis!"

"Name it whatever you want," said Alexander. "You know very well that I'm not interested in names and words. I'm interested in action. Let's win first!" He smiled, well pleased.

"Prepare yourselves, then! It's our first sally alone into war. We're taking on a great responsibility, let's not disgrace ourselves." Then remembering tomorrow's conspiracy, he lowered his head and added softly:

"I'm going to give you a pleasant surprise tomorrow."

"What? What?" they all cried with curiosity, clamoring about him.

"I'm not telling," he laughed. "You'll see."

Night came and the army finally set out for the new war. Philip was riding in the lead with his two brave and prudent generals, Parmenion and Antipatros. Alexander accompanied him out of the capital and rode with him for about an hour.

"Good luck, father!" he said in parting. And remembering what he had told his friends that afternoon, he added with a laugh: "Don't win all the victories. Leave some for us!"

"Don't worry, my son," answered Philip embracing him. "Don't worry! The world is big. You will accomplish things so daring that mine will be erased."

"I hope so. For our country's sake I hope so," thought Alexander to himself, and turning, he headed back to the capital.

At the Palace a young girl was standing at the door of his room waiting for him. When she saw him coming, she lifted her hand in greeting. "Hail, O King of Macedonia!" she called in jest.

"Hail, O sister of the King of Macedonia!" laughed Alexander. "Hail, O Cleopatra!"

It was Cleopatra, Alexander's sister. She was a year younger, a gentle-spoken, cheerful girl with warm-toned skin, black eyes, curly hair and a large beauty mark on her cheek. She didn't look at all like Alexander. She loved to spend her time in the women's quarters learning splendid weaving from the slave women. When she'd weary of the loom, she would sit at her mother's feet and work on her embroidery.

"Were you looking for me?" Alexander took her by the hand.

"Now that father's gone and you've become King, I want you to do me a favor," she said. Then, with a mischievous laugh, "Do I have to fall at your feet and worship you?"

"Don't talk nonsense. I'm no barbarian. Speak freely."

"I heard they brought two slave girls from Asia to sell at the marketplace and I went to the harbor and saw them; they're young like me, and pretty, with big eyes and painted fingernails. They say they know how to weave exotic new designs..."

"Well? What of it?" interrupted Alexander who was impatient to be alone.

"I want you to buy them for me," said Cleopatra in a coaxing voice.

"You'll have them tomorrow, little sister," he said planting a kiss on her. "Good night now. I'm busy."

So saying, he shut himself in his room.

All night he remained awake, plotting the new war that was on his mind. He would have to decide which of his friends and which of the soldiers to take with him. He was impatient, too, for morning to come, to see if the things young Stephan had told him were really true—if the barbarian with the reddish blond beard would really come up to him and shout, "Justice, Alexander!" and pull out a hidden dagger.

33

12

Dawn broke. Alexander was seated on a marble throne between the wooden columns at the Palace entrance. All his friends were gathered about him. The great courtyard spread out before them with its arcades, its statues of former kings, its tall cypresses all around. In the center spired the altar to the great god of Olympos, the god *Dia*.

People had already begun to arrive at the first sign of dawn— nobles to pay their respects, officers to get their orders, common people to report their grievances and ask for justice.

Alexander rose to his feet. Before commencing, he walked with great reverence to the altar to pay homage. The priests had slaughtered a white ram to be offered as sacrifice. He cut off a few hairs from the ram's head and put them in the burning flame of the altar. Then lifting his arms high he prayed: "O *Dia*, father of the gods and men, you who brought order to chaos and defeated the barbarous forces of nature, the Titans, hear my prayer. Help my father defeat the barbarians. Kings are your representatives on earth; they, too, make order out of chaos as best they can. Help my father and his army, and help me, his son. Give me strength to not only match him but surpass him, because what is the supreme duty of a son if not to surpass his father!"

Lifting their arms toward heaven his friends called out: "Father *Dia*, hear the prayer of Alexander!"

Alexander returned to the throne and sat down. He looked about him among the throng to see if he could detect the barbarian with the flaming blond beard and drooping mustache that the Persians had hired to kill him, but saw no one resembling him. "Could Stephan be mistaken?" he wondered. "Could this whole idea of a conspiracy be a figment of the boy's imagination?"

He nodded his head slightly in greeting to the long-bearded Arsites and Artabazos who were standing quietly in the center of the courtyard, carefully groomed and colorful in their spendid dress. "Is it possible they are guilty?" he wondered nailing his eye on them.

Meanwhile, Stephan out among the crowds was looking about everywhere, searching with his eyes, seeking anxiously. His two good friends Leonidas and Hermolaos were with him, looking at him with perplexity.

"What's the matter with you, Stephan?" said Leonidas. "You look like you're standing on hot coals. Are you expecting someone?"

"No," murmured Stephan looking anxiously around at every person who went by. But the barbarian with the flaming blond beard and long hair was nowhere in sight. "Could I have been dreaming?" he wondered to himself. "How shameful...to give the prince such a scare for nothing."

Suddenly, under a portico at the exit of the Palace, he spied a magnificent horse. It was saddled, as though waiting in readiness for someone.

"There's the horse!" he cried under his breath. "There's the horse they were talking about—it's waiting."

And now a wizened old man had gone up to Alexander. He was talking to him about his only son who had been killed in the war and the man was alone now and bereft in his old age. "O my prince," he was crying, "I fall at your feet. Don't let me die of hunger."

Alexander beckoned to the officer of the guard. "Amyntas," he commanded, "take this man's name and give orders that he is to be given a monthly allowance for whatever he needs to live. It's shameful to take men to war and leave their families unprotected. When I become King, this injustice will stop."

As he was talking, a buzz of excitement rumbled through the crowd. A loud hubbub arose and people were turning to look in the direction of the outer entrance where two men dressed in the simple Greek chiton had just arrived from Greece and were at that moment entering the Palace grounds.

"Ambassadors from Athens!" voices echoed.

"Who are they? Amyntas, go and find out," said Alexander to the officer of the guard, half rising from his seat in his impatience.

Shortly the officer returned, in great agitation.

"Ambassadors from Athens!" he called out, "Aeschynes and one other..." The officer hesitated.

"Who is the other? His name!"

"Demosthenes."

13

At the sound of this name a great stir went up among the crowd as they craned to see.

"Demosthenes! Our dreaded enemy!"

The name of the great orator was notorious in Macedonia. Everyone hated him. He was the arch enemy. Wasn't he the one who called the Macedonians barbarians? Wasn't he the one who had prevented the Athenians from becoming Philip's allies? And what fiery speeches he had made against Philip! Now here he was in person, daring to appear in the Royal Court of Macedonia!

Alexander rose to his feet. He didn't like this man at all but he admired his boldness, his formidable rhetorical power and his patriotism. Despite his narrow mindedness and enmity toward them, the man possessed great virtues.

The crowd shuffled to make room and the two Athenians came forward, walking solemnly, in measured step, their right hands wrapped beneath their mantles. The one was about thirty-five years old; the other, a few years older. They approached the throne and stood before Alexander, raising their hands in greeting.

"Which of you is Demosthenes?" asked Alexander, not without some eagerness.

"I am!" answered the elder, and he stepped forward a pace.

Alexander, too, stepped forward a pace. He looked at the other for some time without speaking. He was thin and sickly-looking, with sparse black hair that was streaked with ashen gray, and a lined face that looked tormented and in need of sleep.

"This is the celebrated orator; this is our notorious enemy Demosthenes!" thought the prince to himself, his heart pounding hard. He didn't know what to say to him, how to begin. But quickly he took control of his emotion:

"Demosthenes," he said, "I know how great an enemy of ours you are. I know how you malign us and call us barbarians even though we, too, are genuine Greeks." He started to add, "Indeed, more genuine than you," because he knew that Demosthenes's grandfather had married a woman from Scythia, a barbarian, who had given birth to Cleoboulas, the great orator's mother. For a second he was tempted to add this insulting remark, but he restrained himself, and tossing his head back sharply, as if to fling this evil thought away, he continued:

"...I know all this, but you've come to our Palace as an ambassador of a city that is owed respect by an entire world—an ambassador of Athens. You are, therefore, a holy personage now and I will permit no one to insult you. You are my guest. Welcome! And you, Aeschynes, are welcome, too, as our friend and ally. What have you come to ask of us?"

Demosthenes began to reply but his voice broke off. He who could make entire audiences quake when he orated in public, he who like Pericles flashed and thundered when he spoke, could barely utter a word now.

Aeschynes opened his mouth. His voice was deep and resonant. As a youth he had studied elocution and had played actors' roles in the tragedies of Aeschylos.

"We have come as ambassadors from Athens to talk with your father Philip!" he said.

"And not with me?" said Alexander, his brow darkening.

"No," stammered Demosthenes.

Alexander smiled sardonically. "Do I still seem a boy to you?"

Demosthenes did not answer.

Alexander felt his blood quicken. "I know," he said raising his voice, "that you call me *Margites the dunce*,[8] but you can mark my words the day will come..."

But before he could go on, a colossal giant of a man jumped forward from out of the crowd and stood between him and the ambassadors.

"O Alexander, justice!" he shouted.

The prince drew back a step. He braced himself against the wooden column and fingered his sword remembering the signal Stephan had told him about—this was how the barbarian who was going to assassinate him was supposed to jump at him.

He looked at the shouting giant, but there was no beard or mustache or long hair hanging over his shoulders. He couldn't be the one.

"What do you want?" he said. "Who has done you an injustice?"

"I have an important secret to tell you, my prince," the man replied. "No one must hear it." And he took a step toward Alexander. 37

Stephan, meanwhile, had torn through the crowd and was anxiously scrutinizing this man who had so abruptly broken into Alexander's conversation with the ambassadors. Could he be the conspirator that he had seen at the foot of the plane tree? He had the same build, the same voice, but this one's head was clean-shaven.

"Approach," said Alexander. "Tell me your secret."

The giant turned for a second and looked around, as though to see if anyone were near. There was a deep scar between his eyebrows. Stephan let out an ear-piercing yell:

"He's the one!" he screamed. "Alexander! he's the one!"

But with lightning speed the giant had already pulled out a short dagger from his belt and was lunging at Alexander. The prince dodged, supple as a tiger, and the knife plunged into the wooden column.

With a groan like an animal, the barbarian turned and fled headlong toward the outer door where the saddled horse was waiting. Stunned, the crowd made room for him to pass. He reached the horse, leaped to mount it when Perdiccas and Crateros, bearing down on him with unsheathed swords, got there just as he did and a blow from Crateros split the giant's head in two.

"Don't touch him!" shouted Alexander, "he's not to blame!"

But it was too late. The barbarian collapsed to the ground with a thud. He was dead.

Alexander came down the Palace steps then and walked to the center of the courtyard where the two Persians, Arsites and Artabazos were standing, acting uninvolved. He reached out and placed his hands on their shoulders. "Leave," he said. "Go! You are barbarians, so you fight your enemies in cowardly ways. Go! Return to your country. One day soon we will meet in the gardens of Persia, to measure up with one another like men."

He turned to the crowd.

"No one is to touch them!" he ordered.

The two Persians, ashen and speechless, slithered through the crowd and disappeared.

14

The news made the rounds of the city like lightning.

"The prince narrowly missed being assassinated!"

"We must sacrifice to the gods. He was saved!"

"And do you know who saved him?" an officer was saying to

a crowd that had gathered outside the Palace.

"Who?"

"A boy. The son of Philip the physician."

"Stephan! It was Stephan!" cried some who knew him.

In an hour the name of our young friend had become famous. Leonidas and Hermolaos strutted about town bursting with pride over him, and Alka fell on his neck crying with joy. His mother, the good Elpinice, embraced him.

"My son," she cried, "I suckled Alexander and I love him as my own. Bless you for saving him!" And once again she began to relate the miracles that occurred on the night Alexander was born, how "a huge star had appeared in the sky and how three messengers had arrived all at the same moment, each bringing the good news to King Philip that General Parmenion had defeated the Illyrian barbarians and that the royal horse had won at the Olympic Games, and that Olympias had given birth to a son."

And how a few days later "news had come from Asia Minor that on the very day that Alexander was born the great temple of Artemis at Ephesos burned down to its foundation, and the priests came out and shouted: 'Today a child has been born somewhere who one day will raze and rebuild Asia!'"

These were the things the good Elpinice was saying and she would still be talking if it had not been for a loud knock at the door. She opened it and there stood an officer on the threshold accompanied by a slave who was carrying a large package. The officer handed Elpinice a letter and deposited the package in the courtyard.

"From Prince Alexander!" he said, then saluted and was gone.

"What could it be? What could it be?" wondered Kyra Elpinice aloud, bursting with curiosity.

Stephan opened the letter first. His eyes, brimming with tears of emotion could barely read a thing, but little by little he began to make out the words. His mother, standing before him, was watching proudly. "Read it out loud, my son, so that I can hear, too."

Stephan read and his voice shook:

ALEXANDER, SON OF PHILIP, TO HIS BROTHER STEPHAN, SON OF THE PHYSICIAN PHILIP AND ELPINICE. GREETINGS!
FROM THIS DAY I APPOINT YOU MY ATTACHÉ. YOU WILL SLEEP AT THE PALACE NEAR MY ROOM AND YOU WILL

ACCOMPANY ME WHEREVER I GO, IN WAR AND IN PEACE. YOU PROVED YOURSELF ALERT AND BRAVE, AND YOU ARE WORTHY. AND TONIGHT I INVITE YOU TO THE PALACE TO ATTEND THE SYMPOSIUM THAT I AM GIVING FOR MY FRIENDS TO CELEBRATE MY ESCAPE FROM THE ASSASSIN.

The mother embraced her son, her tears flowing copiously.

"Why are you crying, mother?" asked Stephan with surprise.

"I don't know, my child. I don't know," answered the simple Elpinice. "I'm happy that you will be entering the Palace as attaché to our beloved prince Alexander. But I'm sad, too, that you won't be sleeping in our house anymore and that I'm going to lose you." She wiped her tears and tried to compose herself with a brave smile.

"Open the package now, my child, let's see what the prince has sent you."

Stephan swiftly undid the package, and what should he see! A splendid royal attaché's uniform, complete with a small gold-hilted sword, a brass etched breastplate, handsome leather gaiters, red sandals...

"O my boy, my boy!" exclaimed the poor mother, crying with joy all over again. "May God grant that I see you a general some day!"

Just then the door opened and Stephan's father entered. He was solemn, but if you looked at him closely you could detect in his face a look of deep pride that he was trying to conceal.

"I am pleased with you, Stephan," he said in a sober voice and he placed his hand on his son's head as though he were bestowing a blessing.

"Father," cried the boy, "Alexander has made me his attaché!"

"I know," answered the physician. "And I know, too, that he has invited you to his symposium for his closest friends tonight. That's why I've come home, to tell you some things that you should know if you want to be loved and honored by men."

"I'm listening, father," murmured Stephan, lowering his head. He was deeply moved.

"First of all, my son, I give you this difficult but important advice: Never be satisfied with what you have done. Always tell yourself: 'This is not enough! I must try to be braver, better, more honorable.' Never look at someone who is inferior to you and think: 'I am better than he is,' and rest on your laurels; but always look

40

at the superior person and think: 'I am inferior to him,' and be moved by pride to try to reach him. Do you understand?"

"I understand, father," murmured Stephan.

"Next," continued Philip, "I give you this second counsel: Don't ever be harsh or arrogant toward your inferiors, but always be good and gentle. Toward your superiors don't be timid or fawning, but fearless and honorable. No matter whom you stand before, never forget that you are a free man."

"I will never forget it!" whispered Stephan again.

"And a third injunction," continued Philip. "Always speak the truth, come what may! Never condescend to tell a lie. Whoever lies is a slave. A free man, Stephan, always speaks the truth."

Philip stroked his son's hair. For a moment he was silent.

"I have nothing more to say to you," he resumed. "These three things are enough. Now go put on your new uniform and hurry to the Palace. You have my blessing, and never forget the advice I have given you. Never."

Stephan kissed his father's hand, picked up the precious package and went inside to dress.

When he came out, his mother could hardly recognize him. How her beloved young son glowed like a prince! The brass breastplate, the golden sword, the red sandals—how handsome they looked on him! She embraced him and walked with him to the outer door. There she kissed him.

"Take my blessing," she said in a voice strained with emotion. "I don't know a great many things like your father, so I only ask one thing more of you: Love. Love everyone!"

15

Stephan arrived at the Palace. The tables in the dining hall were spread and waiting. Bronze lanterns glowed in their sconces. He stood for a long while admiring the frescoes that covered the walls, walking back and forth across the room to stare at them.

He knew Homer well. His mother used to lull him to sleep when he was a small child with verses from the *Iliad* and the *Odyssey*. And now here he was, standing before these Palace walls, gazing at those heroes that he loved so well. There was Odysseus tearing through the waters of the sea with his ship; and there was Odysseus 41 returning to Ithaca, to his faithful wife Penelope; and again Odysseus stretching that formidable bow and slaying the suitors...

Farther down at the end of the hall was a beautiful painting of golden-haired Achilles, with his powerful athletic body. "How much he looks like Alexander!" he thought. "How identical they are!" Achilles was sitting on the shore of the sea grieving for his beloved friend Patroclos who had been killed; farther down he was fighting with the great Trojan hero Hector, and was shown in the act of killing him; and farther down from that was a painting of the jubilant Greeks entering their ships for the return voyage to their beloved country.

On the opposite wall, in the place of honor, was a painting of a blind old man with long hair and a broad forehead, holding a lyre on his knee and singing. "Homer!" murmured Stephan. It was Homer, the great poet of the *Iliad* and the *Odyssey*, the father of all poets.

His mother had often talked to him about Homer. No one knew just where he had been born. Seven cities claimed him—Smyrna, Chios, Rhodes, Argos, Athens, Colophon, and Salamis. He was blind and used to make the rounds of the cities, singing at their sacred festivals or at the Courts of the Kings and nobles. He would sing, and all the young would listen in awe and they would thrill and ache with longing to become celebrated heroes some day like the heroes he sang of, and have a poet like him extol their praises.

Stephan stood before Homer and gazed at him for a long time. He was portrayed with his head inclined to one side, his mouth open, his eyes unseeing. To his right stood a beautiful woman with a breastplate and a javelin, looking as though she were going off to war; and to his left another woman in a blue chiton with an oar over her shoulder and sea-weeds covering her feet.

"What were these women supposed to portray?" he wondered. "Who could they be?"

He turned at the touch of a hand on his shoulder. Someone had come up behind him. It was Alexander.

"So, my young attaché," smiled the prince, "you're looking at Homer. Do you know who these women are that are painted beside him?"

"No," answered Stephan lowering his eyes.

"They're *Iliada* and *Odysseia*. See, the one with the javelin is *Iliada* because that poem sings of wars; and the other, with the oar, is *Odysseia*, because she represents the travels of Odysseus, the ten years that he battled the sea to return to his country."

The friends of Alexander were arriving now and servants were bringing in sumptuous foods. The cup-bearer began mixing the wine with water in the kraters, those huge silver wine vessels. The ancients hardly ever drank their wine undiluted. Low couches had been set up around the tables and the friends all stretched out on them now and the symposium began.

"First," said Hephaistion, "let us pour a libation to the Savior *Dia* who saved our Alexander from death."

They all raised their wine cups and spilled a few drops of wine over the tiles on the floor and thanked *Dia*.

Alexander then raised his cup.

"Now," he said in a loud voice, "let us pour a libation to the terrible god of war, to Ares! Tomorrow we begin our preparations, and in a few days we set out for battle. Let the god of war come and fight with us!"

He spoke, and they all tilted their wine cups and spilled fat drops of wine to the glorious god of war.

Stephan was standing erect behind Alexander listening to the brilliant young men as they talked and ate. In his role as attaché to Alexander it was his duty to be at his side always, to be ready to carry out his orders quickly.

When the eating and drinking were finished, Alexander turned to Stephan. "Stephan," he said, "there's an old man sitting in the next room, waiting. Please bring him in."

"I've invited the blind old rhapsodist Phymion," he explained to his friends, "to sing us some favorite verses from Homer. Now that our bodies have been pleasured and satisfied, it's time for our souls to be pleasured and satisfied, too."

The door opened and Stephan, who had hurried eagerly to do the prince's bidding, returned, leading by the hand a venerable old blind man with a big lyre in his arms. Now when Stephan first had laid eyes on this old man sitting in the other room, he gave a start. For a fleeting instant he thought he was dreaming, so identical was the old man to the Homer that was painted on the wall. He must have come to life again, he thought, and was here in the Royal Court of Macedonia again, these five centuries later, to sing the praises of the new Achilles, young Alexander! And now he, Stephan, was holding Homer by the arm, escorting him into the royal symposium.

Alexander laughed, guessing Stephan's astonishment.

"Homer's come back from the dead, Stephan!" he called, pointing to the image of Homer on the wall.

43

Stephan looked at the old man he was escorting, then at the old man who was painted on the wall, and shuddered—this was the same man!

"Don't be frightened, Stephan," said Hephaistion taking pity on our small friend. "Our beloved Phymion here came to sing for us not too many years ago and King Philip was so pleased with him that he commissioned an artist to paint his portrait on these walls portraying Homer. Now do you understand?"

"Yes," stammered Stephan, his voice barely audible, "...for a minute I was startled..."

The friends laughed.

Alexander greeted the blind bard and seated him on a high stool. "If only a new Homer might indeed be born again in Greece!" he said with a sigh. "We, too, want to perform great deeds, but what will they be worth if a great poet isn't around to eulogize them?"

"Is song really that great, then?" said Cleitos who didn't share Alexander's opinion on the subject.

"Of course!" said Alexander. "You do a great thing, but how long will it live after you? One, two generations will remember it and mention your name; then it will be forgotton and your name will disappear as if you had never been born. But if a poet comes along who will sing of you, your name will live and reign eternally! When will Achilles die? Never! Why? Because Homer sang his praises!" For a fleeting moment a sadness clouded Alexander's face. He had been talking heatedly. He turned now to the old rhapsodist. "Open your mouth, beloved Phymion," he said, "and sing of Achilles."

The white-haired rhapsodist bowed. Then raising his head which inclined slightly toward the side, he opened his mouth and began to sing the first verses of the *Iliad:*

> *Muse, sing the anger of renowned*
> *Achilles, the wretched! who fed woes*
> *to all the Achaians and sent myriad*
> *valiant souls to Hades!*

16

The calm in the house of Captain Nearchos was disrupted today.

As we noted, King Philip had summoned him to the Palace at dawn yesterday. "I give you authority," he told him, "to cut down the pines and firs in the forests and to gather together craftsmen from every part of Greece to set up new shipyards so that we can begin to build ships..."

"Has the blessed hour come, then?" Nearchos had asked, deeply moved.

"It has," Philip answered. "We have no time to lose now. I want you to prepare a big fleet for me to transport my army from Europe to Asia Minor. Agreed?"

"Agreed!" Nearchos had answered, and left at once to plunge into the dense forests of Macedonia and to gather thousands of lumberjacks and begin preparing timber for the ships.

And so his house was left to its own devices and, as we said, was out of sorts today. From early morning Alka had been coming and going in silence, engrossed in some busy doings of her own, opening and closing drawers, gathering clothes, collecting threads and rags, and carrying them all out into the courtyard. To these she added a small jar of oil and a jar of wine and then a larger one which she filled with cold water from the well. She had brought out some old dolls that had been stored in the closet and now she was snipping off a curl from her hair and mixing water and flour and pasting mustaches on her dolls.

"What in the world are you doing?" said her mother Kyra Melpo. "Have you lost your senses?"

"I'm expecting my girl friends," Alka answered. "Iphigenia and Cleo and Eleni are coming over to play.

"What are you going to play? Why are you pasting mustaches on your dolls?"

"You'll see, mother, when my friends come; you'll see."

"Is Stephan coming, too?"

Alka pulled at the ribbon in her hair and jumped to her feet. She twisted the ribbon and tied it again in a tight knot. "Stephan who?" she said, tearing a rag in two. "He's gone. He left his house to live in the Palace. He has no time for us now."

Kyra Melpo smiled. She turned to the well in the center of the courtyard and began to draw water. Her jar filled, she stood for a moment again to look at her daughter who was bringing out a small cart now and proceeding to lay out her three thickly mustachioed dolls on it.

"They tell me Stephan's going off to war with the prince..." the mother said.

"I know it! I know it!" Alka's voice sounded shrill. "That's why I'm getting all this ready..."

"What are you going to play?"

"Nurses."

There was a knock at the door and the sound of joyful voices. Alka ran to open it.

"Come in, come in!" she cried through a huddle of hugs and kisses.

Iphigenia and Cleo and Eleni were Alka's age. They were pretty and bright and full of charm and grace. Iphigenia was tall and slender with pale blond hair and blue eyes. She was from northern Macedonia, the granddaughter of General Antipatros. Cleo was petite and brunette, and was always giggling and teasing her friends. She was the niece of Alexander's beloved friend Cleitos.

And the third, Eleni, was from Athens, the niece of Captain Antigonos. She had only recently arrived here last year and was still proud of her celebrated city.

"What's Pella?" she would scoff at her girl friends. "Nothing but an oversized village! You should see Athens. You should see the theaters there, and the temples and gardens and palaces! And you should go up to the Acropolis, to the Parthenon! You'll lose your mind. There isn't a more beautiful temple in the whole world. You can see all Athens from up there, stretching out as far as the sea, and all around you can see Attica, with her mountains—Hymettos, Pentelis, Parnes..."

46

Eleni's friends would listen wide-eyed and ecstatic, and they'd wonder when, oh, when would they, too, be able to go to Athens.

"And did you get to see Pericles?" impish Cleo would tease, and the girls would burst out laughing.

"Pericles! What are you talking about," Eleni would answer testily. "Why even my grandfather wasn't born yet in his day!"

The girls crowded into the courtyard now and the whole house reverberated with shouts and laughter.

"What are we playing...what are we playing?" they clamored to know looking with curiosity at Alka's preparations.

"Nurses!" said Alka solemnly.

"Nurses? Why?" Eleni made a face.

"Because," retorted Alka, "the day after tomorrow the army's going to war again."

"So?" exclaimed Iphigenia. "It won't be the first time. Aren't we always in some war? When did we ever play nurses before?"

Alka wasn't talking.

"It's different now," piped Cleo, always ready with her barb.

"Why?" asked the other two.

"Because this time," Cleo intoned solemnly, holding up her finger for added emphasis, "STE-PHAN is going off to war!" She pronounced our young friend's name slowly, punctuating each syllable with exaggeration and they all broke out laughing. Only Alka didn't laugh. She felt like bursting into tears. She managed, though, to hold them back but smarted with embarrassment and didn't know what to say or do.

Luckily Kyra Melpo came out to the courtyard just then carrying a large plate of sweets that she had made yesterday—little cakes oozing with thick honey and sesame seeds.

"Ooo!" cried the girls dancing up and down, "thank you Kyra Melpo! thank you!" and in no time their girlish faces were covered with sesame seeds and honey.

They ate, washed, and now it was time to play.

"We might as well play nurses," said Iphigenia. "Where are the wounded?"

"Here," said Alka, pointing to the three mustachioed dolls stretched out in the little wagon.

"What's the matter with them? Where are they hurt?"

"Bring bandages..."

"...and wine to wash the wounds!"

47

All four began to shout now and scurry about the courtyard in a great rush, washing the wounds, anointing them with oil, cutting strips of cloth, making bandages, transporting the wounded to the hospital on a litter they fasioned from a broken piece of pottery.

"Do we have any dead?" asked the fair-haired Iphigenia.

"Of course!" said Eleni. "Could there ever be a war without dead?"

"Oh...then let's mourn them..."

"No!" shouted Alka. "Why should we mourn them? They fell in glory for their country. They're not dead anymore; they're immortal."

"Well, then, let's bury them," offered Iphigenia once more.

"All right, that we'll do," agreed Alka, "and let's decorate the graves with flowers."

"And let's ask Stephan to write an epigram to put over the graves praising their bravery," cried Cleo.

"Ha! what makes you think Stephan will give a thought to us now," retorted Alka turning up her nose. "Why should he leave his Palace for our old yard!"

17

Just as she uttered these words there was a knock at the door. The four girls ran to open it and whom should they see? Stephan! For an instant they stared dumbfounded. There he stood in his new red mantle that was bordered with gold all around, and from his belt hung the small sword with the golden hilt that Alexander had given him.

"Welcome, General!" greeted Cleo with her mocking laugh.

"Have you come to inspect your nurses?" joined in Iphigenia.

Alka alone had nothing to say. She hung back a few steps behind the others and kept looking away toward the well.

Stephan laughed. He crossed the threshold and strode over to his small friend. "What's the matter, Alka? Are you mad at me?"

"Why should I be mad?" Alka shrugged feigning indifference.

"Then why are you acting like that? Why have you changed?"

"*Me*? Why have *I* changed? You're the one who's changed. Now that you're living in the Palace and wearing a gold sword and red sandals you can't lower yourself to be around us anymore!"

Stephan laughed. "But I'm here. See, I've come to visit you."

"Sure. You've come," whispered Alka, her throat constricting, "... because you're going away. You're going to war."

"Hey, you two! What are you whispering about over there at the well?" called Cleo. "Come over here. Let's all play together. We've got the war dead here, and we've buried them already. Come on, Stephan, write an epigram for them."

"What kind of epigram?"

"I don't know," shrugged Cleo, "you know better than we do."

"The best epigram I can think of," said Stephan, "is the one the Spartans wrote on the grave of their comrades who fell at Thermopylae. Do you know the one I mean?"

"Of course we know it!" broke in proud Iphigenia:

> O wayfarer who pass this way, go forth and tell Sparta that we are buried here, faithful to her command.

"That's for Sparta!" said Eleni who, being Athenian, didn't very much care for Sparta.

"That's all right," said Stephan, "Instead of Sparta you can write 'Athens' if you like."

"Write 'my country'; then no one can complain," put in Alka.

Just then Kyra Melpo emerged into the courtyard again carrying a beautiful earthenware plate which she had filled with honey cakes for the new guest.

"Welcome, Stephan," she called. "Congratulations!"

"Thank you, Kyra Melpo."

"Have you come to say goodbye to us?"

"What! You know already?" Stephan exclaimed in surprise.

Cleo laughed her mocking laugh again. "Just me and you," she quipped, "and Pella, too."

"It's true," he confessed, "I'm going to war with Alexander."

"I don't suppose you'll be doing any fighting," said Iphigenia.

"He's young yet," said Kyra Melpo. "He has lots of time."

"I have time..." murmured Stephan, "...later, in Asia," he added under his breath.

"When do you leave?" asked Kyra Melpo again.

"Tomorrow."

"So soon!" cried Alka with a start.

"Alexander's in a hurry," said Stephan.

"Why?"

49

"I don't know."

They fell silent. Stephan ate two honeycakes, drank a cup of cool water, and thanked Kyra Melpo. "I must go now," he said, "...until we meet again!"

"Farewell then," said Kyra Melpo, and she embraced the boy warmly.

The girls gave him their hands:

"Goodbye! Goodbye!" they cried. "Come back soon!"

Alka hesitated. "I've made something for you," she whispered shyly, and running inside, she opened a drawer, pulled out a long woolen scarf that she had woven and brought it out to him.

"Wear it around your neck," she said, "and keep warm."

Kyra Melpo followed her daughter with her eyes and smiled.

"Thank you," said Stephan taking the scarf. "I won't be cold but I'll wear it to remember you. Stay well!"

"Goodbye! Goodbye!" cried all the girls again, walking with him to the gate. "Come back soon!" they shouted after him.

When the gate closed, Alka turned to her friends:

"The game is over for today," she said. "We'll play again when Stephan comes back."

18

The mountains were wild, the dense oak and pine forests teeming with foxes, bears, wolves, boars. There were no cities here, just dirty towns buried under snow most of the year. There were no artists and philosophers, no theaters, no noble games in discus-throwing and javelin or running. The people were hairy barbarians clothed in sheepskins, their feet wrapped in thick pelts. They were savage, still eating acorns and roots and raw meat, still growling like beasts.

In these dark forests that lay in the distant northernmost outposts of Macedonia, near today's Bulgarian capital Sophia, lived the barbarian race of the Maedi. A few years earlier Philip had conquered them and put up a fortress and installed his sentinels there. But of late the barbarians had begun to rise in revolt; they had slaughtered the Macedonian sentinels and installed their own king. And now Alexander was setting out to march against them, to punish them and impose law and order again on the rebels.

On the eve before his departure, an old woman who had cared for him as an infant, a faithful slave of his mother's, came to the door of his room and knocked. It was around midnight. Alexander had not yet gone to bed and was sitting at his window absorbed in thought, gazing out at the starry heavens. The galaxy was spilling across the sky from end to end, and Dia was glittering up there brighter than all the other stars, with fierce, red-glowing Ares trailing close behind. Gazing at the stars in the heavens at night was one of Alexander's greatest joys, a joy that stirred his soul profoundly.

He was thinking of tomorrow, and what a crucial day it was for him. For the first time in his life he would be taking up the awesome responsibility of leading the Greek army into war. He had no doubt that he would come out the winner, but his heart was beating loudly and he felt an imponderable tremor throughout his body.

There was a knock on the door behind him. "It must be Hephaistion," he thought. "He's insisting that I take him with me but I don't think I should. The country out there is wild and if we're hit with a harsh winter, how will he ever get through it? He isn't trained and he'll never hold up. No, I won't allow him to come," and he rose abruptly to open, determined to deny his best friend this favor. But at the door he saw old Calliope, wrapped in her familiar black shawl.

"What is it, nurse?" he asked in astonishment. "What is it at this late hour?"

"Your mother wants you, my child," answered the old woman.

"Is she sick?" cried the youth feeling a chill in his blood. He dearly loved his mother and could not live without her. Whenever he was troubled, he would go to her and sit at her knee and she would stroke his curly hair tenderly and at once his heart would grow calm. Nobody, not even Hephaistion, understood him the way his mother did. Whenever those great and noble aspirations that swelled his soul to bursting would come upon him and the whole world felt narrow and too small to hold him, many of his friends laughed at him. Hephaistion would look at him with those great beautiful eyes and not understand what it was that troubled him. His father, Philip, would knit his brows and tell him brusquely: "I don't like daydreams and fantasies. Come to your senses. Face reality and concentrate on what is practical!" And Aristotle, his teacher, would shake his head and say: "The strong man is the one who imposes limits on his desires."

Olympias alone understood him. She not only understood him but she encouraged him further still. "You were born for great deeds, Alexander," she would tell him. "The night you were born I had a prophetic dream in which a grapevine sprouted from my breast and covered the whole world with its branches and grapes. You, Alexander, are the last incarnation of the great god Dionysos!"

"Tell me the truth, nurse," he cried, "is she sick?"

"No, no, my child, she simply wants to see you. Tomorrow you're leaving for war; she probably wants to give you her blessing."

Alexander drew his breath easier. "Tell her I'm coming at once. Go now!"

His mother's apartment was a spacious chamber with costly rugs on the floor and curious paintings on the walls. Olympias had been initiated in the Orphic mysteries of Samothrace[9] and it was there, while she was still a young girl, that Philip had met her and made her his wife.

Her patron god was Dionysos[10] and she worshipped him with a passion. Many were the times when she had been seen dancing at night in the moonlight, with two huge snakes wrapped around her arms. The walls of her room were covered with pictures of the god whom she had commissioned artists to paint. He was portrayed stretched out in a black ship with grapes hanging from masts that had turned into grapevines. She had also commissioned them to

paint the Maenads,[11] followers of Dionysos, who were shown dancing with snakes entwined in their hair and around their arms. And over her luxurious enormous bed they had painted Ammon, the god of Egypt, with two curly ram's horns in his hair. She frequently saw this god in her dreams and had placed Alexander, her only son, under his protection.

"Make him worthy, my God," she would pray, "to some day worship you in your holy altar out there in the desert of Egypt."

19

Alexander opened the door quietly and entered. At first he could see nothing through the smoke that filled the room. As was her custom his mother had lit coals in a large censer and was burning aromatic resins and incense.

But his eyes, adjusting to the haze, quickly made out her form reclining on the bed, a gold ivy wreath woven in her jet black hair.

"What is it, mother?" he asked, striding rapidly across the room to kiss her hand.

Olympias sat up in bed but kept silent for a while. She stroked her son's golden hair and sighed.

"Is something worrying you, mother?" asked Alexander anxiously.

"I am happy," answered Olympias. "I had a dream and I've called you to tell you about it. You know, god often reveals himself to me in my sleep and foretells the future..."

Alexander was listening intently, profoundly stirred. He dared not speak for fear of interrupting her, so impatient was he to learn of her prophetic dream.

"I dreamed," continued Olympias, "that a lion came out of my breast while I was sleeping and went away. I watched it go off in what appeared to be an endless road. It walked on, past Macedonia and Thrace, and came to the sea where it jumped in and eventually came out on the opposite shore. It went on and on and the beasts all around howled with terror and fled before its path. It kept going and going until there was no more land and finally it came, so my dream said, to the end of the world. At that point it turned and looked at me and smiled. And it was then, Alexander, that I could see it was you!"

53

Alexander stood up. His heart, jubilant now, was bursting with pride. He tossed his head back and Olympias gasped in terror and joy at the lion she saw standing before her.

"Give me your blessing, mother," came the tender sound of Alexander's voice. "Your words have given me wings. Tomorrow I will set out and I'll win. And after that I will cross the Hellespont and go to Asia. I will conquer the world. What you have dreamed will be fulfilled."

"You have my blessing, my son," said Olympias, and Alexander could feel the fire of her hand on his head piercing his entire body.

The next day he set out with his army, the cavalry in the lead, the foot soldiers following. Alexander was riding ahead on Bucephalas, among his faithful companions. He could still feel his mother's flame boring through him as he rode with his army through the streets of the capital and out into the fields.

Stephan was galloping behind the fierce Bucephalas, astride his own small horse. He was dressed in his uniform, in the bronze breastplate and red sandals, and at his belt to the right gleamed the small sword with the gold hilt.

They sped northward. Racing by night and by day they cut through forests, scaled mountains, marched across vast plains. Now and then they came upon a village of huts or a herd of sheep. Nights, they would camp and sit around their campfires listening to the wolves howling in the distance.

When they had set out from Pella, the sun was shining and the sky was clear and blue. But as they raced northward, the sky grew heavy with dense clouds. Winter was closing in.

"Forward!" Alexander would prod, leading the way on Bucephalas.

One day they came to a dense woodland. Alexander was riding ahead with his most trusted friends and they had just entered the dark forest when suddenly a howling band of hatchet-wielding savages sprang out at them from between the trees and fell on the horses.

"Hail fellows, well met!" shouted Alexander with glee. "I've been riding all these days to find you." And turning to his companions, "On them, boys!" and they all lunged and began the chase.

"It's like hunting wild boar!" yelled Cleitos plunging his long

54

javelin into a barbarian's ribs.

In an hour they had the enemy on the run. Coinos was slightly wounded in the knee and Crateros had a wound in his right hand from a rock they had thrown at him.

Night came and the army halted. They lit fires and Alexander went from fire to fire where his soldiers were gathered and stopped to talk with them.

"The hard part is over, boys," he announced. "We're approaching the heart of enemy country. The war will finally begin. Let's not disgrace ourselves!"

Stephan remembered this whole expedition like a terrible dream—how they had first come upon the villages one icy morning...how the barbarians fell on them with their hatchets...how the two armies grappled with each other man to man...

He had fallen behind and was watching from a hilltop where Alexander's tent was pitched. All of them, Greeks and barbarians, were one tangled ball and you could barely make anyone out except Alexander on his black horse with his golden hair flying in the wind.

Toward evening the barbarians were beginning to limp away in disorder. He watched the Macedonian horsemen chasing them down and all you could hear throughout the entire plain were the howls of the barbarians and the whinnying of horses.

Then the horsemen galloped into the biggest of the villages and set it to the torch, and the smoke billowed from the huts all through the next day and the next, and by the third day they had all become ashes.

"We must not be content setting fires alone," Alexander told them then. "This the barbarians can do, too. What we must do is build!"

"Let's build a big city!" cried the companions.

"Yes, a big Greek city, and all around it let's put up high walls and leave an army behind so the barbarians don't dare rear their heads again."

"We'll call it Alexandropolis!" the prince's friends shouted raising their swords in the air.

"All right, then, we'll call it Alexandropolis," said Alexander. "And may the gods decree that it not be the last; that we build other Alexandrias and Alexandropoleis as far as the end of the world."

20

PHILIP, KING OF THE MACEDONIANS
TO ALEXANDER, HIS SON.
GREETINGS!

WITH GREAT JOY I HAVE BEEN INFORMED, MY SON, THAT YOU HAVE DEFEATED THE WILD MAEDI AND HAVE FOUNDED A NEW CITY WHICH I AGREE SHALL BE NAMED ALEXANDROPOLIS IN YOUR HONOR. AS SOON AS YOU RECEIVE THIS LETTER, TAKE YOUR ARMY AND COME AT ONCE TO JOIN ME HERE AT THE MOUTH OF THE DANUBE IN THE BLACK SEA. I SEND YOU TRUSTY MEN TO GUIDE YOU. WE SHALL RETURN TO OUR CAPITAL TOGETHER.

When he had read this message from his father, Alexander bit his lip. He put the letter away quickly in his belt and got up. Stephan who was standing nearby watched him uneasily. The prince appeared dejected.

"Stephan," he turned to his young attaché, summon the trumpeters."

In a short while the trumpeters were before him.

"Sound the signal to fall in!" he ordered. "We're leaving!"

The trumpets echoed throughout the camp and the men scrambled into marching formation. Astonished, Alexander's friends gathered about him. "Are we leaving?" asked Ptolemy. "Why?"

"I thought we were going to conquer all the barbarians in these parts," exclaimed Crateros.

"I have orders," said Alexander in a strained voice, "orders from my father that we are to leave at once and meet him at the Black Sea…"

"He's jealous of your victories," muttered Perdiccas.

"Silence!" ordered Alexander and he swiftly leaped astride Bucephalas.

Before riding off he ordered two thousand hand-picked soldiers to remain behind as sentinels. Mounted on his horse, he addressed them:

"I leave you here as guards in this barbarian land," he said. "Hold the name of Greece high. Don't allow yourselves to be conquered by petty squabbling and laziness and fear. If you do, you'll be lost. You are surrounded by the enemy, so train yourselves daily to remain strong. Don't act barbaric toward the barbarians. Behave gently, with moderation and good will. Don't forget that you are Greeks and don't forget that I am leaving you here, not only to guard the country, but also to impart our civilization to it as best you can. I am turning over wild creatures to you; I want you to make men of them!"

The victorious army of Alexander set out and in a short while disappeared into the dense forests toward the north.

Cold. Snow. Packs of wolves dogged them along the way. At night the phalangites could see the beasts' eyes glowing red in the dark. Incited by hunger, whole packs of them fell on the campsite where the horses were kept, and every night two or three horses would be found killed.

"Light campfires!" ordered the officers. "They'll frighten the animals and keep them from coming so close."

By day the sky was filled with clouds so dense that not a ray of sunlight could pierce through. Thick snow fell incessantly. Soldiers, horses, carts all pressed on through stark white snow.

Toward dusk of the fifth day, as they were preparing to camp for the night, the mail carriers arrived from Macedonia. Dismounting, they entered Alexander's tent and laying open a small leather sack they had brought, gave him a handful of letters.

The prince scanned them eagerly and separated two from the others. "My mother's," he murmured pleased, "and Hephaistion's."

Stephan was standing in the corner watching. "Oh for a letter from home of my own!" he was thinking.

Alexander glanced up and saw him. "Is that you, Stephan?" he said. "Here, you have two letters."

Stephan ran to him and grabbed the letters eagerly from the prince's hand. "Thank you," he cried and hastened out of the tent to the fire that the soldiers had lit, and began to read.

One letter was from his father: "We learn with joy, my son," he wrote, "that our army is advancing victorious. I am pleased that you are fortunate to be following the army at such a young age and learning how to become worthy of Greece some day. I know it's cold up there and snowing, but you must not fear the cold. If you do, you will feel even colder and won't be able to endure. You
57

must not fear anything, Stephan. There is no greater shame than fear. You must be enduring in everything—fatigue, hunger, cold—and you must not forget the three injunctions I gave you the day you went into service at the Palace."

In a corner of the letter Stephan made out the handwriting of his mother. She had written him a few words, too. Stephan read and his eyes filled with tears: "My son, take care not to catch cold; if anything happens to you, what will become of us?"

Stephan tightened the woolen scarf around his neck and opened the second letter. "Alka!" he cried joyfully. "Alka's writing to me!" He read eagerly:

"Alka, daughter of Captain Nearchos, to Stephan, son of the physician Philip. Greetings! From the day you left I have been sitting here embroidering a green laurel wreath on a white linen cloth for you. When you come back I will give it to you. At the bottom in the corner I'm embroidering in tiny letters the word ALKA so that you will remember me.

"...but when will you be back? The embroidery is almost finished. They tell me it's cold out there, but I'm not worried because I gave you the woolen scarf to wrap around your neck."

21

"Thalassa! Thalassa!"

The foot soldiers clanged their shields with joy, the cavalry raised their long javelins high, and the whole army gave out a joyous shout:

"The Sea! The Sea!"

For fifteen days now they had been trudging through the snow, battling either the wolves that were growing fiercer by the day, or the barbarian tribes that kept ambushing them along the way and falling on them in surprise attacks from behind. But as they were approaching noon today, their advance scouts finally sighted the vast stretch of gray glistening far out on the horizon and hastened back to the army with the momentous news: "The Sea; the Sea!" By day's end they were entering Philip's campsite.

Soldiers were embracing with joy, Philip's phalangites clamoring to hear what Alexander had accomplished. "We beat the barbarians and built a new city and named it Alexandropolis," boasted the youths, "... and you? what have you been doing?"

"We found the Scythians here terrific archers," said the others. "They have a tough old soldier of a king called Atea who's ninety years old. We told him to surrender but the old man would have none of it; in all his ninety years, he said, he'd never shamed himself and wasn't about to do it now. So he mustered his archers, thousands of them, and took up his ancient bow himself, and attacked us. But he was no match for our phalanxes and we had them on the run in a few days. We took over their harbor and put up fortresses on either side of the entrance, and now at last the Black Sea is ours."

Philip, meanwhile, had sighted Alexander's army from a distance and was hastening out to welcome him. Accompanied by his two old generals Antipatros and Parmenion, he approached. "Hail, victorious Alexander!" he called to him and, embracing his son, he led them all back to the royal tent where the fire was burning and the table was spread for a feast. Philip loved luxurious living. He loved wine and good food and good cheer, and often he had someone around him who was good at telling jokes and could make him laugh.

Alexander eyed the sumptuous table and smiled.

"I'm not hungry," he said. "I'd like to see the harbor first, where you've put up the fortifications."

Philip looked at him in astonishment. "Aren't you tired?" he asked. "Aren't you hungry?"

"No," answered Alexander. "Let me take a look at the harbor."

Philip rose from the table annoyed. "Let's go!" he said.

Father and son walked ahead in the direction of the sea, their entourage following behind. They arrived at the harbor and climbed the two newly-built fortresses. Alexander examined everything closely, without a word.

"Well? What do you think? Why don't you say something?" ventured Philip, looking at his son with a certain testy uneasiness. What was Alexander? Still a mere boy. And yet here was he, Philip, who had waged so many wars and had lived so many years, feeling compelled to ask the opinion of this raw, inexperienced youth.

Alexander thought a while. "Very good," he said at last.

"Very good? And why, may we ask?" Philip's voice was sarcastic now. "Can you tell us?"

"I can," answered Alexander.

"Let's hear it then."

"Because this harbor was indispensable to us," the prince said soberly. "The Persians command the southern and eastern seacoasts of the Black Sea and would be able to send troops by ship to attack us in Macedonia when we're away in Asia—so we would be compelled to abandon the Asian campaign and turn back. But now..."

Philip put out his hand and laid it on Alexander's shoulder. "My son," he said, "I told you once before and I tell you again, Macedonia can never hold you. Find yourself another kingdom, a bigger one."

"I've found one," said Alexander smiling. "Asia. It's there for the conquering."

"All Asia?" Philip laughed scoffingly.

"All of it."

"Asia Minor's enough! We'll liberate the Greeks there. And that's all!"

"That's not enough," murmured Alexander. "That's not enough!"

No more was said and they returned to the royal tent where they settled down at the table. The two old generals were dining with them, along with some officers from the battalion of the "Companions." The Companions were the bravest and most trusted of Philip's officers, all Macedonians from noble and wealthy families.

Philip set to eating with great gusto, the cup-bearer filling and refilling his cup with wine. He was in high spirits this evening, joking and talking in a booming voice, his eyes sparkling. Alexander was silent, eating sparingly, drinking little, his mind far off on distant Asia.

22

Early the next morning Philip summoned his officers. "Our mission here is finished," he said. "We had a purpose and we've achieved it. Now it's time we returned to our capital. The news that I've been getting from Greece is bad; they're starting their internal wars again and our country is going to ruin. It's urgent that I return quickly to restore order."

Stephan heard the King's words with joy. They were going back! He would be seeing his beloved parents again; he would be crossing their familiar street and knocking on Alka's door again. He envisioned her opening it, and seeing him standing on the threshold...

"On the march!" said Philip. "Back to our country!"

The army set out in high spirits. It was still snowing and the cold was fierce, but the soldiers were patient. It would get milder, they knew, the closer they got to their country. Patience.

Philip was marching ahead with his army and Alexander was following behind with his. They crossed more snow-filled plains and mountains and eventually arrived at the outskirts of Alexandropolis. Here one night one of the Maedi barbarians stole into their camp and headed for Alexander's tent. The fires were blazing and the guards were awake, but no one took notice of the barbarian. They thought he was one of them, a phalangite.

Stephan had not yet gone to bed and was sitting outside Alexander's tent near the fire warming himself when he saw a shadow approaching and sprang to his feet. "That's no Macedonian," he said to himself. The shadow was heading straight for Alexander's tent.

"Who are you?" shouted Stephan grabbing the barbarian by his long cape. "What do you want?"

"I must see Alexander," answered the stranger in a barbarian accent.

"Why do you want him?"

"It's urgent. I'm a friend."

"Wait here," said Stephan. "I'll tell him you're here. Don't move."

"Sure, go tell him."

In a short while Stephan came out again. "You can go in," he said to the barbarian, following him inside the tent uneasily.

Alexander, though, was motioning him to leave. "Go to bed, Stephan. Leave us in private."

"Don't be afraid," he added, seeing Stephan hesitate. "He's a friend. I know him."

Stephan went out, but how could he think of sleep? He stood outside the tent and waited anxiously.

Five minutes went by. Ten. He could hear them talking inside but couldn't make out what they were saying. After some time the barbarian came out. He pulled his heavy cape tightly about him and disappeared in the dark.

The next morning Alexander summoned his friends. "I want you to continue riding ahead with my army," he told them. "I will be going up front to keep my father company."

"Are you leaving us? Why?" they asked in dismay.

"Only for today," said Alexander and prodding his horse he galloped off to catch up with his father on his mount at the head of the army.

"What is it?" queried Philip as he turned and saw him. "Why together?"

"Father," said Alexander, "see that black forest out there between the two mountains?"

"I see it."

"The barbarians are hiding in there waiting to attack us."

"How do you know?"

"I have my spies."

Spurring his horse then, Philip spurted ahead and checked his advance guard. He gave orders to his officers and sped back. "We're ready," he said to his son.

It was noon when they finally arrived at the forest and began to penetrate it. The soldiers advanced slowly, carefully, through the first trees, Alexander sticking close to his father's side. Suddenly some dogs that were following the army began to bark and run amuck among the brush, their tails standing straight in the air.

"On your guard!" shouted Philip. "Look sharp!"

They edged forward. All at once savage, blood-curdling yells broke out. Wild, hatchet-waving barbarians were leaping at them from behind the trees. They grappled man to man. Soon soldiers from the rear were pouring in, encircling the barbarians. Seeing themselves surrounded thus, the savages turned into monsters, hacking away desperately with their hatchets, killing left and right. A giant among them who looked as if he might have been a leader, recognized King Philip and lunged at him. He wielded his hatchet, struck, and down crashed the King to the ground, his leg laid open with a gaping wound. The barbarian lunged again and was raising his hatchet high over the royal head when Alexander, hurtling at him like a thunderbolt, cut the barbarian down with a slash of his sword on the head, and holding his shield over his wounded father he fought off the enemy and kept the King's body out of their reach.

When night finally came and the barbarians, seeing their chief killed, finally scattered and fled, Alexander lifted his father in his arms and laid him over his mantle which he had spread on the ground. Then, ordering that a fire be lit at once, he washed his father's wound with wine and bound it carefully.

Philip pressed his son's hand. "Look," he smiled, opening his tunic to show him his body that was covered with wounds from previous wars, "...look, I've grown used to it."

"Sleep, father," said Alexander. "If you want anything, call me. I'll be sleeping here beside you."

23

In a few days Philip and Alexander, at the head of the army, were entering the capital victorious. The entire city was decked out with laurel and myrtle branches that the people had cut to decorate their houses. The whole populace—women, men, children—were out in the streets cheering the King and his son, the two victors.

Stephan was riding behind Alexander, trotting at a smart clip and looking to left and right as if in search of someone. A fat old man in the crowd was following him with mocking eyes and as Stephan caught a glimpse of him, he tightened his lips. "Callisthenes the philosopher," he muttered turning his head away. Suddenly he gave a jubilant shout. There in front of the Palace was a group of young girls, about ten to fifteen years old, with crowns of flowers in their hair. They were dancing and singing.

"Alka!" Stephan yelled. "Alka!"

Alka heard the shout. "Stephan! Stephan!" she wanted to shriek back but was too shy and didn't, and she waved to him and nodded.

King Philip dismounted. He was still limping in pain from his wound, and Alexander took him by the arm and helped him up the stairs. The people cheered lustily. He was wounded again, they noted, wounded to enlarge their country. The King climbed the stairs, stood before the entrance and turned to greet his people.

Stephan hurried home. We can imagine with what joy his parents were awaiting him—his mother beside herself in tears, his father trying hard to keep his emotion hidden.

"Were you cold, Stephan?" he asked him.

"No," laughed Stephan. "I wasn't cold and I wasn't hungry and I wasn't tired. Everything was fine!"

After a while he got up. "I'm going to see Alka," he said. "She'll be waiting."

"Yes, go and see her, my son," said his mother. "She's made you a present."

"I know. She wrote me. She's embroidered something." And in two bounds, Stephan was at Alka's door. He knocked. At once, as if she had been sitting behind the door waiting for him, Alka opened and stood before him.

"Stephan," she whispered, her voice trembling a bit.

"Alka!"

They sat in the garden and talked. They talked and talked and never stopped, like two little birds on the branch of a blossoming tree in the springtime, warbling away unsated. "You must tell me everything!" Alka was saying. "Everything!" And Stephan was describing what he had seen, what lands he had crossed, what forests, what rivers, and what joy he had felt when he spotted the sea from a distance.

At that moment Alexander, too, was sitting at his mother's feet, describing the campaign to her. "It was nothing," he was saying in conclusion. "Just a short jaunt."

"True, a short jaunt, but the day will come when you will set out to conquer the world."

"When? When?"

"Are you impatient? So am I. But the gods are the ones who will decree. They're the ones who know. Let's be ready."

"I'm ready every second, mother. I can neither sleep nor take pleasure in anything. I'm forever standing ready, waiting." He stood up and began to pace back and forth across the room like a lion in a cage. He looked at the frescoes on the walls again, at the god Dionysos floating in the green sea with the black grapes hanging over him, and his heart pounded.

Down below in the royal stables Bucephalas neighed again as though he, too, were impatient. Suddenly a swallow flew into the room; it shot through like an arrow and went out the opposite window.

64

"A good omen," said Olympias.

"The first swallow I've seen this year," said Alexander. "Spring is here already. How quickly time passes." Then, after a pause, "My God, how quickly time passes and I'm doing nothing." He kissed his mother's hand and left the room. Outside he headed rapidly toward the stables. At sight of him Bucephalas lifted his massive head with the white birthmark on the forehead and neighed.

Alexander leaped on the horse and galloped off. He raced through the city and out into the fields. His sister Cleopatra who had been watching him as he was coming out of the Palace gave a start. How pale and tired he looked.

"What's wrong, Alexander?" she asked.

"Nothing, Cleopatra, it's nothing. I'm just going out for a ride."

He galloped and galloped through the fields, his golden hair flying in the wind, and Aristotle who was out taking his usual walk with two of his students, discussing the seven sages of Greece, stopped at sight of him.

"Achilles!" he murmured.

Alexander sped by without seeing him, looking ahead into the distance. Aristotle turned to his two students: "Great and thrice-noble is the race of the Greeks," he said. "Centuries ago it succeeded in giving birth to Achilles, the ideal youth. Now look out there. It has once more sired this youth, perfect in beauty, in strength, and in nobility—lacking in nothing."

"Except one thing," challenged the dark-haired student with flashing eyes who was standing to the right of the great teacher. "Except one thing."

"What?" asked Aristotle. "What is he lacking?"

"A Homer. A great poet to sing his praises and not let him die."

Aristotle nodded his head. "You are right, Theophrastes," he said quietly.

24

The swallows came, they built their nests, the almond trees blossomed, they sprouted their new leaves, the first fruits budded. The earth covered itself with green grass again, and anemones and poppies and yellow daisies.

Alexander, looking out from the Palace balcony, was gazing at the ships in the harbor that stretched out before the capital. They sailed in from all over Greece, hauling in wine, oil, wheat, wool, and fruit, and taking away timber, leather, sheep, and bulls.

He watched them unfurl their sails and put out to sea, following them with his eyes until they disappeared like white seagulls on the horizon. Some sailed southwesterly toward the seacoasts of Greece; others set their course southeasterly, toward Asia Minor.

"When will this harbor spill over with warships full of soldiers?" he wondered to himself. "When will we be ready to set out for distant Asia?"

One day, toward the end of spring, a big ship arrived from Greece. Three men leaped ashore and headed with great speed toward the Palace.

Philip was expecting them.

"King of Macedonia, great ally," they said to him, "the Panhellenic Congress has sent us to ask your help."

Philip's cunning eye gleamed.

"I am willing to do what I can," he said. "I am listening."

The elder of the three began:

"The inhabitants of Amphissa have once again violated the sacred fields of the Oracle of Delphi. The Congress has decreed that they should return the fields and pay damages to the Oracle. But they refuse. They have the Thebans on their side, too. The Athenians and the other city-states dare not go to war against them because they fear the Thebans.

"Who, then, will undertake to punish them? Only you, O King of the Macedonians, have the power to make war and bring about justice. That is what we have come to ask you. Will you accept?"

Now there was nothing the shrewd, ambitious Philip wanted more, but he disguised his delight lest he tip his hand, and he lowered his head pretending to be thinking it over. The envoys watched him anxiously.

66   At last he lifted his head. "It is not an easy matter," he said. "I would have to muster all my army, a tremendous effort, and very

costly. And I have problems here of my own with the barbarian races living in the north."

He fell silent again, pretending to be thinking. The second envoy spoke:

"You are aware, O King, that dissension is destroying Greece. One city is constantly fighting the other. Civil war has ruined us. Only one salvation remains for Greece—you."

Philip sighed. He rose to his feet as though he had come to a decision.

"Very well," he said. "I will make this sacrifice, too, for our beloved country. I accept."

The envoys opened their arms. "We thank you!" they cried. "We thank you!"

"Go tell them I am coming. I will punish the profaners, I will restore order; I will put an end to the dissension. We will all become one Greek nation again and we will all fight together against the common enemy—the barbarians."

The envoys took their leave well pleased, and without further ado they boarded the ship and sailed away to bring the good news to Greece.

When he was alone, Philip rubbed his hands in glee. "Just what I wanted!" he murmured, limping back and forth across the huge throne room. "Just the opportunity I've been looking for to march into Greece and force all the city-states to unite and stop bickering and destroying themselves over their petty self-interests." He looked out toward distant Greece and smiled. "I'll compel them to proclaim me Commander-in-Chief—to get my grand design moving at last."

He clapped his hands. The captain of the royal guard drew the heavy curtains apart and entered. "Amyntas," said the King, "go at once and summon Parmenion and Antipatros."

Philip's two faithful co-workers hastened to him.

"My dear friends," he told them jubilantly, "the sacred moment has arrived! The Greeks themselves have invited me to march into Greece with my army to impose order. Prepare the best phalanxes, select the finest mounted warriors, and let us set out before the month is up. There is still time for Greece to be saved from anarchy!"

67

25

Before the month was up thirty thousand troops and two thousand horsemen were ready. It was autumn. The apple and pear and fig trees were loaded with fruit. The grape harvesting had begun.

Out in the countryside Alexander was returning from his walk with his teacher Aristotle. "Alexander," the sage teacher was saying, "tomorrow is going to be a crucial day in the history of Greece. Your father is setting out to bring harmony and peace to the Greek states which for so many years now have been tearing each other to pieces. If he succeeds, the great dream of every true Greek soul will be realized: Greece will be united. With Greece united the first step will have been taken and then you, Alexander, will one day be able to realize your own dream—the conquest of Asia."

Alexander was listening but kept his silence. All the things his teacher was telling him were true. He knew how important this expedition was. He had begged his father to allow him to take part in it and his father had appointed him Commander of the Cavalry.

"What does it mean, Alexander, to conquer Asia?" the sage Aristotle continued. "Do you know?"

"Of course I know!" the fiery prince retorted. "To wage war, to win, to conquer the cities, to fortify them, and to proclaim yourself King."

"That is not enough!" said Aristotle sternly.

Alexander thought for a minute. Aristotle was right. To conquer the body was not enough. "You must also conquer the soul," he said after a pause. "To truly conquer Asia, you must first conquer her soul."

"And how will you accomplish that?"

"By imparting Greek civilization to the barbarians—by imparting our arts, our learning, our science so that they, too, can live with enlightened minds, with tempered control over their barbarous strength, and with the knowledge that the highest good for man is liberty."

"May the gods grant," said Aristotle then, "that in just such a manner you conquer Asia soon!"

"In the name of the Panhellenic God!" shouted Philip to his army the next morning, giving the signal to set out.

They marched through western Macedonia, advanced through the endless plains of Thessaly, crossed the Pintos River, and arrived at renowned Thermopylae.

When the Greek states heard that Philip had entered Greece and was advancing with his army, a great clamor went up. In the lead was Demosthenes who resumed his inflammatory speeches against Philip. "The barbarian is at our door!" he shouted to the Athenians. "He is going to subjugate Greece and we shall lose our freedom! Let all the Greek states unite against him!"

Demosthenes was a great orator and a sincere patriot but his vision was limited. He did not see that the Macedonians, too, were genuine Greeks and that at this point, if Greece were to be saved, she would have to unite under a strong leader. And only one existed now—the King of Macedonia, where the center of Greek power had shifted. But the tremendous oratorical power of Demosthenes swayed many Greek states against Philip: Athens, Thebes, Corinth, Megara, Corcyra. And having swayed them, Demosthenes now took up his shield and javelin and rushed out to join in the fighting, too.

In vain Philip sent envoys all over Greece with the message: "I have not come to subjugate Greece! I, too, am a Greek and I have come to put an end to the discords, that we may all unite and liberate the Greeks who live in Asia. This is my purpose. Let us not get caught up in war with each other!" But the Greeks, inflamed by the words of Demosthenes, would not listen.

"Drive him out! Drive him out!" they shouted. "Drive the Macedonian barbarian out!"

By now the Macedonian army had crossed Boeotia and was approaching Thebes at Chaeronea. There, under an oak tree near the shores of the River Cephisos, Alexander had pitched his tent.

"Stephan," he said to his young attaché, "tomorrow we're going into battle. Our opponents are many and brave. They're going to fight fiercely. If anything happens to me, take these two letters and give one to my mother and the other to Hephaistion. Understand?"

"I understand," said Stephan, his voice breaking. He hid the two letters in his bosom and his eyes filled.

69

"Hey, little brother," said Alexander thumping him playfully on the shoulder, "don't worry, nothing's going to happen to me. I've a long road ahead of me. But it's a good idea to anticipate all eventualities; to be ready to die any minute."

Just then a man arrived who had been sent by Philip to summon him.

"Alexander," said his father, "I've called you here to confide my plans to you. Tomorrow we engage in the great battle. Our opponents are as brave as we are and there are more of them, so if we want to win we shall have to use a bit of cunning."

"I'm listening, father."

"Do you know how our opponents are arrayed for battle?"

"I do," said Alexander. "I sent out spies. On the left flank, ten thousand Athenians and six hundred cavalry. In the center, nine thousand foot soldiers and six hundred cavalry from the small allied states, and another five thousand mercenaries. On the right flank toward the Cephisos, the Theban phalanxes, twelve thousand foot and eight hundred cavalry. The renowned Sacred Company, the three hundred select youths, will also be fighting alongside them."

Philip listened to his son with admiration. "Your information, Alexander, is more accurate than mine. You have better spies."

Alexander smiled. "Your plan, father?"

"Hear me: You will be in battle formation with your cavalry opposite the Thebans. I, with the best of the phalanxes, will be opposite the Athenians. As soon as the battle starts, I will pretend that I'm retreating and the Athenians will advance to pursue me. At this point you will hurl yourself at the Thebans with all your might. You'll break their line, they'll scatter, and then, when the Athenians are good and tired from chasing me, I will begin the attack. Agreed?"

Alexander thought for a while. "Agreed," he answered at last. "The plan strikes me as clever and daring."

"On with it then! Go and prepare, and may the God of Greece be with us!"

26

And indeed, the God of Greece was with them.

The great battle dawned. With a mighty shout the Athenians led the charge:

"Out! Out with the Macedonian!"

Philip, following his cunning scheme, ordered his men to retreat slowly and the Athenians, taking courage, chased after them, panting to catch up. Philip watched them with his wily eye, laughing to himself. "Athenians, poor things, don't know how to win."

Meanwhile, Alexander charged with Bucephalas into the Thebans. The collision was fierce. The Thebans fought back with formidable valor, most valiant of all the three hundred who made up the Sacred Company. These warriors always fought on foot and had taken an oath to die but never retreat. They died, thus, to a man, under the force of Alexander's thrust, and the remaining Thebans, unable to hold their ground, yielded and began to disperse.

Philip saw, and promptly ordered a counterattack. The stunned Athenians, exhausted from the chase, looked around, saw the Thebans in flight, and, giving in to panic themselves, broke and ran.

With the Thebans routed, Alexander turned at once to attack the center. As he charged at them from the left, Philip drove at them from the right, and before long the center collapsed and took to flight. Spurring his horse, Philip sped after them, hot on their tail, when suddenly his horse riding rampant tripped over a rock and Philip was flung to the ground. Alone among the enemy, his back against a rock, Philip fought to fend them off, but they outnumbered him and he was in great peril. From his mount on Bucephalas Alexander saw, and wheeling around, his comrades close on his heels, he streaked to the aid of the King and scattered the enemy. Philip was saved.

"I gave you life once," said the King, grasping his son's hand, "and you gave it to me twice; twice you've saved my life until now."

"Let's not lose time, Father!" interrupted Alexander, "mount your horse and let our phalangites see you so they don't think you've been killed. After them!" And they thrust forward again in pursuit of the Athenians.

But suddenly Philip stopped his horse. He turned to Alexander galloping beside him. "Alexander, look!"

There in the distance behind a rock where he was caught by his chiton was a fleeing Athenian waving his arms and calling for help.

Alexander stared at the panic-striken deserter.

"Do you recognize him?" said Philip.

"It's Demosthenes!" cried Alexander in astonishment.

Philip laughed and spurred his horse.

"Demosthenes! Demosthenes, dear friend!" he called, "Wait!"

But Demosthenes was out of hearing range. Wrenching himself free of the rocks, he turned for an instant to look back. He could see the Macedonians gaining on him. They would take him prisoner. What should he do? Flinging away his shield the better to run unencumbered, he began fleeing again in his torn chiton, running head over heels.

Philip burst out laughing. "Pick up his shield," he ordered a soldier, "and give it to me after the battle. I'll send it to him as a gift so that he will remember me."

The sun set at last and Philip gave orders to his army to halt. "Enough!" he said. "They're not our enemies to be exterminated; they're our brothers. They've been punished enough!"

They camped along the shores of the river. Philip laid out sumptuous tables and sat down to eat and drink with his friends in celebration of the victory.

Alexander stretched out wearily in his tent. "Stephan," he called, "bring me my mantle."

Stephan hastened to bring it. Alexander took out a cylinder made of soft leather and unrolled it. It was covered with tiny letters. "Do you know what this is?"

"Yes," said Stephan, who had often seen the prince reading it.

"What is it?"

"Homer."

"That's right. My teacher Aristotle gave it to me and I will never part with it. Come, sit on that stool now and read to me."

Stephan sat on the stool and began to read aloud the verses from Homer. Alexander closed his eyes, contented, and before long fell asleep.

27

Philip was now lord of Greece.

"We must punish our enemies without mercy," his brave general Attalos said to him, "so that they will never rear their heads again."

"Hear! Hear!" shouted the other generals.

"What enemies?" asked Philip, nailing his shrewd eye on them.

"Why the Thebans...the Athenians...the Peloponnesians..."

"You consider them our enemies? Are you forgetting that we're Greeks?"

They all fell silent, shamed.

Alexander listened and marvelled at his father. A great mind who could see far, envisioning all Greece united in one undivided kingdom, bonded in brotherhood and invincible...

"My father," he realized, "has begun the grand design; I will complete it. My father is bringing peace to all Greece and uniting her; I will become her commander and will transmit her light to all the inhabited earth!"

"I will punish only the Thebans," said Philip, an angry glint in his eye. "They were my allies and they betrayed me. Traitors should be punished without mercy."

Philip kept his word and punished the Thebans. He sold into slavery all those he had taken prisoner, banished the Theban nobles, supplanting them with his friends, and placed a guard around their acropolis Cadmea.

Toward the Athenians, however, he showed clemency. "Do not fear," he told them. "I will not tamper with your liberty. Athens is the pride of the world, the mother of beauty and wisdom. I love her and respect her, and even my greatest enemy, Demosthenes, will receive a gift from me because he is an Athenian. To him I return the shield he dropped while running from battle!"

He crossed the Isthmus and marched into Peloponnesos. City after city sent their ambassadors beseeching him not to harm them.

"Peace! Peace!" his message went out. "I have no intention of subjugating Greece. I want to bring her peace. Have no fear!"

Sparta alone remained neutral, neither fighting Philip nor acknowledging him as leader.

Arriving at Sparta, Philip asked her to acknowledge him commander, but the Spartans answered him with mockery. "If you think you're any bigger now because you've won, measure your shadow," they jeered.

Philip sent them envoys again. "At least let me enter Sparta as a guest."

"No!" was the Spartan response.

"I'll exterminate you!" threatened Philip.

"Do what you can," the Spartans answered. "No matter what you do, you will never be able to stop us from dying for our country."

"Heaven help you," Philip warned, "if I conquer Sparta."

And ever so laconically the Spartans replied:

"If!"

Philip laughed.

"Sparta is a faded grande dame," he said, "a snobbish has-been. Her powers are gone, but she has hung on to her pride. Let her be."

And he went away without touching her.

His sojourn through Greece continued for a year. He went everywhere, preaching his doctrine: "Peace! Peace! We are all Greeks. Let us stop fighting amongst ourselves!"

Summer passed into autumn again and representatives from every part of Greece arrived in Corinth to attend the Panhellenic Congress.

When he was marching through the city-states, Philip had announced that he would tell them at this Congress of an important decision of his that would give Greece back her former glory. And now representatives from all over Greece, except Sparta, had come to Corinth to hear him. Crowned with the gold laurel wreath that the Athenians had given him, Philip rose to speak:

"Brother Greeks! This is a great day! For the first time all the city-states of Greece are united and at peace. For the first time the frontiers of our country are expanding and are no longer confined to the walls of Athens or Sparta or any other city. They are broadening and reach as far as the sea at one end, and as far as the high, snowy mountains of Macedonia at the other. From this day forward, Peloponnesos, mainland Greece, the Islands, Thessaly, Epiros, Macedonia, Thrace, should be the country of each of us. Let us not say, 'I am an Athenian or I am a Corinthian or I am a Macedonian.' Instead, let's all say, 'I am a Greek.' Nothing more."

This is how Philip began his speech and everyone listened intrigued by these novel words. They all listened and understanding began to illumine their minds and broaden their hearts.

"Behold what I propose," continued Philip. "Three things: Peace, Liberty, Alliance. All city-states are to declare peace with one another; all city-states are to be free; all are to ally themselves with me in the Grand Design."

"What design?" asked the prudent representative of Athens, General Phocion.

"The design to liberate the Greeks who are still under the Persian yoke in Asia Minor!"

And the representatives of Greece all rose to their feet, then put out their hands and shouted: "Long live Philip, the Commander-in-Chief of the Greeks!"

28

Philip had set out from Macedonia to fight the Greeks, and now he was returning as Commander-in-Chief of the Greeks! He could hardly contain himself for joy. The wounds that covered his body were forgotten. He no longer was aware of the pain in his injured foot. He was young again.

As he was riding into Pella, his eye spotted a young woman at the Palace, a niece of General Attalos. Her name was Cleopatra. She was very beautiful and Philip fell in love with her.

"Attalos," he said to his general, "I want to marry your niece Cleopatra."

In those days men were allowed to have many wives.

"I will bring my niece and you can speak to her yourself," Attalos replied.

Cleopatra came. She was tall and golden-haired, with blue eyes and crimson cheeks. Intelligent, too, and ambitious and proud.

"Will you be my wife?" Philip asked her.

"You have Olympias," the young woman answered.

"I also have a right to take another wife."

"But you don't have the right to have two queens."

"No."

"Then divorce Olympias and make me queen. I am a genuine Macedonian, from a royal race, and I am younger and more beautiful than Olympias."

"I will think about it," said Philip.

The news that his father was thinking of divorcing Olympias and making another woman queen reached Alexander. We know how much he loved his mother. He hastened now to find Philip.

"Father," he said, trying to control his agitation, "father, I've heard that . . ."

"Silence!" interrupted Philip. "I know what you want to tell me!"

"Is it true?"

"I don't have to give an accounting to anyone!"

"But I'm your first-born son, I'm your heir to the throne, I have rights, too. If you take a new wife and sire other sons, think of the terrible danger! All those sons will some day kill one another fighting to see who will take over the kingdom."

Philip smiled sardonically. "Aren't you glad," he said "that I shall be giving you an opportunity to beat them all and gain the throne with your own sword!"

Alexander could see that this conversation was getting them nowhere. "Think carefully, father, before you decide," he said, and left with trepidation.

Philip grew angry.

"Imagine!" he fumed at Attalos, "a seventeen-year-old youth, and he has the impudence to give me advice. That settles it. I'm going to divorce Olympias and make your niece my queen!"

"When?" asked Attalos eagerly.

"Tomorrow!"

The next day the stunned capital learned that the King was going to marry another queen, and that same evening the wedding was celebrated in the Palace with great pomp.

All the generals and Philip's friends, the "Companions," were present. Alexander came, too, pale and silent. They laid out the tables, brought in sumptuous food and wine, and the banquet began.

As was his custom Philip drank copiously and got drunk, as did Attalos, the bride's uncle. Alexander sat in a corner, neither drinking nor eating.

Attalos rose to his feet holding a brimming wine cup in his hand. He could hardly stand for the wobbling.

"I drink to the health of the groom and bride," he slurred. "May the gods grant that they have a son, a legitimate heir to the throne."

Now when Alexander heard these words he sprang from his corner, his eyes flashing fire.

"Idiot!" he roared. "What do you take ME for, a bastard?" and grabbing a cup full of wine he hurled it at him.

Attalos ducked and it missed, and grabbing a cup of his own he threw it back at Alexander. Everyone sprang to their feet and ran to the two men, some to Alexander, others to Attalos, to quiet them. Philip, too, got up in a rage, roaring drunk and hardly able to stagger. He lunged for Alexander at the other table to strike him, stumbled, his knees buckled, and he fell in the puddle of spilled wine and broken wine cups.

Alexander laughed sarcastically.

"Look at him," he shouted, turning to the guests. "Admire him! The man who wants to go from Europe to Asia and can't even transport himself from one table to the next." And with that he strode out of the banquet slamming the door behind him.

At his mother's where he went directly, he found Olympias sitting on the floor, her hair disheveled and her eyes swollen from crying.

"Mother," he said, "we're leaving."

"Leaving? Where can we go?"

"To your brother Alexandros, the King of Epiros. We can no longer live here." And he described what had happened at the banquet.

"Are we going alone? He'll pursue us!"

"I'll take my faithful friends with me. We'll leave in secret."

"When?"

"Tonight. At once. Get ready."

Olympias sprang to her feet, determined. "I'll be ready," she said. "Run and collect your friends."

Alexander wrapped his mantle around him carefully, hiding as much of his face as he could, and slipped out of the Palace. Swiftly he made the rounds in the narrow streets, knocking softly on the doors of his friends.

"We're leaving!" he told them. "Take up your arms and follow me!"

By midnight all his friends had furtively gathered in the dark outside the Palace—Hephaistion, Crateros, Perdiccas, Philotas, Nicanor, Ptolemy, Cleitos. All were there waiting. Alexander stole back into the Palace now to get his mother, stopping first in his room to put on his armor and pick up his inseparable companion, Homer. As he was passing the adjoining room, he remembered his young attaché, Stephan. "I'll take him along, too," he thought. "I like him and wouldn't want to part from him," and bending over Stephan's cot where our small friend was sleeping soundly, Alexan-ing he was mounted on a white horse and galloping behind Alexander through wild mountains, he nudged him gently by the shoulder. "Stephan!" he called softly.

Stephan gave a start.

"Get up!" whispered Alexander. "Dress yourself quickly and come with me!"

"At your command, my prince," and Stephan was dressed in a flash.

"Come!"

They went into Olympias' room. His mother was ready and stood waiting, clutching a small ivory statue of Dionysos to her bosom. She was never without it.

"Ready, mother?"

"Ready!"

They descended the stairs stealthily. Light glowed through the open windows of the banquet hall and they could hear the hoarse singing of the drunks.

Outside they headed for the stables. Alexander released Bucephalas and the best of the horses for his companions and soon the small company was galloping across the fields outside the capital.

It was two past midnight. The stars glittered in the sky, the wind blew cold in the deep night.

"Wrap yourself tightly, mother," Alexander called to Olympias, "don't get chilled."

They galloped and galloped and were well up the mountainside when the first rays of dawn began to appear. The sun came up, a brilliant red alongside the morning star that was still glittering in the east.

Alexander turned and looked behind him, down at the big white road in the plain below. No one! Philip had not sent anyone to pursue him. He spurred his horse and they continued to race toward Epiros.

29

It was dawn when Philip staggered to bed to sleep off his drunkenness and already approaching noon when he wakened at last. He sat up in bed trying to remember, and dimly the scene from last night's banquet began to come back to him. He felt shame.

"I behaved badly," he murmured. "I shouldn't have drunk so much wine. What shame! Alexander was right. I must summon him and ask his pardon."

He clapped his hands. A servant entered.

"Go and call Alexander," he said. "I want to see him."

The servant left and returned at once. He looked shaken.

"What is it?" asked Philip noting the servant's fright.

"My King," stammered the wretched man, "...Alexander..."

"Speak up! What is it?"

"Alexander is gone!"

"Gone! Where did he go?" Philip sprang out of bed.

"No one knows..."

"Alone?"

"No, his mother's gone, too."

"The two of them?"

"I don't know. About ten horses are missing from the stables. The whole city's in turmoil."

"Very well. Go now."

Philip dressed hastily. He went to the window. "He's right," he muttered. "I behaved badly." He looked out toward the harbor. Ships were coming in with their cargo; others were leaving with theirs. He realized how wealthy his kingdom had become, how powerful. Beyond, along the shores of the harbor lay his huge shipyards where myriad ships were unloading the timber that Nearchos was sending him for the new fleet.

"I'm Commander-in-Chief of all the Greeks," he thought, "I've imposed discipline on all Greece and yet I have not been able to impose it on myself. What shame!"

Wearily he sat on a throne. "Where could they be going?" he wondered. Suddenly he jumped to his feet. "They're going to Epiros!" he cried aloud, "They're going to King Alexandros to ask for refuge there!" For an instant his mind flashed with anger. "I'll send horsemen," he muttered. "I'll send all my calvary to capture them and bring them back," and he ran to the door to give orders. But there he checked himself. "No," he realized, "Alexander's right."

He leaned against the window again, engrossed in his thoughts. So absorbed in his reflections was he that he didn't notice the door open softly and an officer come in.

"King," said he.

Philip didn't hear.

"King," the officer repeated louder.

Philip turned. "What is it?"

"A friend of yours has arrived from Corinth and is asking to see you."

"What's his name?"

"Demaratos."

"Demaratos!" exclaimed Philip. "Let him in at once!"

A tall, elderly man with a venerable countenance entered.

"Dear friend," said Philip opening his arms. He made Demaratos sit near him. "What news do you bring from Greece? Do peace and harmony reign at last down there?"

Demaratos shook his head. "Why do you ask about peace and harmony, O Philip, when turmoil and discord reign in your own house?"

Philip lowered his head. For a while the two men were silent. A battle was raging in Philip's soul. "You're right, Demaratos," he said at last, raising his head and taking his friend's hand. "Do me a favor."

"I am at your command, my King. Speak."

"I will give you an escort of cavalry. Go to the Palace at Epiros and, here, take my royal ring and give it to my son Alexander. Ask him to come back."

"With his mother?"

"With his mother," said Philip in a low, humbled voice.

Demaratos stood up. "You have made a brave decision, Philip. I shall leave at once. In a few days your son and his mother will be here." He smiled. "And then, O King, you will have the right to ask if peace and harmony reign in Greece."

30

Demaratos was successful in his mission.

In a few days the city's populace were spilling out into the streets waving laurel branches and myrtle to welcome their beloved prince who was returning from Epiros.

It was morning. The stone-paved thoroughfares of Pella reverberated with the clang of horses' hooves as Alexander rode in on Bucephalas, his mother Olympias beside him, and his faithful companions and Stephan riding up behind. Stephan had grown. He had become a handsome, sun-bronzed youth and no longer rode a pony, but a tall white horse given him by Alexander.

Philip was standing erect between the two wooden columns at the entrance of the Palace to welcome them. He embraced his son joyously and spoke: "May peace and harmony reign in our Palace from this day forward," he said. "I acted badly, and I regret it."

Then he turned to Olympias. "Let our two royal houses, that of Macedonia and that of Epiros, be united in bonds of love. I have a proposal to make to you that I hope will please you."

"Let me hear it," said the queen, her voice severe.

"Our daughter Cleopatra is grown and of marriageable age. I am thinking of giving her in marriage to your brother Alexandros, the King of Epiros. Will you agree?"

"If that should come to be," answered Olympias, "then peace will reign between us."

At once Philip sent envoys to Epiros with a letter summoning Alexandros. "Come immediately to the capital, dear Alexandros," he wrote, "to attend the ceremony of your marriage to my daughter Cleopatra. Our two royal houses will become one." When the answer came back from the King of Epiros who wrote that he was fortunate to be taking the daughter of Philip for his wife and that he would, indeed, be coming to the Macedonian capital for the wedding, Philip joyfully notified all the Greek states to send their representatives for the great event. He was impatient to become reconciled with all his enemies and to put all his affairs in order in Macedonia because he had made up his mind that the following spring he would set out with his army and the armies of all the Hellenes to liberate the Greeks in Asia Minor. All was going well. Philip's dream was nearing its fulfillment.

The wedding rites were to be performed in Edessa, the ancient capital of Macedonia. They were to be unsurpassed in magnificence, accompanied with splendid festivities and preceded before all else by the offering of rich sacrifices to the gods. The leading actors from Athens were invited to perform the tragedies of Aeschylos and Sophocles and Euripides, as well as the comedies of Aristophanes. The best athletes were invited, too, to compete in wrestling and running, and Philip ordered costly kingly prizes for the victors.

By August Edessa was teeming with distinguished visitors. Ambassadors were arriving from all over Greece and the seacoasts of Asia Minor, bringing lavish gifts for the groom and bride and King Philip.

Messengers, too, arrived from Delphi. Philip had sent to the Oracle of Delphi to ask Apollo if his expedition against the Persians would be successful. He listened now to the Oracle's prophecy. What did it mean? As was customary with the Oracle, the message was obscure and no one understood exactly what it meant. "Repeat the Oracle's message to me," Philip commanded the messengers.

"The bull is crowned; his end is approaching; the priest who will slaughter him is ready," they said.

"Who is the bull?" wondered the King uneasily. "Who is the priest?"

Suddenly calamitous forebodings began to weigh on his heart, forebodings that would have grown worse had he known what was going on in secret at a certain lordly house not far from the Palace.

In that house lived a young noble, a most handsome bodyguard of King Philip's. His name was Pausanias. Once General Attalos, the uncle of the new queen, had uttered a deadly insult against him, and Pausanias had gone to the King to demand justice but Philip, who favored Attalos, only laughed. "It serves you right," he had said. And from that day on Pausanias had only one purpose in his life—to take revenge on Philip who had acted so unjustly toward him. "I'll kill him!" he told his friends. "I cannot live dishonored."

Now some new Persian spies who had returned to Philip's court and were looking for a way to get rid of this dangerous king heard of Pausanias's hatred for Philip, and losing no time, they got around him, won his friendship, and encouraged him to carry out his plan. "Kill him," they urged. "Have no fear. We'll have horses ready for you and a ship for you to escape. And the Great King will give you his daughter for your wife."

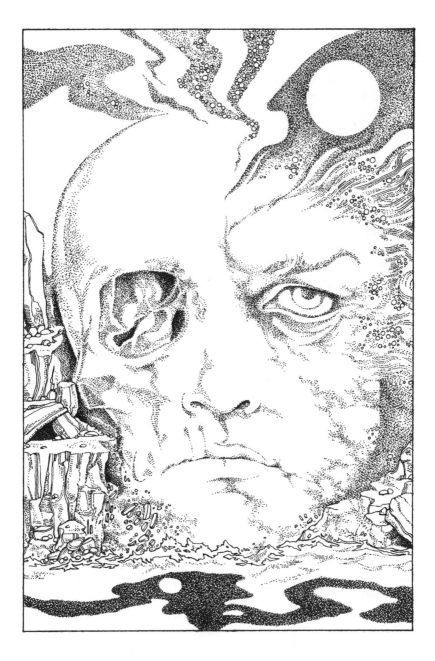

When the day arrived for Philip's daughter to wed, Pausanias had made up his mind. "I'll kill him," he said, "and let come what may!"

The day of the wedding dawned. The huge amphitheater overflowed with people. Twelve splendid statues of the gods had been set up at its entrance, and at the end they brought in a thirteenth— a statue of King Philip.

The sun was up, the trumpets blared, the audience rose to its feet; the royal entourage was entering the amphitheater.

In the lead, handsome and solemn, with a golden wreath in his golden hair, came the heir apparent, Alexander, and at his side walked the groom, the King of Epiros.

Behind them, alone, dressed all in white, came King Philip.

Cheers were tearing through the amphitheater, shaking the very ground beneath it. Philip paused, profoundly stirred. This was the most beautiful moment of his life. He had completed the first phase of his great ambition: the unifying of all the Greeks under his leadership. And now he was about to embark on the second phase: the crossing of the Hellespont to liberate the Greeks in Asia. He felt triumphant and fortunate, like a god, indeed so much so that he had ordered his own statue placed alongside the twelve gods.

"I'm blessed," he exulted.

Just then something horrifying happened. A youth sprang in front of him. It was Pausanias. And before anyone could stop him, he raised his sword and plunged it into the King's heart.

Philip fell dead.

31

When the dreadful news reached the capital, the people shut themselves inside their houses in the grip of fear. What would happen now? For years they had seen the bloodshed that came with every change of Kings. The ambitious gloryseekers would all rush in to grab the power, killing everyone who stood in their way.

Stephan, who had been at the scene of the murder and witnessed it at close range with the other courtiers, had returned with them now to the capital and was sitting in his father's house describing the terrible spectacle.

The neighbors, too, came hurrying over to hear what he had to say, among the first, Kyra Melpo, the wife of Captain Nearchos, and her daughter.

How Alka had grown! And how pretty she had become. Olive-skinned, with long black hair, and such a proud bearing about her. There was none of her former playful familiarity, none of the former laughter as she greeted Stephan now with dignified formality and stood to one side, a young lady, shy in his presence.

Alka's three friends arrived, too—Cleo, Iphigenia, and Eleni. They, like everyone else, were anxious to hear what had happened at the great festivals of Edessa, and how exactly the King had been slain. But more than anything, they were eager to see Stephan. They had heard he had grown into a handsome young man and had seen so many wonderful things while serving Alexander.

The three girls entered in great high spirits, their laughing banter quickly turning sober at sight of him. "O, indeed, what a man he had become!" and they hurriedly edged their way toward the corner where Alka stood.

Stephan's faithful friends Hermalaos and Leonidas came, too. They hadn't seen him in a long time and sorely missed him. Leonidas had become a first-rate athlete and Hermolaos was enlisted in the "Royal Cadets," a military school that would make an officer of him.

Kyra Elpinice had lit the brazier on this cold autumn day and the guests were all seated around it warming themselves. She brought out some chick peas, too, which they put on the ashes to roast and now as Stephan began to narrate the event, the guests listened and munched on the roasted chick peas.

When Stephan finished, Kyra Elpinice sighed. "What's going to happen now?" she queried.

"Alexander is going to ascend the throne and then we're going to Asia," answered Stephan, his voice ringing with certainty.

"What do we want with Asia, my boy?" exclaimed Kyra Elpinice. "Isn't our country enough for us? I'm queen of my humble house here and have no desire to go beyond my doorstep."

The three boys laughed. "We're men!" declared Leonidas, "and our country isn't big enough to hold us."

"...and if we don't go to Asia," joined in Hermolaos in a comically tragic voice, "I'll smother here!"

85

Shouts resounded in the street, cheers and the clanging of horses' hooves, and the boys raced out to the yard. They flung open the gate and joined in the cheers.

Alexander had just emerged from the Palace and was touring the city greeting his people.

"Long live Alexander!" they shouted raising their arms high in salute.

"Stephan," exclaimed Leonidas, "you're not out there with him. He'll be angry with you."

"He gave me the day off to see my family," said Stephan, "...and to see my dear little neighbor," he added with a smile at Alka as they strolled back to the house.

Alka blushed and lowered her eyes. Stephan burst out laughing. "Hey, what's happened to the little tomboy who was always yelling at me and making fun of me? Now she doesn't even raise her eyes to look at me!"

The three girl friends were watching Alka and laughing. "Don't worry, Stephan," called Cleo, "when you leave we'll start making fun of you again!"

The two mothers, Kyra Melpo and Kyra Elpinice, were sitting near the brazier talking in low voices and chewing on the chick peas. "And how's your husband, Kyra Melpo?" the mistress of the house was asking.

"What can I tell you, my dear Kyra Elpinice. He's still chopping down wood, levelling the forests one after the other, and building ships...to do what? Alas, my dear Kyra Elpinice, it's the end of the world!"

"You mean the beginning of the world Captainess," laughed Leonidas whose ear had picked up her words. "A new era's beginning; the old one's gone, closed. It's no longer a world of little villages and microscopic cities and petty family squabbles. It's broadened. All Greece is united now. Macedonia and Greece are all one kingdom. Do you know how far our frontiers reach?"

The captain's wife shook her head but didn't answer.

Cleo laughed. Leonidas turned on her. "And why is the niece of the noble Black Cleitos laughing?"

"Don't call him *Black*!" bristled Cleo. "I don't like it!"

86 "Don't get mad, Cleo," said Stephan, "that's what Alexander calls him, too."

Leonidas moved closer to Cleo. "Why are you laughing?" he persisted. "Do you know where our frontiers reach now?"

"I do," offered the fair Iphigenia.

"Okay, let's hear and we'll see."

"On the one side along the north we have a big river, I don't know what it's called..."

"The Danube," said Stephan. "I've seen it. It's as big as an ocean."

"...and on the other side we have the Peloponnesos and Crete."

"My homeland!" broke in Alka with pride, opening her mouth for the first time.

"And then...to the west?" pressed Leonidas.

"We have Epiros and Corcyra."

"And eastward?"

"The Bosphoros and the Hellespont."

"I'm smothering!" shouted Hermolaos with tragic-comic theatrics again. "You call those frontiers? You call this a kingdom? It can't hold us, I tell you. We'll all be smothered!"

"Look who's aping Alexander," giggled Cleo. "Monkey sees, monkey does!"

Everyone laughed. Hermolaos glowered.

"It's not your fault, it's mine for sitting here talking with women," he muttered. "You'd do well, my girl, to get back in your corner with your spinning and not talk so much."

Just then Kyra Elpinice came in with a tray of glasses and a pitcher of dark wine.

"Come," she said, "drink a little wine to warm yourselves, and stop quarreling. Make up, my children. Drink to the health of our new King. Long may he live!"

"To Alexander's health!" shouted Stephan raising his glass. "And one day may he be called Alexander the Great!"

"To his health! To his health!" they all shouted rising to their feet.

"And to Asia, with Godspeed!" added Hermolaos. "To the capital of the Persian King!"

"What do they call his capital?" Kyra Melpo asked.

"I don't know," shrugged Hermolaos. "But don't worry. We'll find out."

87

The Pythia

32

"Alexander, my boy," Olympias was saying to her son, "the road has opened, you have become King, you have a great responsibility now. When are you going to set out for Asia?"

"I must strengthen my position in Europe first," Alexander answered.

"Aren't you firmly established?"

"Not yet. The barbarians are rising in revolt again, the Greeks are beginning to ally themselves against me, and General Attalos, with part of the army, doesn't want to recognize me as King. I must bring them in line." Alexander's voice was resolute. He kissed his mother's hand and hurried out.

Mustering an army of foot and cavalry, Alexander set out without delay to attack the barbarians, the first of his priorities. Once again he cut through the forests, climbed the snow-filled mountains, and fell upon the wild tribes that dwelled there, subduing them all the way to the Danube.

Next he turned his sights on Greece. He marched past the foothills of Olympos, entered Thessaly, crossed the Vale of

Tempe, climbed the narrow footpaths of Ossa, marched into Phthiotis and Phocis, and finally reached Boeotia.

"I will punish the Thebans harshly for rising up against me," he said, "so that all the Greeks will see who I am." And pouncing on the Theban army like lions, the Macedonians routed them completely.

Alexander entered Thebes. "Raze it," he ordered. "But don't touch the temples of the gods and the house where the great poet Pindar lived." Eight thousand Thebans were sold into slavery; the others scattered and fled. Thebes disappeared. Thebes, which just a few years ago when Epaminondas and Pelopidas were alive, had conquered Greece and humbled Sparta, now lay in rubble.

Fear gripped the Greek states. All sent their envoys to Alexander. "We're yours," they told him, "friends and allies."

Next Alexander crossed the Isthmus and marched into Corinth. There deputies from all of Greece except Sparta proclaimed him Commander-in-Chief of the Hellenes.

Here in Corinth Alexander met the famed cynic philosopher Diogenes. What had he not heard about him! He was the man who had once taken a lit lantern in broad daylight and gone out searching the streets. "What are you looking for?" people would ask him. "A man!" he would answer.

Diogenes had been born in the city of Sinop along the Black Sea and because he had insulted the archons of the city they had sentenced him to be banished. "I, too, sentence you to live in Sinop!" he had answered them, and picking up his walking stick had left.

He wandered from city to city, half naked and fierce, and by the time he arrived in Corinth he was already eighty years old.

"I want to see Diogenes the philosopher," said Alexander. "Where does he live?"

"In an earthen barrel," they laughed, directing him to a garden where Diogenes was lying outside his barrel sunning himself.

Alexander approached. "I am Alexander, the King of Macedonia," the young monarch announced proudly.

"And I am the philosopher Diogenes, the Dog."

"Ask me any favor and I will grant it," said Alexander magnanimously.

"Move a bit and let me get the sun," Diogenes answered. And as his Companions laughed at Diogenes, Alexander shook his head. 89 "If I were not Alexander," he said, "I would want to be Diogenes!"

Alexander returned to Macedonia in great haste, stopping along the way at the famous Oracle of Delphi. There he went into the temple and summoned the Pythia.

"I want you to mount the tripod at once," he told her, "and prophesy whether my campaign against the Persians will succeed."

"My King, it is impossible," replied the Pythia. "I cannot do it immediately. I must pray and fast for three days before I mount the prophetic tripod."

"Immediately!" commanded Alexander, grabbing her by the hair and setting her on the tripod.

The Pythia smiled then. "You are invincible, my son!" she said.

Alexander was pleased. "I want nothing more. The words you have just uttered are enough." And heaping lavish gifts upon her, he left.

When he arrived in Macedonia, winter had set in.

"The great Asiatic campaign will begin in the spring," he said to his two elderly generals, Antipatros and Parmenion.

"May the gods grant that you fulfill the goals of your father," said old General Parmenion.

Alexander lifted his head high. "My father," he declared, "only wanted to conquer Asia Minor, to liberate the Greeks who are under the Persian yoke. This goal is not enough for me. I want to pierce the depths of Asia, to liberate not only the Greeks, but the barbarians themselves. Do you understand now, my general, the difference between a Philip and an Alexander?"

The old general did not speak. But his noble heart shuddered. Only a god could fulfill such a goal.

And Antipatros, who had not spoken until now, looked at Alexander. "With what army?" he asked.

"With all the Greeks that I will muster," said Alexander.

"And how many do you figure on? Bear in mind that you will also have to leave an army behind in Macedonia, to protect your throne."

"Thirty, forty thousand," replied Alexander.

"And how many men can the Great King of Persia enlist? Do you know?"

"Millions," answered Alexander.

"Well?"

Alexander laughed. "All that you say, my prudent brave general, is correct. If I were to consult only my logic I would never undertake such a war. But I don't consult it."

"What do you consult then?"

"My soul," answered Alexander.

"It's madness! Sheer madness!" thought Antipatros.

"Madness! Sheer madness!" thought Parmenion.

But Alexander believed, and he knew that belief creates miracles. "I will win," he said to himself. "I believe and I will win!"

33

Great preparations. Every day new recruits were arriving from the provinces. The barbarians, too, were rushing to enlist.

The Thracians had sent Sitalces as their chief, the man we saw earlier attempting to mount Bucephalas. Another tribe, the Agrianes, sent fierce lancers. Many Greek cities sent armies. The Athenians sent a fleet; Thessaly, her finest horsemen; from Crete came that island's famous archers, along with Clearhos their chief, a true giant with a black curly beard.

In the gold mines of Pangaion,[12] laborers were digging deep in the earth to excavate precious metal. Alexander sent thousands more to dig. Such a campaign needed a great deal of gold.

One day he turned to Stephan. "Do you want to come with me?" he asked.

Our friend's eyes sparkled. "Yes!" he replied.

"Think of the dangers. We may never return to our country."

"Then we won't return," said Stephan.

"You may never see your parents again," persisted Alexander testing him. "Don't you love your father and your mother?"

"I do," murmured Stephan, his eyes misting. "I love them, but I must go."

Alexander put out his hand and stroked Stephan's hair.

"How old are you?"

"Almost fifteen."

"Ah, you're a man then!" he exclaimed laughing. "I'll take you with me!"

Stephan's heart bounded. "Thank you, my King!"

"We leave this coming spring. Prepare yourself."

Alexander ordered Bucephalas brought to him so that he 91 could go out to the shipyards to inspect his fleet.

Stephan hurried to find his two good friends Leonidas and Hermolaos. It was winter now and cold, and Stephan walked briskly. He arrived at Leonidas's house and knocked. Leonidas came out.

"What's up?" he cried at sight of Stephan's beaming face.

"I'm going away!"

"Away! Where?"

"With Alexander."

"When?"

"In the spring...this coming spring."

Leonidas was silent. How he wished he could go, too. "I want to come with you," he said, grasping Stephan's arm, "and let's take Hermolaos, too. Let's not break up!" His voice was choked with feeling; in this iron athletic body was a very tender heart.

"That's just what I came to see you about," laughed Stephan, "to get all three of us to leave together. I'll speak to the King."

"I'll run and get Hermolaos right away!" shouted Leonidas, fairly sputtering with joy and gratitude.

"You can try," said Stephan, "but I'm afraid he won't want to come."

"Why not?"

"He'll never pry himself away from his teacher. I hear he's become a student of Callisthenes' and follows him around learning philosophy and wine-drinking. His nose, they tell me, is already turning red."

Leonidas laughed. "We'll see about that. I'll go right over. So long, now."

"So long."

Stephan continued on his way, basking in the joy he had just shared with his friend. As he was walking briskly along the narrow street, a mocking voice rang out behind him.

"Hey, there! Bon voyage and swift winds in your sails! Where are you headed?"

Stephan turned. Emerging from the door of a tavern was his fat, unkempt old acquaintance Callisthenes. Stephan didn't like this man at all. He was always blustering and poking fun at things. "I'm in a hurry," he called to him as he made to continue on his way.

"Wait, I have something to tell you!" shouted the old philosopher.

What could he do? Stephan waited.

"Have you heard the news?" Callisthenes panted as he approached. "Have you heard? I'm going away with Alexander."

His breath smelled of wine and Stephan pulled back a step. "You? To do what?"

"To do what!" sputtered the philosopher banging his walking stick against the stones. "To do what? Why, without me your Alexander would be lost!"

"You exaggerate, my respected philosopher," Stephan laughed. "He'll be lost?"

"Most certainly. He'll be lost. Who will know him after one or two hundred years? I, though, will save him!"

"How?"

"Like this: I'll follow him wherever he goes. I'll witness whatever he does, how he fights, what he says, and I'll write it all down. I'll write the history of Alexander. Do you understand? So that when Alexander dies, my work will remain, and even if a thousand years go by, men will know what Alexander was."

Stephan was silent. Callisthenes was lording it now.

"You see?" he cried. "Do you see now? I'm not going to Asia to be glorified; I'm going there to glorify! Let's go back to the tavern now," he urged, "Hermolaos is with me. It's cold out here. I'll treat you to a glass of wine."

"I don't drink," said Stephan, "and besides, I'm in a hurry."

"All right, be on your way," said the philosopher. "And listen, if you go off with Alexander, too, I'll write something about you as well. To save you, too, poor boy...to save you, too." And giving him a fatherly pat on the shoulder he shuffled back to the tavern.

And so the winter went in a flurry of great preparations. The cities and villages sent soldiers, the plains contributed horses, the forests gave up their trees to be made into ships and the mountains yielded their gold and their iron.

Winter passed and April came. Spring put on her embroidered green dress again with the multicolored flowers, and Alexander was ready.

"Before we leave," he said to his friends, "I will hold high celebrations to say farewell to Macedonia. Who knows if I will ever

93

see her again." Then after a pause, "To which god do you think we should dedicate these celebrations?"

"To Ares," answered Cleitos the Black. "He'll be our patron god."

"You're mistaken," said Alexander. "We're not going to Asia to kill and burn; we're going to impart Greek civilization. So we'll dedicate these splendid celebrations to the nine Muses."

"The nine Muses!" they all cried in astonishment. "This is the first time a general going off to war has ever offered sacrifices to such goddesses."

"Maybe because it's the first time a general is setting out to conquer a country with such a goal in mind," laughed Alexander.

The friends did not answer. For some time now they knew that this Alexander did not resemble any of the Kings they had ever known. He had curious aims, difficult desires that transcended the aims and desires of men. "Whatever you say is good and has our sanction!" shouted Hephaistion looking at him with unspoken devotion.

"All right, let's sacrifice to the nine Muses then," said Clearhos the Cretan. "And may they be with us throughout the campaign."

And so in the final days of April the brilliant farewell festivities began. The great amphitheater filled again with people, the young in high spirits at the prospect of going off with Alexander to take part in the great campaign, the old somber and sad that their sons and grandsons were leaving, knowing they might never see them again.

Alexander was seated on the throne. He was dressed in a white chiton bordered with silver embroidery, and on his head he wore a gold laurel wreath. Seated to his right and left were the friends, and behind him stood Stephan.

The priests offered the sacrifices that preceded the festivities, and Alexander lifted his arm:

"O Nine Muses, Calliope, Clio, Euterpe, Melpomene, Terpsichore, Erato, Polyhymnia, Urania, and Thalia, hear me! I am setting out for war. Come with me! I am undertaking this great expedition for your sake. I do not want merely to conquer bodies and cities and land. I want souls. And only you, O Muses, can help me in this difficult task. Do not abandon me. Come with me!"

He spoke, and the scent from the sacrifices rose high into the sky. The festivities lasted nine days. The first day was dedicated to

Calliope, the Muse of Epic Poetry. Renowned bards recited verses from the *Iliad* and the *Odyssey*.

The second day was dedicated to Clio, the Muse of History. At this point the philosopher Callisthenes participated, too, giving a speech in which he explained how he imagined history should be written. "What is meant by Truth?" he said. "To believe in what you see. What is meant by Myth? To believe in what you do not see. What is History? The daughter of Truth and Myth." He talked along these lines until he grew tired.

The third day was dedicated to Euterpe, the Muse of Lyric Poetry. Great artists recited the triumphal odes of Pindar, the greatest lyric poet of Greece. Alexander listened to the Pindaric odes extolling the young men who had triumphed in the games, and his heart stirred with longing. Once he had been asked why he, too, did not compete in the Olympic Games. "I would compete," he replied, "if I had kings for rivals." But to his friend Hephaistion he said one day: "I would compete if a Pindar were alive to eulogize my victory."

The fourth day was dedicated to Melpomene, the Muse of Tragedy. The finest actors had come and were performing the trilogy of Aeschylos: *Prometheus the Firebearer, Prometheus Bound,* and *Prometheus Unbound.* "I, too, am like Prometheus,"[13] reflected Alexander. "I am taking the light from Greece and bringing it to the barbarians to be enlightened."

The fifth day was dedicated to Terpsichore, the Muse of the Dance. The best dancers had come from all over Greece to dance. First they danced the wild pyrrhic dance; Clearhos and his Cretans lit the fires, then in full battle dress—breast plate, shield, and javelin—they danced in circles round the fires, letting out mighty war shouts. Then came the dances of peace. Beautiful girls, some crowned with roses and others carrying yellow ears of corn, danced the sedate *syrta* while they sang.[14]

The sixth day was for Erato, the Muse of Erotic Poetry. They recited the songs of the great poetess of the centuries, Sappho of Lesbos. Never had love been sung with such sweetness and passion, and Alexander closed his eyes and listened enthralled.

The seventh day was for the Muse of the Sacred Hymns of War. The priests, crowned with olive branches, sang the ancient hymns of the gods.

The eighth day was dedicated to Urania, the Muse of Astronomy. 95

And finally the ninth and last day, to Thalia, the Muse of Comedy.

At the close of each day Alexander gave a banquet in honor of his friends and his people and on this, the last evening, the banquet was being given in honor of his elderly general Antipatros who was to remain behind in Macedonia to represent him in his absence. Antipatros was a man of courage, prudence, and dedication; and Alexander had great confidence in him. He raised his golden wine-filled cup now to toast his health:

"Antipatros, faithful friend and comrade of my father's," he said, "to you I leave the great seal of the Nation while I am away. I will rest easy knowing that you are here in my place. Viceroy Antipatros, I drink to your health!"

Everyone rose. The symposium was over.

"Wait!" called Alexander holding out his arm. "Tomorrow we leave. Before we set out, I want to distribute all my possessions— fields, houses, clothing, jewels—to all the friends here that I'm leaving behind. I no longer have need of anything."

The guests gasped in amazement. "And what will you keep for yourself, O King?" Perdiccas dared ask.

"Hope!" answered Alexander.

"Then I, too, my King, will keep the same for myself. I will share your hope."

"And I, too! And I! And I!" echoed Alexander's friends, fired with noble passion and ashamed to appear lesser men than their leader on this momentous occasion.

And so they divided their possessions among all the friends who remained behind and prepared to set out the next day, taking with them one possession only, hope.

34

Well before dawn the next morning Stephan was in his humble home saying goodbye to his parents.

His mother stood quietly crying without a word, while Philip the physician, holding back the tears, was giving his final instructions to his son.

"Did you hear what King Alexander said last night to Old General Antipatros? He praised his three great virtues: faith, prudence and valor. Try, my son, to acquire these three virtues." He was silent for a moment, a knot catching in his throat, but quickly he conquered his emotion and continued.

"I don't know if I will ever see you again. I place my hands on your head and give you my blessing. I know you will not shame me."

At that moment in the Palace another son was taking leave of his mother. Olympias, dressed all in white, was holding her son's hand, confronting him with her level gaze.

"My son," she said, "go with my blessing. I know you will meet with terrible difficulties and undergo great dangers, but you will be victorious. I am confident of it. A great god, Ammon, whose oracle stands in the desert beyond Egypt, protects you. He has been your protector from the day you were born. Go and find him. Offer him sacrifice. Ask him about your destiny, and he will answer you. He will reveal to you the great secret of your life."

Alexander said nothing, merely bowed his head and kissed his mother's hand. He looked at her long and intently, as though taking his leave for the last time. Would he ever see her again? Then he turned toward the door and strode rapidly down the Palace halls and out into the great courtyard where his faithful friends were assembled and waiting for him.

"You're late," whispered Hephaistion.

Alexander's voice was choked and barely audible. "I was saying goodbye to my mother," he said.

Stephan, too, had just arrived. His eyes were red as though from crying. On the way he had seen Alka standing on her doorstep waiting for him to emerge from his house. In the bound that it took to cross the alley he was at her side.

"You're on your way?"

"Yes."

"Goodbye!" She was holding back her tears, trying to smile. "My father left, too," she said. "He left last night with the ships."

"I'll be back," said Stephan. "Will you wait for me?"

"I don't know..." Then after a pause, "I'll come to you!" she said, her voice resolute.

"Come! Out there!"

"My father promised to send a ship for me." She knew she

97

would not be able to hold back the tears for long. "Goodbye," she said again. "Goodbye..." and she gave him her hand.

Stephan pressed it hard. "Until we meet again," he whispered. And they parted.

At the bend of the road Stephan met his two good friends, Leonidas and Hermolaos. He had succeeded in getting Alexander to take them with him and make them officers, and they were on their way now, dressed in their armor, to take their places with the army.

"Long live Alexander!" shouted Leonidas.

"Long live liberty!" shouted Hermolaos.

Stephan clasped their hands and quickly strode away to keep them from seeing a tear that was spilling from his eye.

At the Palace courtyard King Alexander and his Companions had assembled on their mounts. Turning for a moment, Alexander paused to look back at the paternal palace. A white-clad woman was standing motionless at a window overlooking the garden. "My mother," he murmured, and waved toward the window. The woman in white opened her arms for an instant, and disappeared.

Alexander reached out then and patted Bucephalas gently on the mane. "Forward!" he said and the proud horse reared and broke into a canter. Behind surged the faithful friends, followed by Stephan astride his white horse. They rode through the streets of the capital, past the old men standing erect calling out blessings from their doorsteps along the way, past the women on the roof-tops who were waving and tossing flowers at them and calling, "Farewell! Farewell! Come back soon!"

Out in the plain the army was assembled and waiting, thirty thousand foot and five thousand cavalry. The springtime field was aglitter with brass breastplates and shields. Alexander, mounted on Bucephalas, moved in among them to inspect his troops. Two huge white wings waved from his helmet.

98   "Comrades!" he shouted in a thunderous voice. "words are superfluous now. The time has come to act! Forward!"

The shields clanged in unison and the plains echoed back. The sun was well up by now in a sky unblemished by clouds. Suddenly an eagle appeared, soaring over Alexander's head. It was clutching a huge snake in its claws.

"A good omen!" shouted the army.

Alexander lifted his head, saw it, and the two white wings on his helmet fluttered with joy.

35

May Day. The crops were swaying in green waves. To the left lay the plains of Macedonia and Thrace; to the right, the Aegean Sea. And between them, beach after beach, marched Alexander's army.

It crossed the great rivers Strymon, Evros, and Melana, and came to the Hellespont. Stretching out along the European coastline lay Sestos, with its huge harbor where Nearchos was waiting with the hundred and sixty Greek warships and the myriad commercial vessels that he had requisitioned to transport the army to Asia.

Alexander arrived with his army toward noon one day. Here he summoned Parmenion. "General," he said, "you will remain behind to oversee the crossing of the army to the Asiatic shore while I, with a few of my friends, go off not far from here to fulfill an obligation," and so saying, he went about at once collecting his closest friends to take along with him. As he was singling them out, his glance picked up young Stephan who was looking at him with pleading eyes. "You can come, too," he said to Stephan. Then catching sight of Callisthenes who lay stretched out in the sun resting his weary body, "Hey, philosopher!" he called, "you, too! Don't forget your duty. We didn't bring you here to lie in the sun and nip on that flask that you've strapped to your shoulder. Open your eyes, open your ears, look, hear, and write!"

The bright youths accompanying Alexander burst out laughing as they watched the roly-poly old philosopher drag himself huffing and puffing to his feet and shuffle after them.

"Is it far?" sighed Callisthenes.

No one answered.

"Where are we going?" asked Hephaistion, a little tired himself from the long march.

"Don't worry," Alexander reassured him, giving him his arm. "It's close by, here at Eleounta."

"What are we going to do in Eleounta?" asked Perdiccas.

"The grave of Protesilaos is there," offered the philosopher.

"He's right," said Alexander. "It's where Protesilaos is buried. He was the first of all the Achaeans to leap on the shore of Asia in the Trojan War, and the first to be killed."

Eleounta was a small village at the edge of the Hellespont Peninsula, that would have had no significance had it not been for the grave of Protesilaos. In an hour they were there. Approaching the grave reverently, Alexander called to the shade of the hero: "Greetings, O Protesilaos! After all these centuries we Greeks have returned to march against Asia. Help us to be more fortunate than you were!" And after offering sacrifice, the small company went aboard the royal ship that had been ordered to meet them at the beach nearby, and seating himself at the helm, Alexander put out to sea in the direction of the Asiatic shore on the opposite banks.

As they approached the open waters, half-way between Europe and Asia, Alexander ordered his men to slaughter a white bull that was tied to the prow of the ship and after offering sacrifice to Poseidon, the god of the sea, and to the other divinities of the seas, especially Thetis, the mother of his ancestor Achilles, he raised his golden cup and spilling a few drops of wine on the waves, threw the cup into the sea, too. "I offer it to you, ancestral goddess," he said, "to remember me by."

When they came at last to the Asiatic beach, Alexander sprang to his feet, and leaping ashore before the others, ran his lance into the ground. "I lay claim to Asia!" he shouted.

His friends, too, jumped ashore then, and last came Callisthenes, a bit unsteady. "Give me a hand, lad," he called to Stephan. "Don't let me fall."

Alexander turned to look at him. "Hey, philosopher," he called, "I know you've been here before to worship at the grave of Achilles when you were young. Come up ahead now and lead the way."

"Let's rest a bit, my King," murmured the philosopher. "The sea has made me wobbly."

"Take a swig of wine and you'll come to," said Clearhos.

"You're right, my lad! To your health!" said Callisthenes downing a long gulp from his flask.

"How do you feel now?" laughed Ptolemy.

"A little better, I think. Let's go," and getting to his feet from where he had collapsed on the ground, he picked up his cane and the whole company set out.

They climbed a hill, went down through a small ravine, then up another hill again.

Callisthenes stopped.

"What's the matter now?" said Alexander sternly. "Why are you stopping?"

"An idea occurred to me, my King," answered the philosopher scratching his head.

"Let's hear it."

"Why should you tire yourself trekking all the way to Achilles' grave? Don't go to all the bother. I'll write in my history that you went, and I'll describe the event so beautifully that all future generations will believe me."

Alexander glowered. "Walk!"

The poor philosopher hunched his shoulders and began climbing the hill again, muttering as he went.

At last they arrived at two knolls, a big one and a smaller one.

"Here they are!" called Callisthenes wiping the sweat from his brow. "There's the grave of Achilles, and the other one's the grave of Patroclos. I'll sit here on the rock and watch what you do."

Alexander took Hephaistion by the arm, and lengthening his stride, moved ahead toward the two hills. The others followed.

He stood before Achilles' grave in silence. A long time went by. At last he lifted his arms and greeted his mighty ancestor.

"O Achilles," he said, "you have been blessed. You had a faithful friend, Patroclos, when you lived. And when you died, you chanced to have a great poet to sing your praises. If only I could be as blessed as you!"

And having said, he threw off his chiton and began to race stark naked round the grave of Achilles.

Hephaistion, meanwhile, had approached the small hill where ˌ ⸴ried. He cut a few wild flowers and scattered them

˶ ˳ke me worthy to remain as

ˌˌˌˌnd to

the death.

The people ⸴⸴

built over the ruins of glori⸴⸴

age as it was approaching from a distance, a⸴⸴ ˌ

hurrying to greet them, bringing with them what they believed would be a valuable present for the King.

"O King of many ages," said the eldest, "we have a gift for you from our city. We bring you this ancient lyre that belonged to Paris who abducted Helen."

"I have nothing in common with Paris," answered Alexander waving the gift away. "If you had brought me the lyre of Achilles, I would have accepted it gladly."

And turning to his Companions: "Friends, we have fulfilled our obligation to the mighty shades. Now it's time to return to the army and begin the great march."

Hardly had he uttered the words when a messenger from Parmenion arrived on the run.

"What are you coming to tell me in such haste?" laughed Alexander. "That Homer has come to life again?"

"O King," cried the messenger, "the Persians are assembled along the banks of the River Granicus and are preparing to attack us. And what's more, my King," he added in a quaking voice, "Darius, the King of the Persians, sends you this!" And unwrapping a packet from beneath his mantle, he gave Alexander a letter and three strange objects: a whip, a ball, and a box of gold coins.

Alexander's friends gathered around and stared with curiosity.

Opening the letter Alexander read aloud:

"DARIUS, THE GREAT KING OF THE PERSIANS AND THE UNIVERSE, TO LITTLE ALEXANDER:
I HEAR YOU HAVE COME TO MY KINGDOM AND ARE CAUSING MISCHIEF. RETURN TO YOUR MOTHER'S LAP QUICKLY AND BEHAVE YOURSELF. I AM SENDING YOU A WHIP BECAUSE YOU DESERVE A LICKING, AND A BALL TO PLAY WITH AND A BOX OF COINS SO THAT YOU CAN GET BACK TO YOUR VILLAGE."

Alexander rolled up the letter.

"Forward, my friends!" he said with a smile. "Let Darius learn that I am a man."

36

He returned to his army and gave orders to disembark quickly and advance to confront the Persians.

Day and night the ships moved back and forth transporting the Greek army from Europe to Asia.

Out in the Persian camp, meanwhile, the enemy was holding council. There were four principal generals and all four are familiar to us: Arsites, Artabazos, Spithridates, and the Greek from Rhodes, Memnon.

"What is the best course for us to follow?" Spithridates was asking the council. "Our spies inform us that Alexander wasn't frightened by the Great King's letter and is preparing to attack us. What should we do?"

"We should not give them battle," advised Memnon. "I know the Macedonian army well. It's small, but it's better organized than ours, and their phalangites are the bravest in the world. I know their King Alexander, too. He's brimming with confidence and spirit and from what he has done up to now, I'm afraid he possesses great military skill as well."

"Spare us the praises of the Greeks," interrupted Arsites testily. "Just tell us your opinion as to what we should do."

"Hear my opinion, then," said Memnon with a look of contempt at Arsites. "We should retreat to the interior and burn all the provisions along the way—all the crops, orchards, livestock. With nothing to eat, they'll starve to death."

Spithridates laughed. "That's good advice for women!" he shouted. "I say we don't leave. We stay and fight. In a few hours that splendid army that you've been idolizing will scatter like mist!"

"He's right! He's right!" shouted Arsites and the other Persians. "War!"

Memnon shrugged. "I gave my opinion," he said. "I bear no responsibility; you're the ones who will regret it."

And so the Persians assembled on the opposite banks of the river and waited. Four days went by. "They won't come," they thought. "They won't come, they've gone."

But toward the evening of the fourth day the first of the Greek horsemen appeared in view. Behind them could be seen the Macedonian phalangites. The two armies were now facing each other.

103

Parmenion approached Alexander: "Your orders, King?"
"Attack at once!"
"It's getting dark. We had better wait until morning."
"At once! At once! Before they get away!" insisted the King racing off on Bucephalas to give the command.

His elite cavalry was to spearhead the crossing, and he ordered them now to be ready to charge across the shallow river and attack the enemy in a lightning strike. The army he wheeled into battle formation turning the left flank over to Parmenion. And taking the lead himself at the head of the right column, he shouted a few words to the soldiers to fire them up and ordered the trumpets to signal the charge.

The Persians were watching it all from the opposite shores. They could make out Alexander by his glittering armor and the two white wings on his helmet. The generals they recognized by the way they were racing back and forth on horseback, wheeling the soldiers into battle formation. All at once they heard the trumpets sound the attack and saw the cavalry shoot out in a lightning charge across the river.

In plunged the Persian horsemen, too, from along their banks to confront the Greeks in the water. But how could they stem the force of the Greek cavalry! On it charged, clear through to the other side. The phalangites, too, who had moved into position behind them were surging across with lightning speed.

The Persians, meanwhile, had concentrated their best fighters on the left flank, waiting to pit them against Alexander, and now as the King was surging up to their shoreline, these choice warriors fell on him with upraised swords and a tremendous roar: "Kill him! Kill him!"

Stephan, mounted on his white horse, was following close behind, taking part in his first battle. It was the hour of sunset and he could see the glare of the rays in the Persians' eyes. They were fighting half-blinded as the Greeks, with the sun at their backs, pressed the assault. Suddenly, there in the swarm of Persian horsemen, Stephan spied his old acquaintances Arsites, Artabazos, and Spithridates. They had caught sight of Alexander and were rushing at him. Spithridates was brandishing his sword and struck Alexander, breaking his spear. It shattered to the ground and now his saber broke, too, and Arsites was swooping in, his sword raised over Alex-

104

ander's head. Sprinting with lightning speed, Stephan hurtled at them. He thrust his spear into Alexander's hand and shielding the King with his body raised a mighty yell. At once the King's faithful friends came rushing to his side with their swords.

But the enemy outnumbered them. The danger was great. Arsites fell; Philotas was wounded in the arm. Alexander's helmet was shattered from all the blows and his head was exposed and unprotected. At one point Spithridates, seeing his back turned as he was battling another Persian general, lifted his sword and was bringing it down hard over Alexander's bare head when a slash from the sword of Cleitos, who vaulted on him like a firebolt, lopped off his arm at the shoulder and Alexander was saved. He turned. "Thank you, faithful friend," he said to Cleitos.

They all fought bravely; but by the onset of night the Persian cavalry was weakening and, no longer able to repulse the attack, the Persians swung their horses around and began to retreat, leaving their foot soldiers exposed to fight without cover. By now Parmenion, too, had crossed the river with his men and was joining in the attack against the Persian foot soldiers who, like the cavalry, soon buckled under, turned their backs and ran. The Greeks, all for giving chase, now were halted.

"Don't advance!" ordered Alexander. "Enough!"

Twenty thousand Persian foot soldiers lay dead in the field, and two thousand five hundred horsemen. "See to it," said Alexander, "that the enemy dead are buried with military honors. They fought bravely."

Of Greeks, one-thousand two-hundred and forty fell, and twenty-five elite horsemen from among the King's friends. Later, Alexander gave orders to his favored sculptor, the great Lysippos, to make twenty-five bronze statues of these fallen horsemen and to set them up at the foot of Mount Olympos.

All that evening Alexander went among his wounded soldiers, giving them medicines, binding their wounds, staying up with them throughout the night, ministering the art of medicine he had learned from Aristotle.

Rich spoils fell into the hands of the Greeks, and Alexander selected the finest and sent them to his mother—a gold cup, luxurious rugs, garments of purple. He also selected three-hundred panoplies of armor that had belonged to the enemy and sent them as gifts to the Athenians to hang in the Parthenon, Athena's temple, commanding that the following inscription be carved beneath the shields:

> *"Alexander, son of Philip, together with the Greeks, except the Lacedaemonians, dedicate these spoils taken from the barbarians of Asia."*

The brilliant victory at Granicus spread terror over all Asia Minor.

"Let's press on," urged Alexander's Companions. "Let's chase the Persians as far as the innermost depths of Asia."

"No," said Alexander. "First we'll take over all the seacoasts from Ionia to Egypt."

"Why?" asked his friends astounded.

"So that we can command the coastlines and keep the enemy from transporting their armies with their fleets to attack Greece."

They set out and soon arrived at wealthy Sardis. There the archons came forth and presented the keys to the city on a gold tray. "Have mercy on us, King," they said to Alexander, falling to the ground. "Don't burn our houses. Don't kill us!"

"Rise to your feet," said Alexander. "I've come to bring freedom, not slavery. You are free. And from this day forward I give to your renowned city its former rights."

From Sardis he proceeded to the Ionic Sea and reached the big Greek colony of Ephesos. The city opened its doors to him joyously and Alexander hastened immediately to the famous temple of Artemis. As we know, this temple had been destroyed by fire the day he was born.

"I must rebuild it," he declared, "and make it even more splendid than before," and summoning his great architect Dinocrates, gave orders to begin the construction immediately. As they were strolling about the burned ruins of the temple, a certain resident of Ephesos approached. "O King," he said, "I am the artist Apelles and I ask a favor of you."

"Apelles!" exclaimed Alexander who had often admired this man's work. "Ask anything! You know how much I admire your work."

"Permit me to paint your portrait mounted on Bucephalas."

"I accept!" said Alexander pleased.

106   When the painting was finished and presented to Alexander, he shook his head with displeasure. "It needs correcting," he said.

"You haven't quite captured Bucephalas." And he ordered Bucephalas brought to him. But as the horse was approaching the portrait, he began to whinny.

"Your horse," laughed Apelles, "understands the art of painting better than you, O King."

Alexander laughed then, too. "I like the way you speak your mind to me so freely," he said. "You're worthy of becoming my friend." And from that day he allowed no other artist but Apelles to paint him, just as he allowed no one but Lysippos to make statues of him, and no one but the engraver Pyrgoteles to carve his image on precious stones.

37

Stephan was sitting outside Alexander's tent binding his wound. He had injured his hand slightly when he was giving his spear to Alexander at the battle of Granicus. "How my mother would shudder if she saw me now," he smiled to himself.

It had been his first exposure to danger, his first active part in battle. He had felt a tremor of fear in that initial moment, but as he plunged into the battle and sensed the horsemen all around him charging fearlessly ahead, yelling the battle cry, he was swept up by a kind of intoxication; all thoughts of danger and death fled, and he spurred his horse on like the others, hurling himself into the assault.

"Wounded, Stephan?"

He turned at the familiar voices. Leonidas and Hermolaos were approaching. "It's nothing," he said, "just a scratch. It'll be healed by tomorrow when we leave Ephesos."

The two friends sat down beside him. They were happy. "Just think of all the things we've seen in these few days!" Leonidas was saying. "Imagine if we were still back in our little houses in Macedonia. What would we ever be doing?"

"We were living like blind mice back there. Here we're living like eagles."

"And we haven't seen anything yet!" exclaimed Leonidas. "Wait, this is only the beginning!"

Stephan was silent. He had been overhearing conversations between Alexander and his generals and knew what monumental difficulties were involved. He still remembered what Alexander had been saying to Hephaistion the other day: "…the Persians outnumber us, and they're brave; and while they don't have good generals, they do have one, and that one's not a Persian. Unfortunately he's a Greek."

"Who?" Hephaistion had asked, "Memnon?"

"Him," Alexander had answered, "He's brave and clever. If they follow his plan, we're in serious trouble."

These were the words that Stephan was reflecting on now to himself.

"Why aren't you talking, Stephan?" said Leonidas. "Does your wound hurt?"

"No," he answered, falling silent again.

Callisthenes went by. The portly philosopher, some manuscripts under his arm, appeared engrossed in thought. At sight of him Hermolaos stood up. "Teacher," he called respectfully, "come sit with us and rest a while."

Callisthenes lifted his gaze and peered at the three friends. "I can't," he said. "I have much work to do. I must keep writing. I'll never catch up. This Alexander is racing too fast, crossing rivers, conquering cities, scattering armies. Now he's here; now he's there. He never stops, and my pen has to keep racing right along with him." He sighed. "I don't even have time for a little sip of wine!" and saying, he raised his flask and downed a few gulps. "Ambrosia!" He smacked his lips appreciatively. "I picked this up in Ephesos. One would think," he chuckled, "that Alexander knew his vineyards. He leads us to the best—Ephesos, Meletos, Halicarnassos, Sardis. What wines! He might think he's Alexander, but I see that he's really Dionysos, the god of wine."

"And you're the fat Silenos who follows with a wineskin on his shoulder," laughed Leonidas.

"Speak to him with respect," rebuked Hermolaos. "Look, he's writing again."

"What are you writing, philosopher?" asked Stephan.

"Listen, my lads, listen." And stooping over the manuscript with his myopic little eyes, he began to read in a high-flown, bombastic style: "Dionysos, they say, set out from India and came to Greece. He was loaded down with costly garments, rings and bracelets. And the closer he came to Greece the more adornments he shed from his body, lessening his load. And when he reached the shores of Greece he was naked.

108

"Now, Dionysos has set out from Greece and is heading back toward India. He started out naked, and the farther he goes, the more he loads himself down with costly garments, rings, and bracelets." He shook his bald head. "I have evil forebodings," he murmured.

"Let's hear them, master," said Hermolaos uneasily. "What kind of forebodings?"

But before he could answer a man on horseback was galloping up to Alexander's tent. The horse, dripping with sweat, could barely stand on its legs from exhaustion. Dismounting, the rider took out a letter from his bosom.

"Where's King Alexander?" he asked the three friends.

Stephan rose. "Why do you want him? He's inside conferring with the generals."

"I bring him important news. Direct me to him."

"Is it good?" asked Hermolaos eagerly.

The man turned and smiled at him. "It's good," he answered, and followed Stephan.

The two friends waited. Before long Stephan came out.

"Well?" they cried impatiently.

"Memnon is dead," answered Stephan.

The two friends shrugged. "Is that all?"

Stephan smiled, but said nothing.

38

The next day the army resumed its march southward, beach after beach. All the cities were opening their gates to Alexander and welcoming him like a liberator. Only Miletos and Halicarnassos resisted, but Alexander conquered them quickly. At Halicarnassos he dispatched Parmenion to the interior to bring his rule into that area and he, himself, went on ahead to Gordium, the capital of Phrygia.

He had learned that the ancient chariot of the first King, Gordius, was kept there, tied by its yoke in a manner so skillful that no one had been able to untie the knot. And there was an ancient oracle which said that whoever would untie the Gordian knot would become lord of Asia.

So the moment Alexander arrived at Gordium the notables of the city came out to escort him to the acropolis where the chariot was kept and where everyone was waiting in an agony of suspense to see whether he would be able to untie the knot.

Alexander walked up to the knot, tried to undo it, and couldn't. So he grew angry, drew out his sword, and cut it down the middle. Everyone started in amazement. Then suddenly a cry burst from all their lips. "Long live the Great King of Asia!"

The rains had begun. Winter was setting in.

"We'll stop here," announced Alexander. "We'll spend the winter in these rich provinces and begin new preparations. We'll have to stockpile food and track down new horses to replace the ones that were killed. We'll have to conscript a lot of new men from the Greek cities of Ionia to help us. I'm waiting, too, for reinforcements to arrive from Macedonia."

The winter was harsh. Alexander ordered daily training for the army to keep it in shape. "There's a long road ahead of us," he reminded them. He kept them active, singling out a task force here, a task force there, and making forays into Asia Minor where he conquered city after city.

Meanwhile, reinforcements were arriving at the beaches from the Ionian cities, and it was only a matter of days now until the army that Alexander had asked Antipatros to send him from Macedonia would be arriving, too.

One day he summoned Stephan. "I'm very pleased with you," he said. "You're brave and faithful and I won't forget how much you helped me at Granicus when my spear broke and you gave me yours. You risked your life for me."

"I did my duty," said Stephan quietly.

"Yes, and I shall do mine. Now that the army is coming from Macedonia, I have arranged a fine surprise for you."

"What?" exclaimed Stephan.

"I'm not telling," smiled the King. "You'll see."

And every day now Stephan trekked up to the city's acropolis to search out the big central road to the west that connected the Ionian seacoasts with the interior of Asia Minor. "What surprise could the King be planning for me?" he wondered.

At last one morning the din of military trumpets echoed from the big central road and an army in Greek battle dress was seen approaching. A squadron of cavalry was in the lead and before long it came galloping into the cobblestone streets of the city.

Stephan was standing guard outside Alexander's door where the King, who had been up all night, was still sleeping. The horsemen pulled up and the commanders rode into the courtyard and dismounted.

Jolted from his sleep, Alexander threw on his mantle and bounded outside.

"Greetings, King!" the commanders saluted.

"Welcome!" called Alexander. "Have you brought me letters from my mother?"

An officer came forward and gave the King a leather pouch filled with letters.

"They're probably bringing me letters from my parents," thought Stephan. "This must be the surprise." But just then someone was entering the great courtyard. Stephan looked up, stared at the newcomer, and let out a jubilant yell. "Father!" he cried, and ran straight into the arms of Philip the physician.

Alexander had invited him to come. He had great faith in this old friend of his father's. "The climate here is very harsh," he reasoned, "I don't want to get sick and die before I finish my work. Philip must stay with me."

"My boy, my boy!" Philip was exclaiming, embracing his son with joy.

"And mother? How is mother?" Stephan was crying, beside himself.

"She's well, she's well, she sends you her blessing . . . and Alka, too, sends you greetings, and all your friends. I'm so happy to see you again, my boy."

"Is Alka coming?" Stephan wanted to ask, but didn't.

The winter passed. The Greek army, rested and burgeoning now, was impatient for the day when the King would give the signal to set out again. They had been living here three months and had learned a great deal about the kingdom of the Persians. It was without end! the natives told them. The sun never set in the regions of the Great King. Two capitals lay out there in the great beyond, they said, one for winter and one for summer, and they were loaded with gold and precious stones and countless treasures.

"When will we set out?" chafed the Greeks, their imaginations on fire, "When will we ever get to those golden palaces!"

111

At last the blessed day arrived. Spring came, the snows melted, and Alexander gave the signal. "Forward! Asia is big; let's not lose time!"

And they set out. They climbed towering mountains and marched down vast plains. Here and there a band of enemy soldiers would attack them; here and there a city would resist. But the enemy was quickly dispersed and Alexander arrived at the great mountain range of Taurus in Cilicia, victorious.

"If the Straits of Taurus are in enemy hands," Parmenion muttered to Alexander, "we're done for."

"They're done for!" retorted the King laughing. "No one will be able to stop us."

But old Parmenion shook his head. He sent out speedy horsemen to the narrow pass to see. They returned jubilant.

"The Straits are free!" they announced. "But the Persians are preparing to burn Tarsus, the wealthy city that lies beyond the mountains."

"Hurry!" shouted Alexander spurring Bucephalas on. "Hurry, before they get there!"

They scaled the high mountain ranges of Taurus without meeting resistance and marched down the plains. The heat scorched, and the soldiers grumbled.

"Let's stop for a while and catch our breath, Alexander," said Hephaistion, wiping away the sweat. "We'll die from the heat!"

"There's no time! There's no time!" and Alexander kept spurring his horse.

One afternoon they came to a small river, the Cydnus, and crossing it arrived at the outskirts of Tarsus. The Persians, watching the host approaching, quaked, and panicking, set fire to the houses. But the Greeks, already entering the city on the run, put out the flames before the fire could spread, and took possession.

Exhausted and drenched with sweat, Alexander dismounted from his horse. "I'm going for a swim in the river to cool off," he said.

"No, my King!" cried Philip the physician at his side. "You could get sick."

"I'm not afraid of danger. I'm going."

"You summoned me from Macedonia to look after your health," persisted the doctor. "Listen to my advice. Wait a while until you've stopped perspiring, and then you can bathe. The waters of the Cydnus spill down from high mountains and are icy."

"All the better," said Alexander.

He went to the icy river, took off his clothes, and plunged in. As he sank into the frigid water he felt a shudder throughout his body. "The doctor was right," he mumbled, but he was too embarrassed to come out and remained in the water and swam a long time.

When he emerged, he was ghastly white. His teeth were chattering and he went to bed burning with fever.

His friends rushed to his bedside. He was delirious, unable to recognize them, and they came away in shock, shaken and fearful.

Hephaistion, who had fallen at his feet, lay there weeping. The terrible news spread through the army: "Alexander is dying!"

For three days and three nights Alexander battled with Charon. For three days and three nights Hephaistion wept at his feet. On the fourth day Philip the physician came to him: "I have a strong medicine to give you, my King," he said. "If you take it, you might be saved."

"Go and prepare it," whispered Alexander, closing his eyes again.

The physician went. But as he was leaving, a man was arriving on the run, a messenger sent by General Parmenion who was still fighting out on the Tarsus mountainside. He entered Alexander's room and knelt.

"My King."

But Alexander didn't hear.

"My King," he said louder, "Parmenion has sent me. I have a letter for you. It's urgent!"

Alexander opened his eyes.

"A letter from Parmenion," repeated the messenger.

"I can't read," murmured Alexander through chattering teeth.

"It's very urgent!"

Alexander summoned all his strength and put out his hand. "Give it to me," he whispered and taking the letter opened it. At first he could make nothing out of the dancing letters. But gradually he began to decipher them: *"O King, this very moment I have learned that your physician Philip has been bribed by the King of Persia to poison you. Be careful!"*

Philip was entering now with the medicine.

"Go," said Alexander to the messenger.

The physician approached.

113

"My King," he said, "Take courage! This medicine will make you well. Sit up a little and drink it." And saying, he helped Alexander raise himself on the pillows and gave him the drug.

Alexander took the medicine. As he was holding it with one hand, he handed the physician Parmenion's letter with the other. And now he began to drink, just as Philip was reading the letter. At once the physician fell to his knees, swearing by the gods that all this was slander. Alexander smiled.

"See?" he said, holding up the empty cup that had contained the medicine. "I have faith in you."

For a few days longer Alexander battled with death; then slowly he began to improve. The army breathed easier and the generals gathered round his bed.

"What news?" Alexander would ask them every morning as he lay, still pale, against his pillows. And the generals would report the information that the messengers brought them daily.

"The King of the Persians is mustering a huge body of soldiers out there in Mesopotamia."

"How big?"

"They say four-hundred-thousand foot and a hundred-thousand cavalry."

"Memnon's dead," mused Alexander, "I'm not afraid of them."

"Who's their commander-in-chief?" he asked one morning.

"Their King. Darius himself."

Alexander started. He could feel his strength return. "At last!" he cried, rising from his bed, "at last I will be battling with Kings!"

"Don't be in such a rush, my King," said Philip, making him lie down again. "You're still weak. Wait."

"He's a distance away yet," said Crateros. "We have plenty of time."

"What sort of man is Darius?" asked Alexander, settling down.

"Everything we've heard about him is good," answered old Parmenion. "They say he's the strongest and handsomest man in all of Persia."

"All the better," murmured Alexander. "I like my enemy to be worthy of me."

"He's a cultured man," continued Parmenion, "and speaks Greek fluently. The Persian nation was in anarchy and he restored order. He has an exalted opinion of himself, though, and thinks he's unbeatable."

"So do I," smiled Alexander. "We'll see who's right."

In a few days Alexander was back on his feet, surrounded by his friends and generals, when messengers arrived out of breath. "O King," they cried, "important news! Darius is here with his army!"

Alexander took a step forward. "Where is he?"

"He's camped in a narrow plain near the city of Issus, where the sea runs along one side and mountains along the other. And his army is so big that it's beyond counting."

Alexander rubbed his hands in glee. "He won't get away!" he cried to his friends. "There where he's wedged himself, he's lost! The place is narrow, he'll never be able to use that huge hulk of an army. Let's hurry before he changes position!"

39

They moved swiftly. By day's end they were on their way, marching in the dark throughout the night without stopping. By dawn they were within sight of the countless enemy host in the narrow plain between the mountains and the sea. They could see the gold armored chariot of Darius glittering in the center of the camp, and the Great King himself standing tall in his purple panoply giving out commands. Alexander's eyes blazed. "I'll break through his lines... I'll get to him and do battle with him... I'll kill him, and Asia will be mine..." He could hardly contain his eagerness as he wheeled his army in battle formation and issued the final commands.

The elite cavalry, always the first to spearhead the battle, charged. On the run behind them surged the Cretan archers, followed by the heavy phalanxes. The collision was devastating. The Persian advance guard crumbled. It broke and scattered. Alexander streaked ahead, his eye on Darius who was standing tall in his chariot, shouting exhortations to his men to fire them with courage. The choicest of the Persians, seeing the danger to their King, sped swiftly to his aid. But Darius, looking up and catching sight of Alexander bearing down on him, shuddered. He who had been so brave wavered at this visage of a god charging at him. "He's going to kill me!" he realized, and pulling at the reins of his horse, he turned and fled in panic. Alexander, hot on his heels, pressed after him, a tail of friends and bodyguards from both camps galloping frenziedly behind to aid their respective Kings.

Parmenion, meanwhile, was holding back the enemy on the left wing. Outnumbered ten to one, he was fighting valiantly, but with the onset of night, he could feel himself weakening. Suddenly a roar went up. "Darius is fleeing!" Stunned, the Persians stopped. They looked out and saw Darius in the distance, streaking away like a bolt of lightning in his gold chariot. "Retreat! Retreat! We're done for!" cries rang out and the terrified enemy turned their backs to Parmenion's phalanxes and began to flee.

Out in the dark Darius's chariot came to a halt. Alexander pounced on it. It was empty. The only things inside were the bow, the shield, and the royal mantle. Darius had vanished, leapt on a horse and disappeared into the mountains. Turning back then, and seeing the entire Persian army in flight with the Greek army in yelling, hot pursuit, Alexander issued the command to the trumpeters to signal the end of the chase.

And now the Greeks began pouring into the camp that the Persians had abandoned. They rounded up the prisoners, bound them, gathered up the costly armaments, the clothing, jewels, horses. The gold-embellished tents of Darius spired tall in the center of the camp. "No one is to touch them!" ordered Hephaistion, stationing soldiers to guard them. "They belong to Alexander."

The battle over and won, Alexander dismounted, exhausted, and entered Darius's tent. The wealth inside astounded him—the silver throne and tables, the magnificent beds, the gold plates and wine cups, the alabaster bottles filled with perfumes that were scenting the air all about. "Let's go to Darius's bath," he said, "to bathe away the sweat of battle."

The royal bath in the adjoining tent was ready and waiting, it, too, with its luxurious, costly appointments: pitchers, tubs, sheets, towels. Alexander breathed deeply of the perfumed air. "So this is what it means to be King," he said.

Darius's laden table awaited in an adjacent tent; and after bathing and rubbing his body with aromatic oil, Alexander called his closest friends and generals and settled down with them to eat. Never had they dined on more exquisite foods; never had they drunk from more costly golden cups.

As they were eating and drinking in exuberent spirits, sudden cries and wailing from a nearby tent broke in on them. "What is it?" asked Alexander.

"Darius's mother," they said, "and his wife and daughters, crying over Darius. They saw his empty chariot and think he's been killed."

"Go and quiet them," ordered Alexander turning to Stephan. "Tell them Darius isn't dead and that they're not to fear. Alexander will accord them royal honors and no one will molest them."

The following day Alexander himself went to visit them. He was with Hephaistion, and the moment Darius's mother saw him she fell at Hephaistion's feet and kissed his hand. "O my King have mercy on us," she said thinking him king since he was the taller. Then, seeing her mistake, she knelt before Alexander: "Forgive me!" she cried.

But Alexander calmed her. "You were not at all mistaken, honorable mother," he said. "He, too, is Alexander."

Then reaching down he picked up Darius's small son in his arms and the child, who was six, wrapped his arms around the King's neck without fear. Alexander turned to Hephaistion: "This child is braver than his father," he said softly.

In a few days Alexander received an arrogant message from Darius who had fled to Mesopotamia.

When he opened it, he could barely restrain his anger.

Here is what the message said:

The Great King Darius to Alexander:
Do not think you are lord of Asia just because you have won. 117
Some god helped you on that day. If you want my friendship,

return my mother, my wife, and my children, and I will give you more gold than exists in all of Macedonia.

If you do this I will unite with you in friendship and I will not punish you for your impertinence in coming to my country without cause, without my ever having harmed you.

Alexander promptly gave orders to send a reply:

Alexander, King of Macedonia and Supreme
Commander of the Greeks,
to Darius:

Darius, your first King from whom you took your name, tyrannized the Greeks who were living on the shores of the Hellespont and Ionia. Then vast armies crossed over and fought Macedonia and Greece.

Then Xerxes himself came, with more barbarians than you could count. He was defeated at sea. He fled, but left Mardonion to pillage and burn our cities and villages.

My father Philip was assassinated by men bribed by the Persian Court. By such means, bribes and iniquities, you fight your enemies.

Therefore, I have not brought the war to your land; I have come to punish old injustices. And the gods who always help the just helped me, and now a large part of Asia is in my hands; and you, yourself, I have defeated in battle.

Therefore, you have no right to ask anything of me. But if you come here in person and fall at my feet and beg me, I will give you your mother, your wife, and your children, without any payment. Because I not only know how to win, I also know how to be magnanimous to the losers. I give you my word that you can come without any danger whatsoever.

And henceforth, when you write to me, don't forget that you are writing to a King, and what's more to your King!

When he had sealed the letter with his royal gold seal, he summoned his favorite musician, Terpandros.

"Terpandros," he said, "I am angry, and cannot subdue my rage. Bring your lyre and play for me. Only music can calm my heart."

40

Philip the physician was sitting in a garden of Anatolia, reminiscing with his son about their distant country. It was late into summer and the trees were heavy with fruit. Enormous black grapes dangled from a grapevine over their heads.

"How rich this land is!" said Philip. "How beautiful! And yet, how I long for our country. For our humble little home."

Stephan was silent. He did not share his father's sentiments. He loved his humble home but he would never be willing to spend his life, even a happy one, within those four narrow walls. He was swept up by Alexander's passion.

"Wouldn't you want to go back now?" asked Philip.

"No, father," Stephan answered quietly, his voice determined. "Forgive me. Our generation longs for great deeds."

"Contentment," murmured Philip, "is to be found in the serenity of the ancestral home, don't you know that?"

"Maybe," replied Stephan. "But contentment isn't man's highest good."

"What is then?"

"Setting up a difficult goal in your life and accomplishing it. Didn't you, yourself, tell me that I should never remain satisfied with whatever I did, that I should always want to rise higher? I'm following your advice."

Philip was silent. He knew his son was right. But then, he was young; he had the strength to pursue a life of danger. It was fitting for the young to be insatiable, to have great ambitions, for the good of their country. Yes, it was proper for them to love danger.

"You're right," he said at length in a quiet voice. "I've grown old." Then, after a pause. "Did you see Alexander today?"

"No," said Stephan, "he was meeting with the generals all night. We'll be setting out tomorrow."

"For where?"

"For where?" exclaimed Stephan. "But surely, father!"

"Until when?"

"Until the end of the world."

"And after that?"

"There is no after. We'll fulfill our duty. After that, we can die." 119

"This is a different generation," murmured Philip to himself. "It's insatiable. Fearless. It pushes forward and doesn't tremble at death."

He rose.

"I'm on my way to see Alexander," he said. "He drives himself too much. I must watch him. Last night he had a touch of fever."

"He's always got a touch of fever," laughed Stephan. "Don't worry about it, father. His blood boils and circulates faster than ours."

"We're expecting messengers today," he added, rising to join his father. "The King wants to continue his route parallel to the sea until he reaches Egypt, and he has sent word to the various cities through which we'll be passing, telling them to open their gates to him. We'll see what response they give."

Stephan's friends Hermolaos and Leonidas were waiting for him outside the Palace as they arrived. Philip went inside to see to Alexander's health and Stephan joined his friends. "Well," they demanded, "when do we leave?"

"You're in a hurry?" laughed Stephan.

"Are we supposed to sit around here and rot?" said Hermalaos. "There's a whole big world out there, waiting for us."

"Shhh, here come the envoys," motioned Stephan.

Two dignified old men appeared, dressed in splendid chitons. Behind them followed a throng of slaves loaded with gifts.

Alexander, too, had just emerged from the Palace with Philip and was standing at the threshold. The venerable old men lifted their arms and addressed him with proud dignity:

"Hail, O King Alexander! We are sent here by the wealthy city of Tyre."

"What answer do you bring me?" asked Alexander impatiently. "Peace or war?"

"You will be the one to choose, O King. But first, the city of Tyre sends you this gold wreath for your hair, and these slaves bring you precious gifts."

"That's no answer," said Alexander. "I presented the archons of Tyre with this question: I want to enter your city to offer a sacrifice to your god Melkart. Will you let me? Yes or no?"

"No foreign conquerer has ever entered our city," replied

the elder of the envoys. "We did not allow the Persians..."

"But me?"

"Not even you, my King."

"I would not be entering as a conquerer. Your god Melkart is our own hero, Heracles. Heracles is my ancestor from my father's lineage. I am a Heraclean, and I want to offer a sacrifice to my ancestor."

"According to an ancient law," replied the envoys again, "whoever sacrifices inside our city, on the altar of Melkart, is considered our master. We do not want to become servants of anyone."

Alexander listened with admiration to the proud words of the old men. He was aware that their city was powerful. It was built on a small island just offshore, and whoever wanted to take it would have to come up with a strong navy. Alexander had none. He knew the Persians would rush their fleet to the defense of Tyre and he would be in peril of being defeated.

"We will give you anything you want, O King," the envoys continued. "There is only one thing that we'll not give you. Our freedom."

Alexander thought for a long time. He would have to conquer Tyre. As long as it remained free, he would not be able to conquer the Phoenician seacoasts. If Tyre fell, the Phoenician fleet would be rendered useless and the consequences would be felt throughout the entire East. Tyre must be his.

"Tyre must become mine!" he said in a loud voice.

"You have no fleet. Our city is built on an island. How will you be able to reach us?"

"I will build a mole in the sea," he answered. "I will fill it with rocks and earth, I will make a road and a bridge, and I will cross over."

The old men smiled mockingly. "That would be rather difficult," they said.

"Nothing is difficult for a man who wills it!" answered Alexander. "Go, now. Until we meet again in a few days. And take your gifts with you."

The old men quietly said their farewells, took back their gold wreath, motioned their slaves to follow, and headed for the harbor where the ship that had brought them was anchored.

"He's going to build a mole in the sea!" marvelled Stephan, who had been listening to the exhange between them. "He's going to build a mole in the sea!" Then after a while: "Yes, of course," he concluded, "nothing is impossible for a man who wills it."

41

Alexander's eyes were flashing sparks this morning as they set out on the new expedition. He would no longer be battling mere men now. He had vowed to tame a fierce element—the sea. He would mole it, build a bridge, and cross over it.

Old Parmenion took note of this daring decision of Alexander's with some trepidation. "These young," he thought to himself, "think there is nothing impossible in the world."

They arrived at the great Phoenician city of Byblos, and from there continued on to Sidon. Both cities opened their gates to the felicitous conqueror Alexander, but he was in a great rush and didn't want to stop even for a minute to accept the honors that they were preparing for him. "I'm in a hurry to punish Tyre!" he said.

At last one morning he arrived before the famous city. Ancient Tyre was built on the mainland, and the new Tyre was on a small island about half a mile offshore.

"It's unassailable!" murmured Parmenion as soon as he saw it. He turned to Alexander:

"My King," he said, his voice low to keep the others from hearing, "I have served your father and you faithfully for many years. I have never cowered. But now..."

"My dear old general," interrupted Alexander, "I have made up my mind. No one can make me change it. I am your King. Obey me."

And old Parmenion held his counsel.

Alexander summoned his engineers. "Recruit thousands of laborers," he told them, "all you can find. And if they don't come willingly, use force. Chop the trees of Lebanon; haul down the trunks. I'm going to dismantle ancient Tyre and give you all the stone you need to mole this narrow sea that separates us from Tyre."

And so the daring work began. They excavated ancient Tyre, hauled rocks to the sea, cut down trees, nailed them to the bottom of the deep, piled up earth, and began to build a road two hundred feet wide.

Alexander carried rocks, oversaw the work, handed out rewards to those who labored best, and soon the road began to rise from the depths of the sea.

At first the Tyrians made fun of them, but when they saw the road taking solid shape amid the waves, they grew uneasy and sent out ships to shoot at the laborers from close range with arrows, to stop them from working.

In response Alexander ordered his men to build two wooden towers at the finished end of the road so that his soldiers could shoot arrows back at the Tyrians, but the enemy ships threw fire at the towers from a distance and burned them down.

Alexander began to grow uneasy. What they needed, he realized, was a big fleet to besiege Tyre from the sea and starve her into surrendering. But his fleet was far away in Macedonia, guarding the homeland. Besides, it was too small. What could he do? It would take a long time to build a navy, and Alexander was in a hurry.

One day Stephan, who was working on the mole, noticed two men talking together in whispers, two Tyrian captains whom they had captured and were holding prisoners. Stephan had learned a few words of the local dialect and cocked his ear to listen. He could hear three words quite clearly. They kept repeating the words "many," "ships," and "Sidon," and he wondered what these two captains might be talking about so furtively. He thought about it and finally around nightfall decided to go to Alexander.

"My King," he said, "I overheard two Tyrian captains today talking in secret. I don't know their language very well, but I understood three words that they kept repeating very clearly."

"What words?" asked Alexander, curious.

"Many," "ships," and "Sidon."

Alexander thought a while. "Maybe what you tell me is important, Stephan. Maybe they're expecting some big fleet to be coming into Sidon. I'll give orders," and he summoned fearless Nicanor and prudent Ptolemy. "Go at once to Sidon," he told them. "We're in desperate need of a fleet. Bring back whatever ships you find in the harbor there."

"And you go with them," he said turning to Stephan. "It will be a lucky day for you if your hunch is right!"

The three deputies mounted their horses and set out at once. There was no time to lose. They knew the entire campaign was endangered by Tyre's resistance.

Arriving in Sidon they sped to the harbor. They took one look and their faces dropped. Instead of the huge fleet that they had been expecting, all they found were twenty-four boats that had arrived the previous day from the various harbors of Asia Minor. "You've brought us here on a wild goose chase," muttered Nicanor turning on Stephan bitterly.

Stephan was silent. His eyes were riveted out on the horizon, searching anxiously. "I mustn't let myself lose hope," he thought. "I distinctly heard the captains' words, and I clearly saw their gestures. I couldn't have been fooled."

"Come on," grumbled Nicanor, "Let's go."

"We might as well take the twenty-four boats at least," said Ptolemy, "They're better than nothing."

But as he was talking, Stephan let out a cry. "There's something on the horizon!" he shouted. Out in the distance where sky and sea meet, dark outlines were coming into view. The sea was deep blue; the sky, cloudless. A crowd of people had gathered at the dock and some began clambering up the two towers that spired to right and left of the harbor's entrance to have a look.

"Ships! Ships!" came cries from high up on the towers.

"Ships!" echoed Stephan, turning triumphantly to his two companions.

The black outlines were growing bigger. Their sails, white and red, could be seen clearly now above the dim outline of the slanted prows.

"They're from Cyprus," a voice shouted.

"No, they're ours," cried others. "They're Phoenician."

Alexander's three deputies scrambled up the tower and stared in disbelief. Surely the gods were sending them. "When will they get here, O when will they get here!" they were thinking, eager to get their hands on the ships and hurry back with them to Tyre.

Along about evening the vessels, warships from the northern coastal cities, finally began to stream into the harbor. The three companions were counting. "Eighty!" shouted Stephan, and they raced down the tower and hastened to find the captains to learn whatever they could from them.

The ships, it turned out, had been conscripted by the Persians and had been given orders to go out and unite with the remaining fleet. On the way, however, they had learned from a passing ship that Alexander had conquered their country, so they mutinied and turned back. "We'll go with Alexander," they said, "as long as our countries have gone over to his side."

Nicanor, Ptolemy, and Stephan set about now, gathering the captains together. "Alexander is waiting for you with open arms," they told them. "He has sent us here to take you with us. We leave at once, tonight."

An old captain smiled. "What's your hurry?" he said. "Wait a while."

"Why should we wait?" said Nicanor impatiently.

"Wait," repeated the old captain, "For your own good."

"Why, what's going to happen?" asked Ptolemy.

"The Cypriot fleet will be arriving tomorrow," whispered the old captain in a confidential tone. "And do you know how many ships that means?"

"How many?"

"Two hundred and eighty big ones, and a whole string of smaller transports."

"Why are they coming?"

"They found out that Alexander is besieging Tyre and they're coming to help."

"To help who?" the three asked anxiously.

"Don't you know how much the Cypriots despise Tyre?" laughed the old man winking at them. "They lost all their trade because of Tyre. Now they want her destroyed so they can have control of their old commerce again. And the Cypriots, you know, are our best mariners."

There was no sleeping for our three friends that night, so great was their joy, so great their impatience for day to break when they would see if, indeed, the Cypriot fleet was coming. "Two hundred and eighty big warships!" they exclaimed over and over again with amazement. "There's no doubt about it, the gods are with Alexander."

By noon the next day the sea was blanketed with ships. Our friends began to count again. They counted, and counted.

"Two hundred and eighty!" shouted Stephan.

"And how many small ones?" demanded Ptolemy.

"Oh, those! There's no end to those!" laughed Stephan.

The captains came ashore. They met with Alexander's three deputies. "The moment has come," they declared, their voices ringing with hatred, "for Tyre, our greatest enemy, to be destroyed. Let us go at once!" And by nightfall, the entire fleet had put up its sails again and embarked.

"What luck! What luck!" Nicanor kept exclaiming, his tune changed now. "You're going back in triumph, Stephan!"

"Three hundred and eighty-four warships!" Ptolemy kept echoing. "What will Alexander say!"

42

Alexander had his arm around Stephan and was thanking him. "Now what favor do you want from me?" he asked.

"I don't want anything, my King," Stephan answered happily. "I don't want anything."

"You don't want anything, but I want to give you something," said Alexander. "From this day forward you will be one of my Companions. You will no longer be an orderly. You will eat at my table, and I will consider you equal with my old friends. And later, later, we'll see."

He spoke, and directed that Stephan be given costly gifts: a gold cup from which he would drink his wine, a splendid horse, and valuable Persian fabrics.

"What should I do with the fabrics?" Stephan laughed.

"Send them to your mother," said Alexander. "Send them to some nice girl you know. Why not to that little girl," he added smiling, "who was with you when you discovered the conspiracy? What's her name?"

"Alka," answered Stephan reddening.

"To Alka, then," said Alexander, slapping his friend on the shoulder.

"To Alka," thought Stephan to himself. "Imagine her joy at my sending her Persian booty."

When the Tyrians saw the huge fleet, they grew alarmed and, losing no time, loaded their women and children into their ships and sent them away to safety, before Alexander could blockade them.

And now Alexander sent the besieged city a notice: "Surrender!"

But the Tyrians, who were awaiting the Persian fleet to rush to their aid any day now, were not to be discouraged so readily. "Never!" they replied proudly.

Alexander admired the enemy's mettle. "They're brave," he thought, "But I will conquer them," and he ordered the building of the mole to continue, and put a tight ring of ships around the tiny island.

But the Tyrians devised a thousand and one artful maneuvers, and resisted with invincible courage. When the wind blew in their favor, they threw burning sand into the eyes of the laborers who were building the mole. They threw burning irons at them, red hot from the fires, and when the mole was finally within a few feet of the tiny island, they threw down heavy nets from their high walls and dragged the workers up and killed them.

But Alexander's will won out in the end. The mole was finished. It bridged the island with the mainland. And now the Greeks erected wooden towers and began to hit the walls with catapults. But the Tyrians had managed to add to the height of their walls on the moled side and the Greeks were unable to break through.

"All our efforts gone to waste," thought the prudent Parmenion. But he dared not talk to Alexander. He watched him running hither and yon, from soldiers to ships, firing up his men with courage, and spending sleepless nights, agitated and uneasy deep inside.

"I will win! I will win!" he kept telling himself.

One night he saw a strange dream. A Satyr appeared before him; he was looking at him and smiling. Alexander wakened but presently fell asleep again. Once more the Satyr appeared. It kept looking at him with that same unchanging smile.

In the morning he summoned his astrologer Aristandros and told him his dream. "Interpret it for me," he said.

Aristandros thought for a while.

"The dream is clear," he said at last. "Sa-Tyros.[15] In other words, Tyre is yours."

"I know it, I know it," said Alexander under his breath. "But when?"

127

The Tyrians were beginning to die of hunger now. They had no food and the water in the reservoirs had run out. And nowhere on the horizon was the Persian fleet to be seen.

"Surrender!" Alexander invited again.

"Never!"

"I will order an all-out attack from land and sea!" Alexander announced once more.

"Do your duty," they replied. "We will do ours."

Alexander could no longer hold back. He commanded his men to attack the walls with all their might and attempt to open a breach. But the Tyrians poured down fire on them, burning their towers.

It was the month of July and the heat was scorching. Alexander was sitting under a date tree one noon, silently looking out at the indomitable city. Old Parmenion was sitting beside him, keeping his silence. "We must find a way," he was thinking, "to retreat without losing face." This is what old Parmenion was thinking, but he dared not voice it.

Just then some Persian messengers arrived, and coming up to Alexander, fell at his feet. "The Great King greets you," they said, "and sends you this letter." They gave the letter to Alexander and made obeisance again while they waited.

Alexander read.

The Great King Darius
to king Alexander.

I offer you peace again. I will give you ten thousand gold talents if you return my mother, my wife and my children to me. I will give you one daughter in marriage. I will set aside as dowry all the land from the Euphrates River to the Greek coastlines, if you want to become my ally.

Alexander showed the letter to Parmenion. The old general read it carefully. "If I were Alexander, I would accept," he said.

"So would I, if I were Parmenion," Alexander replied. Then he turned to the Persian messengers.

"Tell your king I have no need of gold. I have all I want. Tell him to come here and pay me homage and I will give him back his mother, wife, and children, without reward."

The Persians bowed without a word and left.

"We lost an opportunity," murmured Parmenion.

128 "We won an opportunity," answered Alexander, "to show that we are men."

43

One day in August Alexander called to his men. His voice was determined. "Put up the ladders for the siege! And all who are faithful, follow me!"

They set up a ladder against the unconquered wall, and leading the way, Alexander proceeded to scale it. General Nicanor followed behind, with giant Sitalces and our friend Stephan close on his heels. The more valiant of the soldiers, too, began clambering up behind them, but just as the first four were climbing over the top, the ladder collapsed and the rest of the soldiers came crashing to the ground.

The sight of their King standing exposed at the top of the wall with only three Companions sent a shudder of terror through the army. They scrambled for a new ladder and in the interminable time that it took to arrive, stood below and watched as the enemy began to encircle their King. He had drawn his sword and along with the three Companions who were fighting desperately beside him was hacking away at the enemy.

Suddenly a hair-raising thing happened. With a mighty leap and a savage yell, Alexander hurtled into the city below, thrusting himself alone against the enemy. The three brave Companions, seeing their King in peril, leaped into the city after him, first Stephan, then Nicanor and last Sitalces.

The Tyrians fell upon them. An arrow pierced Sitalces's heart and the giant fell dead. Another struck Nicanor lodging in his neck. Stephan made a dash for Alexander. He was braced against a tree, mounting his offensive against the enemy with rocks, and now he was fighting them off with his sword. The enemy recognized him by the two flashing wings that waved from his helmet and had rushed at him with a roar. Blood was spurting from his chest. Stephan threw himself in front of him and held up his shield to give him some protection, but a Tyrian, with a slash of his sword, wounded him in the arm and the shield fell from his hand. He turned to look at the King who was now in imminent peril.

"Don't be afraid, Stephan!" gasped Alexander in a strangled voice. "They're not going to beat us! Fight!" and he lunged at the enemy again with his sword.

But how could he ever come out of this alive? One, two minutes more, and surely they were done for.

On the other side of the wall soldiers were scaling the new ladders with lightning speed. Some had already leaped into the city and had begun to form a circle around their King. Others, jumping in after them, were rushing to open the gates and in minutes the entire army was pouring into the famous city. The fleet, too, having fought tenaciously, had begun streaming into the harbor and the men were surging into the city to join in the attack. After a siege of seven months the Greeks were in a rage, thirsting for revenge, and by battle's end eight thousand of the enemy lay dead. Thirty thousand were left to be sold as slaves.

Exhausted but unyielding, Alexander turned then from the battlefield and set out, just as he was, wounded and covered with blood, to offer sacrifices at the ancient temple of Heracles. He approached the site, and standing before the gigantic wooden statue, he lifted his arm in greeting. "Well met, O ancestor!" he called to him. "Well met!"

Hundreds of sheep and bulls were slaughtered and the smoke rising from the altars covered the sky.

When the celebrations and games were over, Alexander gave the signal to set out again.

"Rest, my King," Philip the physician admonished. "You're exhausted from all your wounds."

"I have no time, my dear doctor," Alexander replied. "Egypt is waiting." And they set out again.

They marched through Phoenicia without resistance. On hearing that Tyre had fallen all the cities quaked with terror and opened their gates to the victor. Gaza alone resisted. But Alexander defeated this heroic city, too. He entered and found countless treasures. Most notable were entire storehouses filled with fragrant incense. Alexander laughed, remembering his stern teacher Leonidas who used to scold him when he was a boy because he would burn too much incense to the gods. "You must be more frugal," he would chide. "Incense is expensive!" And now here were mountains of incense at Alexander's disposal. Loading a ship with twenty-eight thousand pounds of it he sent it to his teacher Leonidas who had remained behind in Macedonia. With it he sent this letter. "I send you a ship full of incense so that you won't have to be miserly any more when offering sacrifices to the gods." He filled other ships, too, and sent valuable gifts to his mother and his sister Cleopatra, and to Antipatros and all his friends. To his teacher Aristotle he sent curious animals and plants that he found along the way, and rare minerals and metals that did not exist in Greece.

Among the treasures that fell into his hands was an exquisitely carved gold box. "What should I put in this?" he asked his friends.

"It's meant to hold aromatic scents," said Philip. "Fill it with perfumes."

"Perfumes don't go with soldiers," answered Alexander.

Everyone began to offer his opinion then as to what he would consider the most valuable thing to be kept in the box.

"I'll put the *Iliad* in it," said Alexander smiling at them. "I have nothing more valuable than that."

Resuming their march the army entered the desert. The heat was unbearable. Water was scarce, not enough for their thirst, but they endured without grumbling, knowing that in a few days they would be in wealthy Egypt—Egypt with her vast gardens and plentiful foods and ancient mysterious temples. Here as they were crossing the desert Alexander suffered a bitter sorrow. Parmenion's son Nicanor, the bravest of all his Companions, died. The wound he had received in his neck while protecting Alexander at Tyre was too deep and, unable to hold out any longer, he died. Alexander had grasped his hand in farewell and Philotas, his brother, embraced the dead body and wept. "Until we meet again, Nicanor," Alexander said to him, and closed his Companion's eyes.

They continued the march. Each morning the sun would rise out of the desert, fiery red, and each night it would sink back into the desert, fiery red.

"We're almost there! It won't be long now. We're almost there!" the men would encourage one another. What had they not heard about Egypt! The wisest men of Greece had come here to find out about the mysteries of life and death. For centuries sophists, scientists, merchants, soldiers, had travelled to Egypt and marvelled at her riches and her power and her wisdom.

And approaching now, more profoundly stirred than anyone who had come before, was Alexander. He would finally be fulfilling his mother's great desire: he would visit the Oracle of Ammon in the desert and put his question to him, and the god would reveal a great secret to him. What secret? Alexander could not guess.

Seven days went by. At last they were coming upon green, cultivated fields. Half-naked dark-skinned peasants were stooped over, working the earth. They raised their heads, looked at the army impassively, then stooped over the earth again and continued their hoeing.

"A good sign," thought Stephan. "We won't have any resistance here."

At the entrance of the first big city, white-garbed priests hastened out to greet Alexander. The eldest of the priests came forward: "O King," he said in a deep voice, "ancient Nectanebo was our last King. The accursed Persians banished him, but our mighty god Ammon, at his Oracle in the desert, told us that he would return, not as an old man again, but young and handsome, with golden hair and blue eyes. O King Nectanebo, welcome back to your country—in your new form and your new name!"

On hearing the priest's words, Alexander was greatly pleased, and his joy increased even more when he entered the vast city and saw the people waving palm branches in their hands and welcoming him like a liberator with their shouts, "Hail to our King!

Hail to our King!" They all knew the prophecy of the god Ammon and believed they were seeing their old King returned to his kingdom in another body, young and handsome, and no longer called Nectanebo, but Alexander.

44

In Memphis, Egypt's capital, Alexander ascended the lofty throne of Pharoah, where the priests dressed him in the ceremonial royal vestments and proclaimed him Pharoah, that is, King of Egypt. They gave him brilliant, flattering titles. They named him *King Falcon,* and *Sovereign of Victory.* They named him *King Reed,* because the reed was the symbol of Upper Egypt, and *King Wasp,* because the wasp was the symbol of Lower Egypt. And finally, the High Priest gave him the most exalted title of all: *"Meri-Ammon-Satep-En-Re,"* which means "Most Beloved of Ammon, Chosen of the Sun God!"

Pharoah, King of Egypt now, Alexander boarded a golden ship and sailed to the mouth of the Nile. Following the curve around Lake Mareotis, he reached the small island of Pharos. There he steered the ship along the island's coastline, all the while his eyes darting about as though in search of something extraordinary. The friends who were accompanying him felt the suspense.

"You're troubled, O King," they said. "What are you searching for?"

Alexander didn't answer. He held the rudder and continued to coast very slowly, eyeing the coastline intently. A small, humble village was coming into view along the edge of the sandy beach, perched on a narrow neck of land adjacent to Pharos. Alexander put out his hand. "Here!" he commanded.

All went ashore. The flustered little village gaped at the sight of so imposing an entourage. Alexander looked about him. "I like it," he said.

"What is it?" queried Hephaistion.

"I'm going to build a great city here. The location is perfect. With ships coming in from the sea on the north, and from the Nile River on the south, one day this will become the greatest port in the East. I'll build temples and palaces; I'll pave wide roads; I'll found great Schools, a Library, and a Gymnasium, and Theatres.

133

And I'll summon great sages, artists, scientists, poets, so that this city will become not only a mightly commercial center, but a great intellectual center as well."

"Long live Alexandria!" shouted the King's Companions. Swept up by his fiery words, they were already envisioning the new city spreading before them, vast, teeming with people, bursting with wealth.

He summoned his architects and engineers, staked out the plan himself for the walls, avenues, market places, roads, and when he had completed all the preparations and laid the foundations for his beloved Alexandria, he took his seven favorite Companions and old Callisthenes, who was to write down all he saw, and set out for the desert to worship the famous Oracle of Ammon and ask the god about his fate.

The small caravan headed into the endless stretch of desert, the horses' hooves sinking deep into the sand, bogging them down. On the third day out a violent wind swept in, hurling the sand in great waves all about them like a storm at sea and the guides lost their way. Toward evening Alexander, sighting birds returning to their nests, ordered the caravan to follow the birds. They were showing them the way, he reasoned, guessing their nests would have to be in trees near water at the Ammon oasis.

Taking their direction from the birds, they journeyed on, through scorching days and freezing nights. The heat and cold were unbearable. Their water ran out. They were plagued with thirst. Perdiccas and Crateros, who had been wounded at Gaza, were suffering terribly, in pain from their wounds that had opened again.

Cleitos, looking blacker than ever, with a white turban on his head against the sun, was riding ahead. He had started to sing to relieve the boredom, tired of seeing nothing but sand all these days. Ptolemy who was riding alongside, was looking at him and laughing. Behind them rode Philotas, his thoughts on his beloved brother Nicanor who had just died. He was inconsolable. Nothing pleased him anymore; everything looked black. He turned to the Cretan leader, Clearhos, who was riding beside him. "My father's right," he said. "Alexander's acting like a madman. He should have accepted Darius's offer. Imagine! Darius offers him ten thousand gold talents, his daughter, and the whole expanse of land from the Euphrates to the shores of Ionia, and he doesn't accept! What would you have done?"

"I wouldn't have accepted either," answered the proud Clearhos. "All or nothing!"

A heavy sigh sounded from behind. The two generals turned and saw old Callisthenes mounted on a bony horse, shaking his head dolefully.

"What's the matter, philosopher?" said Clearhos. "What do you think of our life here?"

The philosopher spurred the wretched horse and drew up to the two young men. *"Miden aghan!"*[16] he said in a low voice. *"Miden aghan!"* and he pointed to Alexander who was riding ahead with the two white wings waving in the wind.

Philotas threw a quick glance at Clearhos, but didn't speak.

Clearhos looked angry. "All things in moderation, eh?" he snapped at the philosopher.

"That's right," answered Callisthenes. "Why were our forebears great? Because they knew the golden mean. They knew one must not be overly rich or overly powerful or overly fortunate. *Pan metron ariston...*"[17]

"Nor overly brave?" shouted Clearhos who detested poor Callisthenes.

"Nor overly brave either!" retorted the philosopher. "That's madness too. Always follow the golden mean. Know what harmony is. Everything else is madness..."

"In other words," put in Philotas, winking at the philosopher, "...Alexander..."

"Shhh!" cautioned Callisthenes nervously. "Don't let him hear us."

45

At last one morning trees came into view in the distance, and they could see a tiny lake and a stark white temple out on the edge of the desert.

"We're here! We're here!" shouted the guides spurring their horses on.

"Wait!" called Alexander. "I will go first." And riding ahead, before long he came to the green oasis of the god. The priests, in their ceremonial dress, were standing erect at the temple entrance, awaiting him. The eldest, who was the "prophet," stepped forward and welcomed him. But as he was welcoming him, Alexander's friends began to arrive, too.

"Only the King has the right to enter the temple," said the prophet. "All the others must remain outside in the garden."

Alexander followed the prophet in silence. He strode across the sacred threshold and his Companions watched him disappear inside the dark interior. Never in his life, Alexander confessed to them later, had he been moved by so profound a holy feeling. "It was as though I were not a man," he told them, "but a god!"

Inside, the stony wooden statue of the god spired before him. In the darkness Alexander could barely distinguish anything but the two ram's horns that protruded from its head. But he could feel the powerful stirring of his soul in the divine presence.

"The god permits you to ask him your question," said the prophet.

Alexander's voice rang out:

"I ask the god if he is going to give me dominion over the world."

The god's head moved.

"The god answers yes," said the prophet. "Do you have another question?"

Alexander hesitated.

"About my father," he said after a pause. "I would like to ask..."

"O son of *Dia*,"[18] said the prophet, "you are standing in your father's presence."

"Father!" Alexander cried out then and fell to worship him. Thereupon began the dialogue between the god and the man. What transpired? What was said? No one has ever learned. In a letter that Alexander wrote to his mother that evening he said: *I heard many important, mysterious things from the god, but I cannot write you about them. I will tell you in person when I return to Macedonia.* But he never returned to Macedonia, and so Alexander took the secret with him to the grave.

When he emerged from the temple, he was immediately surrounded by his friends who rushed up to him.

"I learned what I wanted," he told them.

And now Hephaistion went in to the Oracle and asked if they should bestow divine honors upon Alexander.

"Yes," the god answered.

Philotas scowled. He turned to Ptolemy. "I pity men who have a demigod for a King," he said under his breath.

But inaudible as the words were, Hephaistion heard, and when they left the oasis and were heading back to Egypt, he went to Alexander and told him what Philotas had said.

"I'll be careful of Philotas from now on," said Alexander, angered, and he fell silent for a long time. Then he turned and looked at his Companions who were following behind in the sand. "My position is very difficult now," he said quietly to Hephaistion.

"Why, Alexander?" asked his faithful friend uneasily.

"I can't tell you what the god told me," Alexander answered, and was silent again.

They galloped on for some time without speaking. Finally Alexander broke the silence. "From now on," he said, "I shall be wearing two small silver ram's horns in my head."

"Like the god Ammon," thought Hephaistion, and a strange terror seized him. He could sense something in Alexander had changed. He had come out of the god's sanctuary a different man.

After some time Alexander turned and looked at Hephaistion. A warm tenderness was in his eyes. "Hephaistion," he said gently, "you alone understand me."

46

Great celebrations awaited Alexander in Egypt. But he was in a hurry. "No, no," he declined, "I must be on my way."

"Hasn't the campaign ended yet?" muttered Philotas.

Alexander turned, saw him, and his eyes darkened.

"No," he said coldly.

Old Parmenion approached. He looked at Alexander and saw, buried in his golden hair to the right and left of his forehead, two small curled horns sticking up. "What are those things in your hair, my King?" he asked startled.

"The god Ammon gave them to me," answered Alexander. Then presently, mastering his anger, "I don't permit anyone to question me!" he added.

"When do we leave?" asked Crateros.

"Immediately!"

Alexander had learned from his new spies that King Darius had finally assembled his entire army in Babylonia and was preparing to march out to find him. "I'll go find him myself," he announced, and gave orders now to his armies to set out.

Summer had arrived. The heat was scorching and the troops were grumbling. Alexander's friends pleaded with him. "This isn't the proper season," they implored. "How will we ever be able to march such a distance through so much desert in such a furnace? The army will be exhausted."

"I'm in a hurry," was Alexander's reply. "I'm in a hurry," and he spurred his horse onward.

They marched through Gaza, then Tyre. They crossed Syria and turned eastward. The months went by and they reached the Euphrates, built bridges, crossed over, and headed for the Tigris River.

Hundreds collapsed from the heat; thousands fell ill. At intervals along the way Alexander sent Stephan back to the chariot that was carrying the family of Darius, to ask how they were faring, and to see if they were in need, and he would send them whatever he had—food, water, fruit.

When they reached the banks of the Tigris River, they stopped to rest. Here Alexander found time to establish a new city— Nicephora.

139

The weather turned cooler, autumn came, and Alexander set out again. He crossed the Tigris River, and soon the scouts that he had dispatched up ahead arrived to report that Darius had encamped in the plain near the village of Gaugamela, and that the entire plain was blanketed with troops too numerous to count.

Fear gripped many of Alexander's soldiers. "We'll never get out of this alive," they muttered among themselves. "Out there in the plain he could spread out all his might—a million men. And what do we have to put up against him?"

"Our soul!" said Stephan angrily one day when he heard the soldiers' grumblings. "Our soul, and we'll win!"

That evening Parmenion came to Alexander. "My King," he said, "our position is precarious. If we want to win, we'll have to attack in secret, after dark."

"I will not steal the victory!" said Alexander proudly.

That same evening, in the fullness of night, the moon disappeared. A total eclipse. The soldiers leaped to their feet in fear. "A bad omen!" they cried. "We're done for!"

But Aristandros, Alexander's astrologer, was jubilant. "It's a good omen!" he shouted to them. "The moon is the symbol of the barbarians. Ours is the sun. The Persians are the ones who are done for!"

By the next day the advance guard of the Greeks had arrived within sight of the advance guard of the enemy. "Capture some prisoners!" Alexander called to Stephan who, as vanguard commander, was riding ahead, "and bring them to me."

In an hour Stephan was bringing in some ten Persian captives. Alexander interrogated them: how much strength did the Persians have? where were they encamped? where was Darius? Then he released them. "Go," he told them, "and tell your King that I am eager to meet him in battle where the two of us will fight it out."

For the next four days Alexander continued to remain opposite the enemy camp, preparing. This time he didn't rush. He knew that his entire campaign was dependent on this battle. Whoever won would take Asia. But on the second day the wife of Darius fell ill. No matter how well Alexander had cared for her during the long march, the hardships were so severe that the delicate queen finally took sick and died. Alexander himself went to her tent, saw her dead, and ordered that she be buried with royal honors.

And now a Persian who had been serving the queen, finding an opportunity, slipped out of the Greek camp and fled to the

Persians. He hurried at once to the tent of Darius and told him of the death of his wife.

Darius beat his breast in despair. "What wretchedness," he cried, "that a wife of the Great King should suffer such humiliations and die and be buried without honor like a slave!"

"No, my Great King," exclaimed the slave, "Alexander has behaved with great respect toward the queen and has ordered that she be buried with honors," and he described to Darius with what nobility Alexander had behaved toward the royal family that had fallen into his power.

"O gods of my country," Darius cried out then, "help me save my kingdom, but if it is written that I lose my throne, give Asia to Alexander, as a more just and magnanimous victor does not exist!" and he forthwith sat down and wrote a new letter to Alexander.

"I express my gratitude to you," he wrote, "for the nobility with which you have behaved toward my family and for the honorable burial that you gave my unfortunate wife, the queen. I again offer you peace. Take one of my daughters as your wife, take also my kingdom from Mesopotamia to Greece, and let us form an alliance. This is the last time that I will be writing to you; do not reject my offer."

But Alexander did not want to share his world rule with anyone. "Ammon gave it to me," he reasoned. "It's mine. I will not share it with anyone."

"The war will decide who will take Asia," he responded to Darius. "Peace can no longer exist between us."

47

That night he summoned Stephan again. "I have learned," he said, "that the Persians have dug pits between our campsite and theirs and have covered them with earth and branches. Take the best officers and soldiers and go out and examine the terrain. Keep in mind the danger and be careful!"

Stephan collected his good friends Leonidas and Hermolaos and some choice Companions, and well before midnight was ready to set out. "Take a dark lantern," he told them, "and a whistle and a pick-axe. And be on your guard. If you spot anything suspicious on the ground, hit it with the axe and see if it's hollow. If it is, whistle, and we'll all come running to fill it up."

"Are we going far?" one of them asked.

"As far into enemy territory as we can," answered Stephan.

A hot wind was blowing and a din like the roar of the sea was resounding from the infinite enemy camp on the opposite plain. The stars were glittering with a brilliant intensity in the moonless sky as they set out in the night, furtive, crouching low over the small lanterns that illumined the ground.

Stephan was walking ahead with Leonidas. "Who would have told us," Leonidas was saying, "that some day we'd be travelling together in the depths of Asia? Remember that day in your house, Stephan, when we were drinking a toast to the health of King Alexander, and none of us knew the name of the Persian capital? and now..."

"Let the reminiscing go for now," said Stephan sharply, "and pay attention to the ground. Don't talk; the enemy guards across the camp might hear us."

"Someone whistled!" Leonidas cocked his ear. They stopped. No one breathed. A second whistle sounded from the right.

"It's coming from here!" said Stephan and crouching forward they crept another hundred paces to where they saw a light. They moved close. It was Hermolaos, the whistle still in his mouth. "What is it?"

"A pit," indicated Hermolaos, uncovering some leaves at his feet. The others arrived, too, and they all fell to digging and had the hole filled in no time.

"Let's go," said Stephan, "on to the next one, with luck," and they scattered and began searching again.

But Leonidas would not leave Stephan's side. He looked as though he wanted to say something but didn't dare. "I have a suggestion," he ventured at last.

"What?" said Stephan.

"Let's do something daring."

"We'll have time in a day or so," laughed Stephan. "Don't be in a hurry."

"I want to do it tonight; I have a plan," persisted Leonidas.

"Let's hear it. But talk under your breath; we're getting close to the Persian camp."

"Okay, here it is. I've heard that the Persians have built some monstrous chariots. They say bayonets and swords and scythes stick out all over them and they're drawn by four horses and mow down everyone in their path. Do you know about them?"

"Yes. Our scouts have seen them. They're stationed in front of the cavalry—two hundred of them. So, what's your plan?"

"Let's go in and capture one tonight and bring it back to the King. We can see how it's made and make one ourselves. What do you say?"

Stephan reflected. "I like your plan," he said at last, "but it's difficult."

"That's why it's a daring act!" said Leonidas proudly. "What do you say, shall we go?"

"Just the pair of us?" laughed Stephan.

"No, we'll take Hermolaos, too. He'll be angry if we don't."

"Three aren't enough," said Stephan. "Wait here," and he disappeared in the night. Before long he was back with seven Companions, among them Hermolaos.

"Ready," he said in a low voice. "I explained your plan to them, Leonidas. Let's go!"

The nine proceeded with snuffed-out lanterns. The fires in the opposite camp loomed bigger and bigger, and the voices grew louder and louder as they approached. "Careful!" whispered Stephan. "We're here. Get down and crawl on your bellies, four to the right about fifty paces, and the other four to the left. I'll crawl along the middle and when you hear a sound, 'whoo-whoo,' like an owl's, stop and come and join me. Understand?"

"We understand," said the brave Companions falling in formation.

They crawled forward stealthily. The voices ahead were clearly audible now and they could see large shadows moving about the campfires.

Suddenly Stephan discerned a dense black shape outlined against a fire directly ahead of him and heard the neighing of horses. "It must be one of the two hundred chariots," he thought, inching closer as fast as he could. Someone was throwing more branches on the fire, and flames were leaping high, lighting up the ground all around. "It's a chariot with four horses. We're in luck!"

"Whoo-whoo!" he signalled, and halted. At once he could feel the eight Companions closing in on him from right and left.

"What is it?"

"Look straight ahead, in front of that big campfire."

"A chariot!" cried Leonidas. "On it, boys!" and he made to get up and dash for it.

"Wait!" whispered Stephan grabbing his arm. "Not so fast!

143

One of us will go in alone, just to scout around and see if it's guarded and find out how many guards there are and come right back."

"I'll be the one who goes," said Leonidas.

"Let me! Let me!" clamored the other Companions.

"It was my idea," said Leonidas. "I want the reward, Stephan. Let me go."

"You're right," said Stephan. "Go, but be sure you follow orders. You're to take a look only, do you hear? Just a look, and come back and report to us. Don't do anything foolish."

"Don't worry," said Leonidas. "Wait for me here," and he crawled away speedily through the grass and before long disappeared.

Five minutes passed, ten minutes.

"He's late," fidgeted Hermolaos.

"It's not time yet," whispered Stephan, "We'll wait."

Suddenly, in the flashes of light that the campfires were throwing off, Stephan noticed the four horses rear with a start and begin to whinny.

"Ohh!" he groaned.

"What's the matter?" asked Hermolaos anxiously.

Stephan didn't answer. His eyes were riveted on the horses, watching intently as a shadow leaped into the chariot. More shadows sprang up from the adjoining campfire. Shouts and whistles rang out.

"Brothers," Stephan turned to his Companions, "Leonidas is in danger. Let's go!"

In a flash they were on their feet and silently sprinting toward the heavy chariot that was armed with the swords and scythes. Some five or six men were already grappling inside. For a second they heard the voice of Leonidas, cursing.

"Attack the chariot, but don't make a sound!" commanded Stephan. "Leonidas is in there fighting. Don't let them hear us!"

Like lions the eight Companions sprang on the chariot. The five Persians had knocked Leonidas down and were beating him.

Stephan called to him under his breath. "Leonidas," he whispered, "Don't be afraid. We're here!"

"Take the chariot and leave," gasped a dying voice.

144   "Are you wounded, Leonidas?" cried Hermolaos beside himself.

"Farewell, brothers," came a faltering voice, almost lifeless now. "I'm dying!"

In a frenzy, Hermolaos and his friend Haricles lunged at the Persians, Stephan and the others right behind with upraised knives, hacking away right and left in the dark. Pressing forward, Stephan reached for the seat at the front of the chariot and grabbing the whip, lashed at the horses. Off they bolted, dragging the chariot with its load of friend and foe alike in the direction of the Greek camp.

The Persians let out a yell. Myriad shadows leaped up from the campfires and began to chase the chariot. But they were no match for the four frenzied galloping horses. Arrows were whistling all about the Companions. One hit Hermolaos in the neck. Another cut Stephan's ear off, clear to his head. It stung fiercely, but he held on to the reins and lashed and lashed away at the horses, beating them mercilessly, until he found himself entering the Greek campsite and pulling up before Alexander's tent.

Phalangites rushed up with lanterns. Stephan leaped to the ground. Three of the Persians were lying dead in the chariot, the other two had rolled out before the horses bolted. Leonidas was sprawled at the back of the chariot, dead.

Hearing the commotion, Alexander bounded out of his tent. He took one look at the scythed chariot, glanced at Stephan and his Companions, and understood. "Bravo, Stephan! You've brought me one of the famous armored chariots. You're a brave lad."

"I'm nothing," Stephan answered, trying to stem the blood that was flowing from his ear. "Here's the brave one," and he pointed to Leonidas whose wound-riddled body lay swimming in blood.

48

Alexander slept soundly throughout the remainder of the night. When dawn broke at last, the generals gathered outside his tent for their orders, but still he slept on, serenely, as if he had not a care in the world.

Finally Parmenion decided to go in and wake him. He entered the tent and stood by his bed.

"Alexander," he called softly.

But Alexander was sleeping soundly and didn't hear.

"Alexander!" called Parmenion again.

Nothing.

Parmenion reached down and grasped him by the shoulder and shook him. Alexander wakened.

"What is it?" he asked rubbing his eyes.

"You're sleeping," laughed Parmenion, "as though the battle were over and won already. Get up, it's morning."

Alexander laughed. "So what," he said springing out of bed. "We're going to win. All this time we've been chasing after Darius and, look, now he's come of his own accord to surrender." And dressing swiftly in his battle panoply he went outside to his assembled generals.

"It's a great day!" he shouted. "Today is the day the fate of the world will be decided. The barbarians on one side, we Greeks on the other, and Asia in the center. We'll fight and whoever wins will win her!"

"We will! We will!" shouted the generals forming a circle around him. In the waking glow of the dawning day he stood in their midst like a dazzling sun himself. His belt was gold, a gift from the island of Rhodes; his sword, a slender blade of steel with a splendid hilt, a gift from the King of Cyprus. His bronze breastplate was decorated with a carved eagle clutching a writhing snake in its talons. In his hand he held an ancient shield that the notables of Troy had given him from the ruins of their ancient celebrated city. And on his helmet waved the two huge white wings.

The sun came out. It shot its rays down on the plain and brought to light the thousands of men who were preparing to fight. King Darius, dressed in gold, was offering sacrifices to the gods.

"Forward!" shouted Alexander. "The God of Greece be with us!"

The elite royal cavalry, always the first to spearhead the charge, surged forward. At their head sped Alexander, straight for Darius. All around waited the enemy host, too numerous to count.

Darius

But who among them could stop the fury of Alexander's thrust! They crumpled in his path and scattered, leaving their Great King exposed.

On streaked Alexander, directly toward him, javelin at the ready. And once again, at sight of this god-like youth bearing down on him, Darius felt his knees and courage buckle. Panic seized him and, bolting from the chariot, he leaped on a horse and ran, with Alexander and his faithful entourage in hot pursuit.

Shocked at seeing Darius in flight, the Grand Army's central core wavered and began falling back, and the Greeks, taking courage, pressed their assault. The slaughter that followed was horrendous—Persians dropping their arms and fleeing, Greeks chasing them down, and Alexander and his men leaving Darius no quarter to catch his breath. On he ran; on they ran.

But as they were chasing him, a breathless horseman, a messenger from Parmenion, caught up with Alexander. "My King," he shouted to him, "the army's left wing is in danger! Parmenion needs your help!"

Abandoning Darius, then, Alexander spun his horse around and raced back to his army. Parmenion was indeed in great peril. Twenty-thousand cavalry were attacking him from the flank and the Greeks were falling back. Alexander was barely arriving in time.

"Courage, men!" he shouted. "Fall on them! All together now!"

The Greeks went at them, but the Persians, too, fought valiantly. Fifty of Alexander's elite horsemen fell dead. Hephaistion was wounded.

But then a startled cry went up along the enemy lines. "Darius is gone!" The soldiers turned, looked, saw the central core of their army where the Great King had been fighting in disordered flight, and fear gripped them. The battle was lost. Bridling their horses around, they turned and fled, and by nightfall the too-big-to-be-counted Persian host had all but vanished in the dark. Thousands of them were lying dead in the vast plain. Of the Macedonians, only five hundred were slain.

The Greek army began striking their shields now in triumph, and when they caught sight of Alexander riding past them on Bucephalas, their cheers rose to the heavens.

148

"Long live Alexander, King of Asia!"

But there was no response from Alexander. He dismounted from his horse soaked in blood. His jaw was set. The victory was enormous but he wasn't satisfied. He bathed and changed his clothes. "Darius got away from me," he brooded angrily. "He got away from me again. As long as he's alive, Asia isn't mine."

49

"And now," Parmenion was asking, "where are we headed?"

"Darius has gone ahead and is showing us the way," Alexander answered. "Toward Babylonia."

"Two hundred and sixty thousand meters," muttered the old general.

"Since when have you started measuring the distances?" laughed Alexander.

"You're the King of Macedonia," murmured the old general. "I obey you."

"I am the King of Asia," corrected Alexander proudly, and Parmenion was silent.

The army headed south. Envoys were sent ahead to the renowned city with this message from the King: "Have no fear. I come as a liberator, not a conqueror. I will free you from the Persian yoke and give back world-renowned Babylonia her former rights and her past glory. Open your gates to me!"

When they arrived, the gates to the colossal city were open. The Babylonians, who hated the Persians for subjugating them and taking away their rights and treasures, welcomed Alexander joyfully. The notables came forth, bowed to him, and presented him with the keys to the city. The flower-crowned populace cheered him in the streets and women showered him with flowers from the rooftops. In the temples they were lighting incense, and priests were giving sacrificial offerings of thanks to the gods.

"Let no one harm this city and its inhabitants!" Alexander ordered his army. "I am distributing money to you so that you can pay for anything you buy. We are not conquerors, we are liberators."

And surrounded by the Babylonian priests, Alexander, with his silver ram's horns in his hair, twenty-five years old and lord of

149

an infinite Empire, went forth daily to offer sacrifices to the gods and to see to the welfare of his subjects.

He dispatched heralds to Greece to announce his victories and sent costly gifts to the Athenians and to the Plataeans and to the other cities that had first taken the lead over a century and a half ago to expel the Persians from Greece. "I am marching to Susa," he notified the Greeks, "to the great capital of the Persians, to avenge Greece for all the humiliations she has suffered."

And indeed, how many times in the past had not Greek envoys been compelled to hasten to the proud palaces of Susa and beg for an audience with the Great King. And now, the Greeks' Supreme Commander would be entering those sacred courts, mounted on his horse!

"On to Susa!" he commanded.

"Three-hundred and seventy thousand meters," muttered Parmenion again. Alexander turned and looked at him but did not speak. "Parmenion has grown old," he thought, "and has begun measuring the distances."

He had sent men on ahead to Susa to allay the people's fears there. "I liberate," he notified them again. "I do not conquer. I will not harm Susa. I will respect your lives, your honor, and your property. Let your notables come forth and turn over the keys to me."

Some twenty days later, when Alexander arrived at Susa, the notables had assembled at the gate and were waiting to worship him and present him with the keys. And once again Alexander sacrificed to the gods, issued money to the soldiers and gave orders they were not to lay a hand on the city or its citizens. And when he entered the royal palaces he marvelled. Never had he imagined such wealth. The King's reservoirs were brimming with gold and precious stones. His chests were filled with luxurious fabrics.

In all the dazzling triumph Alexander did not forget the mother and daughters of Darius whom he was dragging with him on these long, tedious marches. They were exhausted, and he felt compassion for them. "Prepare the luxurious apartments in the Palace for the royal family," he ordered, and went himself to personally tell the old mother of Darius what provision he was making for them. The poor queen fell at his feet and kissed them. But respecting her rank Alexander reached down and raised her up. "I ask only one thing of you," he said to her.

"I am your slave," answered the old queen. "Ask whatever you want of me."

"See to it," said Alexander, "that your grandson and the little princesses learn Greek."

Alexander did not remain in Susa long. He was in a hurry to continue his march, to conquer the other two capitals that belonged to Darius—Persepolis and Ecbatana—and to proceed even beyond. To where? To the end of the world.

Old Parmenion, the voice of reason who was constantly saying, "Enough! Stop!" approached him again. "My King," he said, "our frontiers are secure now, from the mountains of Armenia on the north to the Persian Gulf on the south. Beyond that on the east stretches Persia, exhausted and harmless. Our soldiers are glutted with all this conquering. They're tired now—stop!"

But Alexander ordered Bucephalas brought to him. "On to Persepolis!" he shouted. "Forward!"

And the army set out again.

"Six hundred thousand meters," muttered old Parmenion again, "six hundred thousand meters from Susa to Persepolis! What madness!"

They were trudging through formidable mountains four and five thousand meters high. There were no roads, no level plains, no sandy deserts on this march. It was December, the heart of winter. The icy mountain cliffs were covered with snow, sending soldiers skidding and plummeting to their deaths. The cold was unbearable. The men were beginning to grumble. "We're following a madman," Philotas muttered to Cleitos. "Why should we be setting out in the dead of winter to cross the mountains?"

"He put us through the same ordeal when we had to cross that blistering desert from Syria to Mesopotamia," answered Cleitos. "Instead of waiting for winter, he made us set out in the heart of summer."

"Well? Isn't he crazy then?" said Philotas.

Cleitos shrugged. "Maybe."

Alexander, wrapped in his mantle, was riding ahead alone, oblivious of the hardships, engrossed in his thoughts. He was the descendent of Heracles—and he, too, had to perform all the labors.

At last he arrived before the holy city of the Persians—Persepolis—the winter capital of the Great King. "So this is where they came from," he thought to himself, "This is where those barbaric armies that profaned everything Greece held sacred came

151

from. I must avenge her." And giving orders to his soldiers to plunder this wealthiest of cities he, himself, hurried to the Palace to take possession of the royal treasures. "Twenty-thousand mules and five-thousand camels are not enough to carry away the treasures that I have found in Persepolis," Alexander wrote to Antipatros in Macedonia.

And when he seated himself on the all-gold throne of the Persian King, many of his Companions could not hold back the tears. "O holy shades of Marathon and Salamis," Alexander murmured, "rejoice and rest at last! Behold! one of your descendents has succeeded in sitting on the throne of the great enemy!"

It wasn't long before Alexander's Companions began to grow accustomed to the luxury and wealth. Each had his own private transport wagons, loaded down with plunder, and soon they were all dressing like lordly Persian magnates in gold-embellished purple. They came to disdain the old practice of anointing their bodies with oil after bathing and began using costly perfumes instead. Now one would ornament his sandals with silver nails, another would import special sand from Egypt to spread on the ground to do his gymnastics, and Philotas had even ordered nets made up, the size of twenty kilometers, to use for hunting birds and animals.

Alexander took pleasure in lavishing his wealth on his faithful Companions. He enjoyed having them ask him for gifts, and he was generous not only with his friends but with the humblest and most insignificant of his soldiers as well.

One day he noticed a Macedonian soldier leading a mule with a load of gold coins that were destined for the Palace. The mule was exhausted and ready to collapse, and the soldier took the pack off the animal's back and loaded the treasure on his own back. Alexander laughed. "Hey, comrade," he called to the soldier, "haul that load over to your tent. It's yours."

He scolded his friends about one thing only. They possessed a great many servants now and did nothing for themselves, and during all the time they were living in Babylonia and Susa and Persepolis they lived like effete Asiatics. "I'm amazed," Alexander would harp at them, "how you fail to understand a thing that's so simple, that the person who works sleeps better than the one who's lazy.

"It's not enough that we defeat our enemies in battle," he would chide them. "We must also keep from falling into their weaknesses and habits."

He, himself, set the example, working constantly, tiring himself endlessly, never allowing himself to slip into laziness. No sooner was a war over than he would turn at once to hunting, in order to keep his body hardened, or he would compete in games, or go on long marches.

And so one day when his friends were carousing and the soldiers were comfortably settled in the luxurious homes that they had appropriated for themselves, Alexander ordered the trumpets to signal the call for assembly. Everyone rushed to the Palace, the generals clamoring about Alexander.

"What is it, Alexander?" asked Hephaistion in his gentle voice.

"We're leaving."

"Leaving!" they all exclaimed in dismay. "But we're getting along so well here."

"That's why we're leaving!" answered Alexander.

50

There was no resting for Alexander until he had Darius in his hands alive or dead. There could not be two Kings of Asia. "On to Ecbatana!" he ordered. He had learned that Darius had fled there and was mustering an army again to attack him.

But when they arrived in Ecbatana, Darius was gone. The gates of the city were open and they sped through the streets straight to the Palace, but Darius had fled eight days earlier. Alexander was enraged. "I'll track him down!" he vowed. "he won't get away!"

He set about at once gathering the royal treasures that he had found in Babylonia and Susa and Persepolis, and bringing them all to Ecbatana, he summoned his old general Parmenion. Parmenion must have been all of seventy years old now and was always grumbling, tired after so many years of fighting.

"My venerable general," Alexander said to him, "my faithful co-worker, the time has come for us to part. I am going to entrust you with an important, confidential office. You are to remain here in Ecbatana to guard my treasures."

Now Parmenion could see that Alexander no longer wanted him around. He knew Alexander would rather dispense with his

153

opinions which were often at odds with the King's. "I'm still able to fight," he said, betraying a tremor in his voice.

"I know it. I know it," said Alexander grasping his old fellow warrior's hand respectfully. "But I cannot entrust the treasures of the Empire to anyone else. I ask this last service of you. You're a soldier, you won't refuse."

Parmenion lowered his head. "What you say will be done," he murmured, and brusquely wiped a tear from his eye.

Alexander threw himself into the chase after Darius, unfettered now. He rode into Persia and there one night he learned that the satrap Bessos, who was with Darius, had compelled the Great King to abdicate and wanted to be proclaimed King of the Persians himself. Choosing his best horsemen, then, Alexander rushed off to catch Darius and his company. He no longer wanted Darius's death now that he had stepped down from the throne. The big enemy was Bessos, the general who planned to be proclaimed King.

He raced his army up the mountains, galloping by day and by night, stopping only toward evening to rest a bit, then setting out again in the dead of night, racing on like this without sleep until he finally picked up Darius's tracks. Town after town was reporting that Darius had passed through, a prisoner of Bessos's, but by now Alexander's Companions had begun to tire. After fifteen days and nights of riding without sleep, they had come to the end of their endurance.

Singling out five hundred horsemen, Alexander pressed on. "Onward! Onward!" he shouted. "There's no time for rest. There's no time for sleep! Follow me!"

The five hundred sped through the mountains and plains in hostile, unfamiliar lands, undaunted; but as the days flew by, many began to collapse, falling off their horses, near death. After three days and nights only sixty horsemen were still riding behind Alexander, among them Stephan, worn to a frazzle, but too ashamed to stop. The others had all dropped along the wayside, half dead from exhaustion.

At last one noon they sighted Darius's company. The sixty Companions took one look at the King's chariot, stared at the thousands of horsemen and foot soldiers surrounding it, and cowered. "On them!" shouted Alexander spurring his horse. And too ashamed not to, the Companions, skeletons now from all the fatigue and sleepless nights, spurred their horses and charged, barely able to hang on to their mounts.

The Persians turned, saw the Greek horsemen approaching, and started with fright. "They're coming!" shouts went up. "The Greek army's caught up with us!" and at sight of the Greeks galloping toward them, Bessos, fearful lest Darius slow down his escape, pulled out his sword and plunged it into the King's heart. Then scrambling on his horse, he turned in headlong flight, his entire company following behind in panic.

Alexander, speeding toward them, arrived at Darius's chariot, looked inside, saw Darius collapsed on the floor, and bent over him to grasp his hand. "I didn't intend to kill you," he said. "That was not what I wanted."

Darius's eyelids fluttered. They opened. He saw Alexander, recognized him, and pressed his hand—as if to say "Thank you" for the way he had behaved toward his mother and wife and children. Then he closed them again. "Alexander..." he murmured faintly, and died.

Alexander, deeply moved, reached down then and laid his royal purple mantle over Darius's body.

51

"The war is over at last! Darius died with Alexander's name on his lips. Our goal has been achieved. Now let's enjoy the fruits of our victory!" So went the jubilant talk among the soldiers and officers.

The great campaign had ended in triumph. Their eyes had witnessed an unbelievable spectacle, they had covered themselves with glory and riches, and now, how good it would be to return to Macedonia and the rest of Greece, settle down in their own homes again like men of rank, and pass away the hours relating their great exploits to their friends and children.

Philip the physician was rubbing his hands in glee. "It won't be long now," he was saying to his son. "We'll be heading back to Macedonia soon. Before long we'll be happily settled in our little home again."

Stephan shook his head.

"What? Aren't you young ones glutted yet?" exclaimed Philip. "What more do you want?"

Stephan smiled. "When we were chasing Darius, we crossed a high mountain, and when we were at the top I looked out toward the east. What a rich land, father, what infinite plains, and out in the distance beyond, I saw a blue sea."

"What are you trying to say?"

"Isn't it a shame not to go there?"

"You've got the same sickness," laughed Philip, "that Alexander has."

"What sickness?"

"Conqueritis."

"It's the sickness of youth," laughed Stephan. "When I get old, I'll be cured."

"I'm on my way to put Alexander to bed," said Philip. "He's exhausted. He's a man, not a god, and in the long run he's likely to collapse. Then what will become of his infinite Empire?"

But as he was talking, Alexander appeared, mounted on Bucephalas. He was in battle dress, and the white wings were waving on his iron helmet again. "We must set out!" he called to his generals. "Get the army ready!"

Philip stared at him in amazement. "He's got nine lives!" he murmured.

Alexander passed in front of Stephan. "Come," he said. "On your horse!"

The army scrambled to fall into position. "Where are we off to again?" they grumbled. "When will it end? He's King of Asia now; Darius is dead. What more does he want? We've been fighting four years now. Enough!"

Our friend Hermolaos's eyes were shining. "Here's wishing us good journeying!" he shouted with glee to Stephan as he rode up. "Where to this time?"

"We're off to track down Bessos who killed Darius and wants to become King."

"Let's track him down! By all means let's track him down!" cried Hermolaos. "And may we never catch him and never have to stop!" Then sighing, "Poor Leonidas," he murmured, his eyes misting, "if only you were still alive!"

"Take your position," said Stephan, "and leave off the crying. We're all going to die. We'll be lucky if we can die like Leonidas."

Alexander went by again, reviewing the troops. All at once he stopped. He looked at the myriad wagons loaded with treasures and the mules weighed down with loot, and he frowned. Each of his generals had his own personal convoy, and each was dragging along the loot he had plundered from the Persian palaces and noble estates. He looked at his own personal convoy, at his chariots and the carts and wagon trains loaded with treasures. "This won't do," he muttered. "I must save myself from all this wealth. I must be free."

He summoned his generals. "My friends," he said, "It's shameful to be slaves to wealth. Of what use is all this excess baggage that we're dragging along? An infinite Asia still stretches before us. We'll find all the treasure we want. Let's free ourselves. I'll set the example." And saying, he ordered his servants to burn all his baggage.

The generals hesitated. They hated to see such treasures go to waste.

"Go ahead," said Alexander. "Triumph over your petty interests. Free yourselves."

The generals felt shamed, and collecting their rich baggage, set the torch to it themselves. Philotas, though, held off until the end, reluctant to burn all that precious loot.

"Burn it!" ordered Alexander.

Philotas bit his lip, and cursing under his breath, he set fire to the treasure-laden wagons.

"Now!" said Alexander. "Forward!"

They set out. The astounding chase began once more, across mountains and valleys, through green fertile plains or sun-blistered deserts. Crossing the desert they suffered terrible thirst. One day Stephan, who was riding ahead of the others with his scouts, spied a bit of water in a hollowed-out rock, and gathering it up in his helmet raised it to his lips to drink. He was parched. They had been without water for two days. But just as he was about to drink, he checked himself, ashamed to be drinking while his leader was dying of thirst, and he hurried with it to Alexander.

The King took the helmet brimming with the precious water and opened his parched lips, but as he was about to drink, his eye caught sight of the Companions standing about him watching eagerly, and tilting the helmet away from his lips then, he spilled the water on the sand. "Either we all drink, or no one drinks!" he said and with that the soldiers struck their shields in pride. "Lead us wherever you want, Alexander!" they shouted, "even if we die of thirst with you!"

52

They passed through Tehran, today's Persian capital, then marched into Hyrcania, and on to the Caspian Sea. Was it an ocean? a sea? a lake? No one knew.

"Let's go! Let's go!" prodded Alexander. "Leave it to the sophists to figure out. We have other matters to solve. More important matters. Let's go!"

They raced on and on, chasing Bessos, and Asia kept unfolding before them without end.

One day Alexander turned to Philotas with a laugh. "If your father Parmenion were here, he'd be scolding me again. Do you know how many thousands of meters we've covered these past months?"

"Yes," said Philotas. "Eight hundred and eighty thousand. I checked with the pacers yesterday. They've been keeping track."

"Correct! And we're only beginning."

"Only beginning!" cried Hephaistion startled. "Alexander, when are you going to be satisfied?"

158 "When I die," said Alexander, a mournful tone in his voice, "because one day I, too, shall die."

They arrived at what is known today as Afghanistan. Here Alexander halted for a few days at a brilliant site that pleased him and laid foundations for a new city. This, too, he named Alexandria.

They scaled new mountains, crossed more rivers, traversed new plains, built more cities. By now they had covered more than two thousand four hundred kilometers. The soldiers were dropping by the wayside exhausted. Their feet were frozen. Many were stricken with snow-blindness. But they arrived at last in Bactria, today's Turkestan. Here Alexander learned that barbaric tribes had captured Bessos and were bringing the satrap to him. And when indeed they laid the murderer of Darius before him, bound in heavy ropes, and Alexander denounced him as a traitor and had him killed, the army breathed a sigh of relief.

"Now at last the war is over," they muttered among themselves. "Darius is dead, the satrap who tried to take his throne is dead, Persia is ours. Now we'll return to our country."

But Alexander mounted his horse again and gave the familiar signal.

"Forward!"

"Where to?" cries went up among the soldiers. "Where are we headed for now?"

Alexander spun Bucephalas around. "Which of you raised your voices?" he thundered. "Step forward and stand before me!"

The Macedonian phalanxes stirred, moved a few paces, and presented themselves in formation before Alexander. The King looked at them for a long while in silence. They were his old comrades-in-arms, brave, faithful, covered with wounds. He loved them. He had subdued Greece and Epiros and Thrace with them. Together they had marched through Asia, conquered a whole world. And now they were abandoning him?

He held his emotion in check. "Companions," he said in a gentle voice, "you've grown weary?"

An old Macedonian stepped forward. His face was carved with sword wounds. "King Alexander," he said, "enough! We've served you faithfully and courageously. We've done all we could. We're men, not gods. We can endure no more. Allow us to return to our country."

Alexander was silent. A terrible battle was raging inside him. He felt a savage anger because his faithful ones were abandoning him, and at the same time he felt compassion because he knew that they were human, and were tired, and longed for their homes.

Hephaistion drew close. "Alexander..." he whispered entreatingly, bending over him and gently taking his hand.

But Alexander had made up his mind. He raised his head.

"My faithful comrades-in-arms," he said. "I thank you for your devotion and your valor. We have worked well together up to now. I have no complaint. You are tired. Others will come in your place, younger and fresher men. I will continue my mission with them. Now, return to your homes with godspeed. Those of you who can no longer endure following me, leave! I will pay all your wages, and I will give you valuable gifts so that you may return to your country like noblemen."

He spoke, and the valiant old warriors broke down and wept.

"Forgive us," they said. "We shall leave."

"Godspeed! Godspeed!" repeated Alexander, and dug his heels into his horse.

53

They had been travelling northward for three days. Where were they going? No one knew anymore—only Alexander. When his devoted friend asked him, Alexander merely answered, "I'll tell you later, when we get there," and fell silent.

At night three of Alexander's commanders, his devoted Hephaistion, Crateros, and Cleitos, were sitting around a campfire, talking.

"Did he tell you anything, Hephaistion?" Cleitos was asking. He was beginning to grow angry that Alexander no longer confided in his friends the way he used to, growing more distant every day, surrounding himself now with Persian magnates who worshipped him like a god.

The outspoken Cleitos was simple and rugged. He didn't like these Anatolian mannerisms of Alexander's. "What's all this?" he would say boldly. "What's all this? Alexander is forgetting that he's Greek. He dresses up in fancy clothes and puts on bracelets and earrings and lets men worship him like slaves."

This particular evening he was even angrier because Alexander had ordered them to continue the march without telling them for what purpose. He turned to Hephaistion, the King's most trusted friend. "Did he tell you anything? Did he tell you where we're going?"

"No," Hephaistion answered in a hurt voice. "Some profound anxiety is tormenting him, but I don't know what."

The cold was stinging. Crateros threw more wood on the fire. "I have faith in the King," he said quietly.

"I have faith in Alexander, too!" said Hephaistion, his voice warm with tender feeling.

"I have faith in no one," said Cleitos. "No one."

"Why?" asked the trusting Crateros.

"I have my reasons," answered Cleitos, and rose to his feet.

Summer came. There were days when they marched sixty and seventy thousand meters at a stretch. One day they arrived at the famous city of Samarkand in Sogdiana. Alexander installed a garrison here and, pressing on another three hundred kilometers northward, came to the Jaxartes River where he built another city, another Alexandria. Here one morning he took Hephaistion and set out to climb a high hill. He was restless, hardly able to contain himself, and they were climbing rapidly.

"I'm wrestling with a big problem," he said. "When we set out from Babylonia, heading south, we came to an ocean. And when we set out from Ecbatana and headed northeast, we came to another ocean. These must be the boundaries of the world.

"We know from our teachers," he went on, "that the Earth is a disc that floats in the ocean. So I've reached the end of the Earth on two of its sides, and now I've set out to go farther, to find the world's other end. There, that's the secret of this last march. And now, when we get to the top of this hill, what do you suppose we're going to see? Ocean? Or more endless land?"

Hephaistion was silent. He felt a strange agitation as he looked at Alexander, like the time when Alexander had come out from the Oracle of Ammon. "This man isn't human," he thought. "He's not human like us. Some great god dwells in his breast."

"If the end of the Earth is out here," resumed Alexander, still plunged in his thoughts, "then there remain the western boundaries. We'll turn back and circle around Africa until we find the end of the world."

Hephaistion shuddered. Until now he had thought that he knew even the most secret corners of his friend's soul. Now he saw that this Alexander walking beside him was filled with mystery, like a god.

161

As they neared the top of the hill Alexander broke into a run, and with swift, leaping strides he bounded to the highest vantage point at the crest. He looked, and bit his lip.

"What is it?" Hephaistion cried, scrambling up behind him.

"Take a look," said Alexander. "There it is. Endless land. The Earth has no end."

"What do we do now?" asked Hephaistion in agony.

"We have fresh soldiers," said Alexander. "The old ones who were grumbling are gone. With the new army we can continue the march."

Hephaistion didn't speak. Alexander, too, said nothing more and they turned and headed back to Samarkand.

Myriad envoys were waiting for them there, hatchet-carrying envoys sent by wild, unknown tribes who lived beyond the Caspian and the Caucasus, out beyond the River Jaxartes. They were dressed in sheepskins and smelled like horses. Alexander looked them over thoughtfully. "Is the Earth so big, then?" he pondered in silence. "Will I be able to conquer it all? There's no time to lose. I must hurry."

Envoys had also come from the distant east, from India. They were dark, half-naked, with faces that reflected great dignity and serenity.

"Is your country big?" Alexander asked them.

They smiled. "Infinite, O King," they said. "Our country is infinite. What is Persia compared to our country!"

"And eastward, beyond your land?" pressed Alexander with a pang of agitation. "What's out there?"

"Another country, O King, bigger even than our own, and wealthier, too, with even more people."

"What is it called?"

"China. And its people are yellow."

Alexander asked no more. "The Earth is large," he thought to himself again. "There's no time to waste."

But the next day a frightful thing happened. Cleitos, as we learned earlier, was one of Alexander's best friends, and one of his bravest generals. He was a bit brusque and didn't mince words, and when something displeased him, he spoke his mind out loud and clear, afraid of no one. But Alexander understood him and never grew angry with him. "Black Cleitos," he would laugh, "has permission to be insolent."

It so happened that on this day Alexander had organized great celebrations in Samarkand, and that evening he invited his friends to a banquet. Cleitos, of course, was among the first. They began drinking and talking about all the great things that Alexander had accomplished up to now.

"There's still a lot more that I must do," Alexander was saying. "The Earth is big. In a few days we'll be leaving here."

"Leaving! To go where?" asked Cleitos who had been silent up to now, listening with irritation to all the others heaping accolades on Alexander.

"Eastward, where the sun rises. Toward India."

The flatterers broke into applause, and some pseudo-philosopher called Anaxarhos, who had a crown of roses on his head, stood up. "You are greater than Heracles, King Alexander," he said, "and I will prove it." And he proceeded to sing Alexander's praises so shamelessly that the philosopher Callisthenes burst out laughing.

"Silence!" ordered Alexander. "Why are you laughing?" And the flatterer continued with his unctuous fawning, and now Ptolemy and Perdiccas were embarrassed and so were the Cretan chieftain Clearhos and the physician Philip and even Hephaistion. But most annoyed of all was Cleitos.

"Sit down! For shame!" he shouted at the philosopher, banging his wine cup against the table.

Alexander turned and glared. "What's the matter?" he demanded.

"It's shameful to be listening to such brazen flattery," said Cleitos angrily. "You're not a god, Alexander, you're a man. And who should know it better than I, I who saved your life at Granicus, remember?"

"How dare you talk back to your King!" flared Alexander. "I've put up with you long enough. You've gone too far!"

With that Cleitos exploded. He got to his feet, knocking over the wine cup and spilling his wine and began giving vent to all the things that had been festering in his heart. "We're not your slaves!" he shouted. "We're Greeks! You've changed. We helped you conquer Asia and it went to your head. You think you're a god now. You've stuck two ram's horns on your head and make as though you're the son of the god Ammon. You dress yourself in those ridiculous Anatolian clothes and strut and preen. You allow your-

163

self to be worshipped by barbarians and let them kiss your feet. You've lost all concept of moderation and want us free men to worship you, too!"

"Down! Down! Get him out of here!" voices rang out from the tables all about.

On his feet now, Alexander grabbed an apple from the table and threw it at Cleitos's head.

Crateros and Ptolemy, too, had leaped up and were rushing to get hold of Cleitos to quiet him. But Cleitos was burning and went on raging, and Alexander, snatching up a spear went to throw it at him, but Hephaistion and Perdiccas grabbed his arm and held him back. "Let me at him! Let me at him!" he shouted, and turning to a trumpeter who was standing at the door, ordered him to sound the trumpet. "Call my army! I'm being betrayed!"

But the trumpeter hesitated, and Alexander struck him a blow with his fist and the trumpet rolled to the ground. Then grabbing the spear again he ordered everyone to leave the banquet and leave him alone with Cleitos to battle it out. But Crateros and Ptolemy had managed to drag Cleitos away, out into the corridor.

Alexander sat down at the table. He was ghastly white. He filled his wine cup and downed it in a gulp. He filled it a second time and drained that, too.

Suddenly, there was Cleitos again, coming through the door, raving and shouting. This time there was no holding Alexander back. He snatched up the spear and before his friends could stop him, he flung it at Cleitos and pierced his heart. Cleitos collapsed writhing to the ground.

Everyone froze with horror. In a flash Alexander came to his senses and with a cry fell upon Cleitos, pulled out the spear from his breast and started to plunge it into his own heart. But Hephaistion was in time to grab his arm, and Perdiccas wrenched the spear from his hand. "Cleitos! Cleitos!" groaned Alexander then and slumped to the ground beating his head against the tiles in despair.

54

The army was in chaos. They splintered into factions and fell to quarrelling, some taking the part of Alexander and others that of Cleitos. The more prudent of the commanders, among them Ptolemy and Stephan, tried to impose discipline. "It's not your business to judge and criticize what the King does," they admonished. "Stop quarrelling among yourselves. No one's to blame. Blame it on the wine."

But Callisthenes the philosopher had grown bolder and could no longer restrain himself. "We're Greeks," he shouted. "We're not barbarians. We don't prostrate ourselves worshipping. We came here to conquer the Asiatics, to bring them our civilization. We didn't come to have them conquer us and make barbarians of us. We don't want luxurious dress and perfumes and servilities. I'm going to write all this down in my History. I'm going to enumerate every detail so that future generations will learn the truth. God take pity on you!" he shouted, brandishing his pen high in the air like a spear. "I'm writing it all down!"

Callisthenes had attracted a large following of disgruntled Macedonians and Greeks and a few commanders.

"Calm yourself," Stephan urged the fired-up philosopher. "For your own good, quiet down and stop all this agitating."

But Callisthenes was beside himself. For months now he had been watching Alexander behaving like an Asiatic monarch and he was seething inside. Now he could no longer hold back. "I'm a Greek philosopher," he shouted, "the disciple of Aristotle. I have a responsibility!"

"Callisthenes is right," yelled a voice in the crowd. "We didn't come here to lose our liberty!" It was Stephan's friend Hermolaos, defiantly waving his scarred arm in the air. Haricles, too, was beside him angrily yelling, "Down with the tyrant! Down with the tyrant!"

"Hermolaos!" Stephan called to him.

But Hermolaos went on shouting. "He's right," he was saying. "You all know how much I love and admire Alexander. He expanded the frontiers of our country, took them to the ends of the world. But he wants to narrow the frontiers of our soul. I'd rather be free in a small village than a slave in an infinite Empire!"

A crowd of Macedonians had rushed up to Hermolaos and were standing around him, listening approvingly.

"We're with you! We're with you!" they yelled, waving their spears. "Freedom!"

Stephan took his friend by the arm. "Let's go," he said. They walked a few steps and went into a garden. The evening air was redolent with scents. They sat beneath a rosebush.

"Hermolaos," Stephan said in a gentle voice, "calm yourself, don't carry on so. Listen to me." And he began to talk to him

165

about Alexander, what Macedonia had been like before him, what all Greece had been like. "And now, look how far our frontiers reach! Just look." And with the tip of his spear he etched out the new map of Greece on the ground. But Hermolaos was shaking his head.

"Just think back at how you were suffocating in narrow Macedonia," Stephan continued. "Just remember that day at my house in Pella when you were ranting about how you were suffocating in our tiny land and how we all laughed at you. And yet, you were the only one who felt the things that Alexander felt— that our country was small and had to grow to keep us from smothering. Do you remember that?"

"I haven't forgotten any of it," Hermolaos answered heatedly. "I haven't forgotten anything. But what does it all mean? I'm still raging that I'm suffocating! And not because our country is narrow any longer, but because this Alexander of yours is trying to take away my freedom."

"Don't listen to that crackpot philosopher," said Stephan. "He's always drunk. He knows how to talk, how to pick things apart, but he has no common sense."

"Callisthenes is a free man," retorted Hermolaos, his voice fired with passion. "Don't insult him!

"Remember back in Persepolis, at one of the King's banquets when everyone, Greek and barbarian alike, fell prostrate and worshipped him as they were leaving, and how he kissed each of them? There was only one man who stood erect—and that was Callisthenes. And for that, Alexander refused to kiss him, but Callisthenes laughed. I lost a kiss, he said, but I won my freedom."

It was the first time that Stephan had ever seen Hermolaos talking with such vehemence. He looked at him intently.

"What's happened to you, Hermolaos?"

"Nothing. I listen to my heart, Stephan. I see what's happening every day, I watch how Alexander is slowly changing from a Greek and becoming an Asiatic. At the beginning, remember, he didn't even want the Persians to worship him. Later he said it was all right for the Persians to worship him but not the Greeks. And now he wants us Greeks to fall down and kiss his feet, too. No! I have only one life, and if I must, I'll lose it—but I'll die for freedom."

166   "What do you have in mind?" Stephan asked uneasily, looking his friend in the eye.

"Nothing," said Hermolaos, and got up to leave.

"Where are you going?"

"There's something I have to do."

"Would you be going to find Callisthenes?"

"Am I not a free man?" snapped the other, and left hurriedly without shaking his friend's hand.

55

Night. Callisthenes was sitting in the small house he had taken over and was writing. A fire had been lit in the hearth and the former owner of the house was moving about, seeing to Callisthenes' needs, preparing the evening meal for his master. Outside, the little garden smelled of roses and jasmine, and a fountain in the center was murmuring and spouting water high in the air. A goldfinch had fallen asleep in a tiny cage, tired out from warbling all day.

Callisthenes was writing. He was angry. Until now, what flattering eulogies he had written about Alexander. Unrolling his manuscript he began to read: "We are crossing Pamphylia; and at his passing the waves of the sea fall and worship him." And further on at Gaugamela: "...then Alexander raised his hand to heaven and said, 'If I am the God's son, let victory be granted to me so that the name of the Greeks will be glorified.'"

Callisthenes slammed the manuscript down. "Just look at the things I've been writing about him," he muttered. "I, who fear no one and always speak the truth. Look at these oratorical exaggerations that I've been setting down. I used to think that Alexander was a sacred personage. I used to think the gods had sent him here to spread the light of Greece. But now. . ."

A soft knock sounded at the door, three times.

"Who is it?" called Callisthenes.

"A free man," came a youthful voice.

This was their signal. Callisthenes hastened to open. A young man entered, wrapped tightly in his mantle so that his face barely showed.

"Is that you, Haricles?" asked the philosopher.

"Yes, master."

"And Hermolaos?"

"He's coming."

"Sit down," said Callisthenes. "Tonight we must come to a serious decision."

The young man flung off his mantle. "I'm listening, master," he said respectfully, sitting down on a low stool.

The former owner came in again. He eyed the young man intently, then bowed and made obeisance to him.

"Who's that?" asked the youth.

Callisthenes laughed. "My landlord. A good man. His name is Bogas. He's a little simple, poor wretch, but I've managed to teach him a bit of Greek, and now he's acting as my servant. Don't look at him so suspiciously, Haricles, I trust him."

"It's best that we talk softly," said Haricles.

"Master," he continued after a pause, "what is the most glorious thing that I can do?"

"Kill the most glorious," answered Callisthenes in a solemn voice.

A knock was heard at the door again, three times; then a voice. "A free man!"

"Hermolaos!" said Haricles, and hurried to open. But Bogas had already got there and was opening the door.

"Good evening, Bogas," said Hermolaos.

Bogas bowed to the ground without speaking and made obeisance to Hermolaos.

"You're late," said Haricles to his friend.

"I was with my friend Stephan," Hermolaos replied. They went inside. Callisthenes closed the door securely and dimmed the small lamp.

"Well?" he turned questioningly to Hermolaos. "Tomorrow, then?"

"Yes," answered Hermolaos in a low voice, "tomorrow," and turning to Haricles, "Are you ready?"

"I'm ready!"

Callisthenes pressed each youth's hand. "*Harmodios* and *Aristogiton*," he said, "the two friends who killed a Tyrant of Athens once. You saw the two colossal statues of them in Susa; Xerxes had them seized and brought here to decorate his capital, and now we've found them after all these years. A good omen."

"One day soon," he raised his voice now, his tone solemn, as though he were uttering a prophecy, "two new bronze statues will tower in the great square of Samarkand; two other friends with

168

sword in hand will be depicting two new heroes who liberated not only Athens from the tyrant, but the whole Universe. And new generations will stoop over the names at the base of the two statues and read HERMOLAOS-HARICLES."

The two youths were listening, profoundly stirred. Haricles put his arm around his friend Hermolaos. "Let it be so, then, that we die," he murmured, "that we die for liberty!"

Callisthenes wiped away a tear. He filled three glasses with wine and they drank.

"See this manuscript?" he said, pointing to the history that he was writing. "Here's where I'll make you immortal. Here's where I'll describe what took place this evening. I'll write it all with great imagination. . .how you came to my house tonight. . . and then tomorrow's scene, the avenging murder scene. I'll describe how the sacrifice began, where you were standing, Hermolaos, how you were holding the ram that was to be slaughtered, how your face glowed and your dark hair played in the wind. And then I'll describe how the tyrant came out of the palace, like a ram himself with two curly horns in his forehead, and behind him Haricles, holding the censer and perfuming him with incense. And then I'll describe the moment that he was approaching the altar, and how he bent over it, and how the two knives glistened and how the tyrant rolled in the dust. And I'll describe Hermolaos, springing up, raising the bloodied knife before the shocked multitude and shouting: "Behold the altar of liberty, the tyrant is offered as sacrifice! Long live Greece!"

And as he talked, the flame in Callisthenes kept igniting, and his voice kept growing fiercer. Haricles glanced at the door uneasily; it seemed to have opened a crack, he thought, and someone was out there eavesdropping. When Callisthenes finished, Haricles stole over to it quietly and looked, but no one was there.

"Go now, my lads," said Callisthenes. "I'm going to sit down and write tomorrow's scene at once. My imagination is on fire now and I'll write well."

He looked at the two youths for a moment. "You're blessed," he said, "in that you're not only killing a tyrant, but that you also have a Homer around to eulogize your deed."

56

It was late when Stephan entered Alexander's room. The King was tired and had slept long. Stephan's father was sitting at his bedside. Stephan greeted them and stood aside to wait while his father talked to the King.

"Take pity on your body, my King," he was saying. "Don't exhaust it. Our body is the horse, our soul is the rider, and each soul has but a single horse. . ."

"I have faith in my horse," said Alexander smiling. "Have no fear, my doctor." Then turning to Stephan, "Has Nearchos arrived from Greece?" he asked impatiently. He had summoned him to come at once to build a new navy with countless ships so that they could cross the Ocean.

"Not yet, my King," answered Stephan, his heart pounding. He, too, was eagerly awaiting Nearchos.

"Do you like Samarkand?" Alexander asked again.

"Very much," replied Stephan warmly. "Very much, indeed!"

"Good," said Alexander smiling. "One day I'll remember what you just said."

The Officer of the Guard entered:

"My King," he said, "there is a native here who wants to see you. He says it's urgent."

"Let him come in."

Presently, Bogas, Callisthenes' landlord, was kneeling before the royal bed, face to the ground. He didn't know Greek very well and Alexander was having difficulty understanding what he was saying, and when the native finished Alexander turned to Stephan.

"What did he say? Did you understand anything?"

"From what I could make out, this man is reporting some kind of conspiracy," answered Stephan. "It's supposed to occur today, as you're offering your accustomed sacrifice to the gods. Two youths—I didn't understand which—are going to raise their knives against you."

"Very well," said Alexander to Bogas, "open your hands. Reach into that chest, Stephan, and fill his hands with gold."

Bogas grabbed the gold and disappeared.

Alexander laughed. "Every day someone comes here to inform me of a conspiracy. I've stopped believing them anymore.

People's imagination works overtime here. And then, again, they love the gold."

But the physician was uneasy. "My King, you must be careful. Some day the conspiracy might be real, and then. . .This man seemed sincere to me. Be careful."

"All right," said Alexander, "I will for your sake." And turning to Stephan, "Keep an eye on things, Stephan, while I'm offering the sacrifice," and he rose and went to bathe.

Philip looked at his son. "Do you know which two young men are going to be attending the King at the sacrifice?"

"No, they keep changing. Today the Macedonian phalanx gets to choose them since they're the ones who are presenting the King with the ram that is to be slaughtered."

"Be on the alert," said Philip in a low voice. "I have a bad premonition about this."

"Don't worry, Father, I'll take every precaution. There's nothing to fear." And he left, to issue his orders.

The altar was ready in the great Court. The Macedonian phalanx assembled. Callisthenes, too, appeared with his long staff. Stephan was looking about impatiently to see which two youths would be bringing the ram and assisting the King in the sacrifice today. He had posted his most dedicated soldiers around the altar. "On the alert!" he told them, "when you hear me whistle, charge! It means the King is in danger!"

Alexander was taking long at his bath this morning and the Macedonians standing about were stamping their feet impatiently. Suddenly Stephan tensed. The soldiers had opened an aisle and two young men were leading in a fat ram with curly gilded horns.

"Hermolaos," he murmured with dread. "It's Hermolaos and his friend Haricles!" He made a move toward them. "I'll talk to them," he thought, "maybe there's still time."

"Hermolaos! Hermolaos!" he shouted.

But his friend never turned to look at him.

Alexander was coming out now, striding rapidly up to the altar. Stephan moved close, his eyes nailed on the two young men.

Alexander admired the ram. It was large and fierce, stark white, with a heavy head that was painted red, its horns gilded and gleaming. The King bent down to pet it. "What a beautiful ram," he murmured, "like a King."

The two youths darted quick glances at one another. Suddenly, in a synchronized flash, they thrust their hands into their belts and pulled out their knives. Stephan whistled. The guards sprang forward like lions, and as the two knives were bearing down mid-air over Alexander's bowed head, the two youths slumped and rolled on the ground, dead.

The soldiers gave a triumphant yell. But some left angry, among them Callisthenes who disappeared.

Alexander calmly went on with the sacrifice, and Hephaistion, who arrived on the run with his heart in his mouth at the sound of all the shouting, took one look at Alexander serenely continuing the ritual, and his heart settled back in place.

Stephan picked up his friend's body. His knees were shaking. "Hermolaos! Hermolaos!" he murmured, "why did you do it?" and turning to the soldiers he ordered that they pick up Haricles's body, too. "Bury them," he commanded.

"No, let them be eaten by the ravens!" some shouted angrily.

"Bury them!" he repeated. "We're not barbarians; we're Greeks. And they, too, were Greeks."

That same day the soldiers seized Callisthenes and brought him before Alexander.

"He's the one who's guilty," they shouted. "He's the one who influenced the younger men. He was always with them, always talking to them about freedom, always urging them to kill. He's the one to blame!"

Alexander turned and looked at him. "Do you have anything to say?" he asked.

"I do," answered the philosopher boldly.

"You speak as though you're not afraid."

"I'm not," answered Callisthenes. "There's one virtue that is higher than life."

"And what is that?"

"Freedom!"

57

If some Greek were suddenly to come from Greece to Samarkand and see the Palace of Alexander and go inside to the huge throne room, he would rub his eyes. He would think he was dreaming. Was this the Palace of the Greek Commander-in-Chief or was it perchance the legendary royal palace of the Great King of the Persians?

Alexander was seated on a gold throne. He was dressed like a Persian monarch, in splendid robes and jewels. The floor was sprinkled with perfume, and costly frankincense burned in bejewelled censers before the throne.

And what strange throngs from all the races of the world! Phrygians, Cappadocians, Cypriots, Cretans, Persians, Egyptians, Scythians, Arabians, Phoenicians, Syrians, giants from Afghanistan and Turkestan, swarthy Indians in white turbans. Each was wearing the dress of his country and spoke the tongue of his land, and as they all entered they would kneel, face to the ground, and worship the King who sat immobile, all in gold, like a god on the high throne.

In the midst of this throng stood the Macedonians and Greeks, erect and proud, in their simple dress. And in the corner of the Palace, in a cage, like a dangerous animal, the jailed philosopher Callisthenes was looking out on all this magnificence and shaking his head.

"Clear the room!" ordered Alexander this morning with a wave of his hand. "Everyone leave! The only people who are to remain are the ambassadors from India."

Everyone left, the multicolored costumes disappearing in the dark corridors. The ambassadors from India, two colossal men in thick white turbans, with large almond-shaped eyes and red painted nails, fell prostrate and worshipped.

"God has given me dominion over the world," said Alexander. "I have a duty to reach as far as the ends of the Earth, out there where the great Ocean begins, beyond India. Go tell your King to await me. Spring has arrived; I shall set out."

"You will be welcome, King," said the ambassadors with dread.

"I will send twenty-four camels loaded with gifts for your King, and this ring as a token of our friendship," said Alexander, handing the eldest a heavy gold ring with a green stone. "Send me guides to take me to your King."

The two ambassadors did obeisance and, rising, retreated from the room without turning their backs to the King.

Alexander summoned his generals. "Spring has arrived," he said to them. "The eastern boundaries of the Earth are not far off. Let's go and conquer them! Prepare the foot soldiers and the cavalry. We shall be entering a new world, with enormous rivers and virgin forests. India, they tell me, is teeming with learned men. I'm in a hurry to get there. See that you are, too!"

The preparations began. One day in April the army set out on its southeasterly march. It passed Sogdiana and Bactria, reached the Indian border between two towering mountains, and entered India.

There twenty-four Indians from royal families were waiting to escort Alexander. With them were twenty-four military elephants which they had brought as gifts for the Greek King. These towering animals astounded the Greeks who were seeing them for the first time. They stared in wonder at the formidable tusks, at the trunk, the tiny clever eyes, and tough wrinkled skin.

"What manner of country is this!" the soldiers wondered with a hint of apprehension. "Look at the monsters it spawns!"

Before crossing the border into India Alexander offered great sacrifices to Athena. " O goddess of wisdom," he said, "we are entering a country that is famed for its wise men. Triumph over them! You are the pure light of Greece, enlighten them! Take up your shield, O Commandress, raise your spear and march in the lead!"

They marched through the gates of India and entered a fertile plain where the Indus River flows tranquilly and majestically. Here the King, who had sent the two ambassadors, hurried out to welcome Alexander. He was wearing on his finger the gold ring that Alexander had sent him as a gift. Together, then, they marched through his kingdom, quickly, without resistance, and when they reached the border the Indian King turned to Alexander:

"My King," he said, "at this point the land of the enemy begins. Be careful. You will meet some naked old men, ascetics, holy men. Be wary of them. They are very powerful, and the people heed them. Don't provoke them; get on their good side."

"What is their King's name?" asked Alexander.

"Poros."

"What manner of man is he?"

"Good and brave, but proud. He has a big army, and a great number of horses and elephants. Beware of him!" He spoke, did obeisance to Alexander, and returned to his kingdom.

58

At dawn they were entering the kingdom of the great adversary, the land of King Poros. A violent rain had broken out. It was beating down with great force and in a matter of minutes the earth had turned to mud and the army was straining with difficulty to press on. Through the thunder and lightning and fury of the elements that were thrashing the trees, threatening to uproot them, they could hear the roar in the distance of the great Hydaspes River rushing down in foaming torrents from the mountains. It was the monsoon season, and the torrential rains that last three months in India had started.

The Indian King was camped on the opposite banks of the Hydaspes, with several thousand foot soldiers and horsemen, some two-hundred battle elephants, and three-hundred scythed chariots. He was pleased. "With such rains," he was thinking, "how will this notorious Alexander be able to cross the river? He'll drown."

But Alexander was urging his men forward. "It's shameful," he shouted at them, "to allow ourselves to be defeated by rain. Keep moving!" And muddied and soaked, they pushed on until they finally arrived at the banks of the river.

The Hydaspes had swelled and its waters were cascading down in tempestuous waves. "It's impossible to cross," whispered Ptolemy.

"Nothing's impossible!" answered Alexander. "Haven't you understood that yet, Ptolemy?" and he summoned Crateros. "Stand here with the army," he commanded. "Order the trumpets to sound and pretend that you're preparing to attack—first at one point, then at another—to trick the enemy. I'll take five thousand of the horsemen and seven thousand foot and search out some shallow spot in the river where I can cross without their noticing, and I'll attack in a surprise move. At that point, you rush in, and we'll surround their army."

"At your orders, King," said Crateros. "A difficult maneuver. . ."

"Difficult, yes," replied Alexander, "and just what you should be praying for. Now the glory will be greater." And saying, he gathered his choicest Companions and with the onset of darkness struck out southward to find a shallow place to cross the river.

The rain was coming down in torrents. The night was dense. Nothing could be distinguished in the blackness except the countless fires in the enemy camp on the opposite banks. Thunderbolts were crashing all about them and streaks of lighting, coming one atop the other, were knocking the soldiers to the ground, killing them by the scores. Alexander was walking ahead with Hephaistion. At one point Stephan could overhear him laughing. "If the Athenians could see me now," he was saying, "they would understand what I go through for their sake." He had thought of Athens because he considered that city the center of Greek civilization. And it was for this Greek civilization that he had come all the way out here to the ends of the world.

They came at last to a shallow part of the river where it was somewhat calmer. By now signs of dawn were appearing. "Here!" ordered Alexander, and they plunged into the water but the current was treacherous, imperiling man and horse alike. Many were swept away by the waters and drowned, but the others got through, soaked to the bone.

Water-logged and weary from the all-night march, the exhausted soldiers pushed on in the mud. The rain had let up with the approach of morning and just as the first rays of dawn were breaking through, the enemy could make out the Greeks, on their side of the river now, advancing toward them.

"How many are there?" asked Poros.

"Just a few—ten to twelve thousand."

"And the rest of the army?"

"They're still on the other side."

"Then it's not worth using all our army," said the King. And calling his son, "take foot soldiers and cavalry," he told him, "a hundred chariots and fifty elephants, and attack them."

Poros's son hurled himself against Alexander. The Greeks, too, rushed at them. Four hundred Indians fell, and with them the prince, the son of Poros. The others began to flee.

Swiftly, then, Poros sent in his best soldiers to help. Alexander, mounted on Bucephalas, his select cavalry right behind him, charged at them. The enemy wavered; the elephants started in fright and began to stampede, trampling the Indians underfoot.

Meanwhile, Crateros, too, had crossed the river with the army and now the enemy was surrounded. They fought valiantly. Bucephalas was wounded—he let out a mighty neighing and collapsed to the ground. Alexander embraced him and tried to lift him, but the famous horse looked at his master for a moment as though he were saying farewell, and closed his eyes. He was dead. Alexander leaped on another horse and continued the battle, his eyes clouded with tears.

Poros, mounted on his elephant, fought fearlessly. He was a giant, a handsome man, and a great King, but he could not hold out against Alexander. Ten thousand Indians fell dead on the battlefield. By sundown the legendary army was fleeing en masse in terror, and Poros, full of wounds and unable to fight anymore, fell into the hands of Alexander.

Alexander looked at him with admiration. He had never seen such a tall and handsome man, such majesty and calm in the face of a defeated King. "How do you want me to treat you?" he asked him.

"Like a King!" answered Poros.

"You're worthy of being my friend," said Alexander admiring his pride and dignity. "I'll make you my friend. And I leave you your kingdom. You're free."

And so saying, he took off to find the body of his inseparable friend, Bucephalas. He found it amid the enemy corpses, his head buried in the mud. He ordered his men to lift him up and wash him, anoint him with perfumes, and crown him with gold laurel. Then he dug a deep pit, the battle trumpets sounded, and they buried him. And on the spot where he fell, he built a city. "I name it Bucephalia," he said, "in honor of my beloved companion!"

59

It rained and rained and rained, and everywhere the earth was nothing but mud and swollen rivers and thunder and lightning. Night after night, day after day, soaked and shivering with cold, they marched onward, plunged in mud, their clothes torn to shreds, their knees buckling under from the strange ailments that attacked them.

"Where are we going?" they grumbled. "We've been marching for months and months. Where are we going?"

But no one would give them an answer.

"The soldiers are grumbling," Ptolemy said to Alexander one day.

"Let them grumble," answered Alexander. "It's enough that they obey."

But after a few days Hephaistion came to Alexander. "They don't want to obey any longer," he said. "They've halted."

"What do they want?"

"To go back."

"Where?"

"To Greece."

"Greece is here, Greece is everywhere," shouted Alexander. "Don't they understand that?"

"No," answered Hephaistion. "They want their homes, their fields in Macedonia and Thessaly and Greece."

"I've given them palaces and infinite lands—Lydia, Phrygia, Cappadocia, Egypt, Syria, Mesopotamia, Hyrcania, Bactria, Sogdiana, Afghanistan, India—isn't that enough?"

"They don't want the world," said Hephaistion, "they want their humble homes."

"Summon the ones who are complaining and have them come before me. I'll speak to them."

The rains had stopped that day. The army was gathered on a huge plain. All those who had complaints and wanted to return to their country came forward. Alexander climbed atop a tall elephant that Poros had given him, so that everyone could hear him.

"Do you have anything to ask me?" he shouted to the soldiers who were gathered before him. And then a cry rang out from ten thousand throats:

"Where are we going?"

Alexander stiffened. "Hear this!" his voice thundered. "We are on our way to find the eastern boundaries of the Earth. A short distance from here we will cross a vast river, and we will be there. Then we shall turn back to the Persian Gulf where we will build a huge fleet with which we'll enter the Ocean. We'll sail around Africa, reach the Pillars of Heracles, enter the Mediterranean, and arrive at Greece from the opposite direction. Thus the circle will be completed, and our march will end. This, my faithful and valiant Companions, is my plan. We are Greeks; that is, we are free men. Speak openly. What is your opinion?"

Dead silence. Exhausted, pale, riddled with wounds, grown old in a few years, the old Companions of Alexander were silent. They stared at him astounded, through bulging eyes, and remained silent.

A tremor went through Alexander. Why weren't they speaking? What was wrong with them? Why did they stare at him like that? He looked at his more trusted generals who were standing around him. Big, silent tears were streaming down their gaunt, wasted cheeks.

"Speak! Answer!" shouted Alexander uneasily. "Choose someone among you and let him speak!"

They chose General Coinos. He was one of the more dedicated and valiant of Alexander's generals.

Coinos stepped forward, his face stern and solemn.

"My King," he said, lifting his hand in greeting to Alexander, "I speak because, as you assure us, we are free to speak our mind. Hear me then. You know how well I have served you. I never flinched at any of your orders, no matter how dangerous they were. I never said no. Now, however, I and all your old warriors tell you, No! This is as far as we'll go! We've travelled eighteen thousand kilometers from Macedonia to here. We're worn out. Look at us, we can hardly stand on our feet. Our bodies are like sieves from all the wounds. Our souls are glutted, exhausted. We can't go on, my King. We want to, but we can't!"

Coinos spoke and all the old warriors began to applaud. The officers extended a beseeching hand to Alexander. But he, with a wave, adjourned the meeting and shut himself inside his tent, alone. No one saw him the rest of the day, nor the next. Around evening of the second day he called Stephan. "Assemble them all outside my tent again," he said.

They assembled. Alexander came out. He was making a violent effort to control his anger. The words came strained from his tightened lips:

"Those of you who want to leave may leave! Go at once! Return to Greece and tell them you've abandoned your King among the enemy! I have spoken!" And storming back into his tent he flung himself on the ground and beat at the earth with his fist in a rage. He would see no one and refused to eat or drink or sleep.

But the army, too, stuck to its anger. It refused to follow its King. "Back to our country!" they shouted. "Enough!"

On the third day Alexander came out. He was white, like wax. His lips were ashen and his eyes were shadowed with bluish rings. "Get ready," he said in a hollow voice. "We're turning back!"

The shouts of joy that exploded from the army reached to the very heavens. Trumpets blared, shields clanged, soldiers shot arrows shot into the sky. But Alexander felt a knot in his throat and quickly went into his tent.

Stephan was inconsolable. He assembled his men without a word, drew them up in marching formation and then went and sat under a giant fig tree. The rains had stopped and the sun was scorching. "Alexander must conscript new men," he thought to himself. "The old ones have given all they could. He must make up a new army of Greeks, and must add Persians now, and Egyptians and Indians. He must instill the same dream in all their hearts and set out all over again. What's there for us to do in our little villages now? How will we ever be able to tolerate that simple, hum drum life?"

He lifted his head at the sound of someone approaching. It was his father.

"We're off!" Philip called to him joyfully. "We're on our way!" But Stephan's mouth was set.

The trumpets sounded the call to assemble and he hurried to his post.

Hephaistion was making an announcement: "King Alexander has decided that we should erect twelve altars on the banks of the river before we leave, to show to the coming generations how far we have come."

The soldiers received the announcement in high spirits and fell at once to building the twelve altars that would show the future generations how far the great conqueror had come.

Each altar was dedicated to one of the twelve Olympian gods. It was fifty yards tall and resembled a strong tower. In the midst of the twelve altars they erected a huge bronze pillar:

ALEXANDROS ENTAFTHA ESTI
(Alexander stood here)

180   When the altars were completed and they had put up the bronze pillar, they began the magnificent sacrificial rites to the

gods. Hundreds of bulls and sheep were slaughtered. Tournaments were held, horse races, farewell banquets.

Some Indian princes who attended these splendid celebrations watched everything with awe. And such an impression did these Greek sacrificial rites and festivities make on them that many centuries later the Indians, in commemoration of this great day, still crossed the river and sacrificed on the twelve altars that Alexander had built.

And even today, after more than twenty-two-and-a-half centuries, the legend of Alexander, or *Iskender,* as they had named him, still exists in those faraway places. And many Indians boast that they are descendents of the famous army of the Greek conqueror.

60

And so the return march commenced. Alexander, recovered from his great anger, travelled alone, mounted on his gigantic elephant, weaving daring new designs in his mind. But he divulged them to no one. Not even to Hephaistion. "I'll build a huge fleet," he thought to himself, "I'll have Nearchos cut down the trees in the forests and build ships, and I'll fill them with soldiers. We'll cross the Ocean, and I'll sail around Africa and enter the Mediterranean through the Pillars of Heracles. I have set out from the East and I shall return from the West; I'll conquer the whole world!"

When they reached the shores of the great Indus River in the kingdom of his friend Poros, they halted. The mountains were covered with dense forests and the country was thickly populated. Here were all the timber and laborers that he could want.

He called Stephan. "Nearchos hasn't arrived yet," he said. "He should have been here. I need him. Take five-hundred good horsemen and hurry to the gates of India where we entered. Surely you'll find him there. Bring him back quickly." And looking at Stephan with a sly smile he seemed about to add something, but held back. "On your way now," he said. "You're in for a fine surprise."

Stephan saluted. He was dying to know what Alexander meant by his remark but dared not ask, and he hurried off to carry out the royal command.

By dawn the next morning he had selected the five hundred horsemen and was off. Alexander watched him set out. "If he knew what joy awaits him," he chuckled, "he wouldn't be galloping; he'd be flying like a bird."

The soldiers had fallen to chopping down the trees in the forests. They were chopping with great zeal. "We'll be returning by ship," they buzzed among themselves. "We won't have to wear ourselves out in the mud and the mountains and the endless plains."

And so as they were chopping away at the forests, and Indian laborers were hauling log after log down the river, Stephan was speeding westward to meet Nearchos at the gates of India. He, himself, couldn't say why his heart was pounding so. Was it because he was leading a mission alone? Was it because he was going to see Alka's father and would be hearing about his young neighbor? Or could it be... but Stephan didn't even want to venture a thought about this last possibility.

At last one noon, just as they had passed the deep chasm that joined India with the Persian kingdom, a company of horsemen appeared on the distant horizon. They were riding fast, kicking up dust that was covering them like a cloud. "There they are!" yelled the comrades, spurring their horses and breaking into a gallup. And in half an hour the two groups were within a few hundred meters of each other.

"They're Greeks!" shouted Stephan's comrades. "Look at the gleam of their shields and breastplates!"

Breaking away from the others then, Stephan galloped ahead. In a few minutes he was riding up to the small company. Another man had broken away from his group, too, and was coming toward him, and as they met, two joyous shouts rang out.

"Captain Nearchos!"

"Stephan!"

The two drew close and grasped each other's hand. "King Alexander has sent me to get you!" shouted Stephan. "It's urgent that you come back with me at once!"

"And didn't he tell you anything else?" asked Nearchos.

"No, nothing else."

Nearchos turned and looked back at his company. "Alka!" he called.

A young girl mounted on a white horse moved forward from the other horsemen. She raised the whip; the horse neighed, broke into a canter, and Stephan's heart bounded. "This is the joy!" he murmured. "This is the joy that Alexander promised me!"

The girl was before him, extending her hand. "Stephan," she said blushing, "well met!"

Stephan reached out his hand. "Well met, Alka!" he said, and his voice trembled with joy.

61

Evening had settled over Alexander's tent. A sumptuous banquet was spread on the table. Roasted lambs were steaming, wine in abundance sparkled in the deep copper urns.

The King was seated on his throne, his face beaming tonight. To his right in the place of honor sat Captain Nearchos, and to his left the physician Philip. The generals, in full ceremonial dress, were seated all around. And directly across from the King, at the center of the table, sat our two friends Stephan and Alka, on two flower-bedecked thrones. Their hair was wreathed in gold crowns, the one on Stephan's head resembled gold laurel, the one on Alka's gold olive branches bearing fruit.

The sacrifices had just been completed, and the wedding ceremony had just been performed, the King himself having placed the nuptial crowns on the heads of our two old friends. He had bestowed costly gifts upon them and now all the invited guests were settling down to partake happily of the wedding feast.

Alexander rose to his feet. "May you live happily and be fruitful," he said raising his wine cup and levelling his eye on the two blissful newlyweds. "May you have children and grandchildren who will bring glory to Greece, just as you have done." And turning to Stephan: "Three times you have saved my life until now, and have never accepted a single reward. You were proud. 'I don't want rewards,' you said. 'I am doing my duty.' But I knew of one great reward (the King knows all) that you would not be able to refuse, and I wrote to my beloved Captain Nearchos to bring his daughter Alka. And now I drink to your health. May you both live to a ripe old age in good cheer and good fortune." He turned then to his generals, and raising his voice announced: "I appoint my valued co-worker and friend Stephan, son of Philip, and husband of Alka, to be Governor of the province of Sogdiana!"

184

Applause and cheers broke out. "Worthy! Worthy! Worthy!"

They ate and drank. Dancers came; they danced. Old bards came with their lyres and sang brilliant verses from the *Iliad*, that splendid epic of Homer's that Alexander cherished so.

Around midnight the King rose to his feet again. "Beloved friends and co-workers, we've enjoyed ourselves well tonight, and have wished the new couple good health and good fortune. It's time now to give our bodies over to sleep and rest. Our battles are not yet over. A great deal of work is ahead of us. We must be ready." And turning to Captain Nearchos:

"When dawn breaks, beloved Nearchos, come to me. I'll not be sleeping. I have something to discuss with you."

62

By the first morning light Nearchos was entering Alexander's tent. The King, awake through the night, was seated on his bed deep in thought. A gigantic, enormously difficult plan was ripening in his head. At sight of Nearchos entering he sprang to his feet to welcome his faithful Companion. "Sit down," he said indicating a low chair at the foot of the bed. "We have much to talk about."

Nearchos sat. "I'm listening, my King. I am at your command."

Alexander was silent for a minute, still engrossed in his thoughts. At last he opened his mouth. "You've heard the bad news, Nearchos. The army's tired. It cannot go on any longer. It's sated with victories and I am compelled, alas, to turn back." He sighed.

Nearchos listened without comment. How well he understood Alexander's agony—he who still wanted to press on to the ends of the Earth was finding himself abandoned now, his army exhausted and no longer wanting to follow him. How his colossal, insatiable soul must be suffering!

"You've seen the river that we're passing—the Hydaspes," continued Alexander. "Until now I had thought it was the Nile. I had noticed they both had the same vegetation on their banks and the same crocodiles in their waters. I had thought that the river we're passing originated in the high mountains of India and came down to the plain, passed a long stretch of desert and reached

Egypt where it emptied into the Mediterranean Sea, and that here it's called the Hydaspes, and there the Nile. That's what I had thought."

Nearchos smiled. "I don't think that's so, my King. . ."

"I know, I know!" exclaimed Alexander. "I learned the truth only a few days ago. The Hydaspes empties into a larger river, the Indus River, and that in turn empties into an unknown ocean that isn't the Mediterranean at all. It's far away, toward the south, and not toward the west. The Earth is much larger than I had imagined, Nearchos, and oceans and seas exist that no one has ever seen. This discovery has turned all my plans upside down."

The King was silent again, resting his head against the frame of the bed. His face had suddenly grown pale and two big blue circles were visible around his enormous eyes. He looked tired.

Nearchos, too, had inclined his head forward and was thinking. He had made a thorough study of an old explorer, a certain Skilakas, who had been sent out by a Persian king to circumnavigate the coasts of India and to report to him what he saw. He had taken a navy with him and for many months explored the mysterious coasts of Asia, and when he returned, he wrote a brilliant almanac of his travels, the *Circumnavigation*. Nearchos had read this almanac and he knew the truth long before Alexander had discovered it, and he smiled now as he listened to Alexander telling him he had thought the Hydaspes spilled into the Mediterranean.

"What are you thinking about?" asked the King, noting his admiral's stooped head and silence.

"A great deal, my King. But I'm waiting first to hear what decision you've made. Or perhaps you haven't made up your mind yet?"

"I have," said Alexander. "That's why I've summoned you—to execute my plan. There are two roads that we can take to go back. We can turn westward and retrace our way along the land that we've already covered and reach Susa and Ecbatana where our new capitals are located—that's one road."

Nearchos shook his head.

"You don't like it?" Alexander smiled. "I don't either. First of all, I don't like to travel over the same road twice; secondly, I would want, even on my trip back, to encounter and conquer new lands. I've decided, therefore, to return by another road. Can you guess which?"

"I can!"

"Which? Speak!"

"We'll be going by way of the river, and we'll arrive at the Indian Ocean."

"You've guessed it!" shouted Alexander. "That's the road I've chosen. You're in agreement, then?"

"Most assuredly, my King. That way we'll see new lands, we'll investigate vast seas, and we might even find opportunities to perform great exploits at sea so they won't say that Alexander was a great conqueror only by land, but by sea as well."

"Yes, yes, you're right, Nearchos!" echoed Alexander enthusiastically. "But this plan has a colossal difficulty. We need. . ."

"a colossal fleet!" interjected Nearchos before Alexander could say it. "We'll make one, my King. We have wood in abundance here. The shores along the river are teeming with virgin forests. We have good carpenters, both among our own and among the local people. I've learned, too, that we have rich iron mines. We'll put local craftsmen to work weaving cloth for our sails. We lack nothing. We have thousands of men in your service, my King. In a few months everything will be ready."

The King stood up. He paced the floor of the tent for a while. He was extremly pleased with his friend's words. Suddenly he stopped in front of him. "Nearchos, stand up!"

Nearchos rose.

Alexander laid his hand on his friend's shoulder. "Will you undertake the task of building this colossal fleet, and will you assume its command?" he asked in a solemn voice.

Nearchos was silent. His heart was pounding.

"I appoint you, Nearchos, Commander of the new grand fleet. Do you accept?"

Nearchos raised his head. "I accept, my King," he answered simply, his eyes blazing with joy and pride.

"On with it, then! Let's not waste time. It's dawn already. Go now and gather as many thousands of workers as will be needed, and send them out to cut down timber and dig the mines to get at the iron. Get the huge shipyards set up along the river banks, and start the project. How many ships will we need?"

"Will the entire army be going in the ships?"

"No, half the army will march on land along the shore following the current of the river, parallel with the fleet. The other half will go in the ships. How many ships will that take, large and small?"

Nearchos thought. "About two thousand," he answered at length.

"Let's get on with it then. Make me two thousand. How long will it take?"

"About six months," said Nearchos.

"Then let's not lose a second."

Alexander opened the flap of the tent. The first rays of sun lit up his face. He didn't look tired now; his cheeks were ruddy, and the two blue shadows around his eyes had disappeared. "A great day is dawning!" he exclaimed. "May the gods of Greece be with us!"

63

In a few short days all had changed. Mile after mile of river bank had been converted into a huge shipyard. Thousands of local lumberjacks had invaded the virgin forest and were cutting down pines and firs and cedars. Thousands of mules and carts and elephants were transporting lumber, and other thousands of laborers and craftsmen—carpenters, blacksmiths, ship-builders—were hard at work building the new ships. All through the villages, men and women of India were working the coarse cloth for the sails, weaving and dyeing the fabric in various colors.

Nearchos was everywhere at once, giving orders, overseeing the work, supervising the making of the sails which the workers were instructed to dye in various colors. The fleet was to be divided into trireme groupings and each trierarch would be assigned his own color to avoid the possibility of confusion at sea.

By September's end the fleet was ready and Nearchos presented himself to Alexander. The King pressed his great co-worker's hand in gratitude. "You kept your word," he said. "Your name will remain immortal alongside mine."

He summoned his best Companion officers then and, dividing the fleet into thirty-three trireme groupings, he selected and appointed thirty-three trierarchs,[19] thirty-two of whom were Greek, and one a Persian named Bagoas.

When all was ready he called for sacrifices to the gods. "New battles await us," he said. "Let us beseech the gods to be with us."

They offered great sacrifices to the twelve gods and to Alexander's two divine ancestors, Heracles and Dionysos. Then, after a series of athletic tournaments and competitions in music, Alexander gave the final orders. He divided the army into three large phalanxes and called his trusted and valiant general, Crateros.

"My valiant general," he said to him, "I entrust you with the command of the first phalanx, which will march on the right bank of the river. You are to follow parallel with the fleet and if you should come up against any enemies, you are to repulse them."

Then he called his friend Hephaistion. "Hephaistion, my brother, you I entrust with the command of the second phalanx, which will march on the left bank of the river. I am placing in your care the largest segment of the army—foot, cavalry, and two hundred elephants. I and my aides and Companions, along with the darters and Cretan archers, will go in the ships and we'll all proceed down the river together."

Then he turned to Nearchos.

"Nearchos, take charge of the fleet! Give your commands!"

At once Nearchos assembled the thirty-three trierarchs. "Friends, the great moment has come to embark," he said. "The waters are dangerous. We don't know the currents. Be ever vigilant! Pace your rowers to avoid collisions, and keep your proper distances. I demand order and discipline. When perilous situations arise, pay strict attention to my commands. You know the codes. Keep your eyes on the signals on the flagship's mast.

"Now let us proceed, with the power of the gods! Don't disgrace Greece!"

Dawn was at hand. All were ready. Alexander was standing at the prow of his ship. The sun came up, it, too, ready to embark with joy in a cloudless sky. Alexander filled his golden wine cup with wine and poured a libation into the water. "Olympian gods of Greece," he shouted, lifting his arms to the sky, "I have fulfilled my obligation. I have conquered the world. Now I am returning. Come, sit in my ships, march at the head of our armies, assist our return!"

A hush had fallen as the army listened in silence. Many of the men were weeping.

"O Muses, beauty, harmony, truth," shouted Alexander, "come with me once more!" Raising his right arm, then, he signalled the order to embark.

Trumpets blared, shouts rang out, and the forests and mountains resounded with the din of the jubilant Greeks. Thousands of Indians emerged from the forests to see them off, chanting and playing on flutes, beating on drums, shouting farewells to the glorious conquerers.

King Poros, too, came to say goodbye to his magnanimous friend. With him was a silent, scrawny, half-naked old man. Alexander eyed him with curiosity. He had seen many gymnosophists[20] in India, but this one seemed even more eccentric.

"My Great King," said Poros to him, "what gift can one give you who possess the whole world? Your palaces are filled with gold, your chests are spilling over with magnificent clothing, your tables are loaded with all the good things of earth, sea and air. I thought, then, that I would make you a gift of this old teacher of mine, Calanos, the wise priest of my country. Let him come with you as companion, advisor, and father."

"He is welcome," said Alexander, "since you, my beloved friend, give him to me."

The two Kings embraced and parted forever.

Alexander turned to the soldiers who served him. "Bring me the cage with Callisthenes," he said. "I'll take him along with me in my ship and while away the time listening to him talk with this Indian sage."

"If he's still alive," thought the soldiers to themselves. He hadn't eaten in three days. In a short while the soldiers returned with the cage. "He died," they exclaimed, half laughing and half in tears. "For three days now he wouldn't eat, and he died."

Alexander bent down and looked at the dead philosopher. He had dropped his head on his breast and looked like a bird fallen asleep.

"Bury him with military honors," he said. "He, too, fought valiantly, even if he was my adversary." And so saying, he boarded the royal ship that was being piloted by Onisicritos and gave the command. "Forward!"

The ships raised their anchors, the sails unfurled, and they embarked. Alexander turned for a moment to look back at India, at the distant mountains in the east, the chanting people crowding the banks, the proud King Poros erect on his elephant. "Farewell!" he called. "Farewell!"

Parallel along the shoreline the army, too, began the march, Hephaistion and Crateros at their head.

They advanced along the river. To the right and left stretched endless plains, dark forests, towns, cities. Now and then a savage tribe would offer them resistance, and Alexander would bound to shore and mete out punishment without mercy. Now and then they would pass sage ascetics sitting cross-legged along the river banks, staring out at them with their look of irony as they watched the golden-crowned conqueror of the world going by in all his proud mien.

"Why do they look at me like that?" Alexander asked Calanos one day.

"Because they know that it is meaningless for one to conquer the whole world and not conquer the evil and passions in himself," said the sage Indian.

Alexander didn't answer. He knew he had not conquered his passions. He still gave vent to anger, and there were times when he acted harshly and did things that made him ashamed afterward. He remembered Callisthenes in the cage and sighed.

"Onisicritos," he said, turning to the captain of the ship who was also a learned man and was writing down all Alexander's exploits, "come and read to me how you've described my battle with Poros."

The erudite captain brought forth his manuscript with a pompous air, cleared his throat, took a deep breath, and began to read. Alexander listened, half smiling, as Onisicritos went on in his high-pitched, womanish voice: "...and then Alexander came charging like a god of war, and with one stroke of his sword, split Poros in two from his head to his waist!..." but before he could finish Alexander grabbed the manuscript away from him and angrily threw it overboard. "I'll throw the writer in the water after it," he muttered, and Onisicritos, fleeing in terror, made himself scarce in the hold of the ship.

They continued along the endless-seeming river, the Greeks looking out with burning curiosity at the rich mysterious country they were traversing. Such strange plants and animals. Alexander constantly collected them along the way to send to his teacher Aristotle.

"Do you love Aristotle that much?" someone asked him one day.

"How could I not love him," he answered. "My father gave me life, but Aristotle taught me how to live."

He sent men out to investigate the land round about. He discovered gold and silver mines and enormous salt quarries. He studied the manners, customs, religions of the people in all the countries that he passed. "How vast and rich the Earth is!" he thought to himself. "Indeed, I must create a new army that is fresh and rested, and continue the expedition!"

64

All was going well, the current of the river rolling smoothly, calmly carrying the ships southward. They were in their fifth day at sea when suddenly a frightening din broke out, like the crash of waters falling from a tremendous height.

Abruptly the sailors ceased their singing. The crew tensed with fear.

"Signal the fleet to stop!" shouted Nearchos leaping to his feet.

The signal was hoisted on the flagship's mast and the rowers quickly checked their oars. The fleet halted.

"Send a landing party ashore," ordered the Admiral. "Have them proceed along the riverbank and investigate the noise!"

Ten choice men leaped overboard. They picked two local interpreters to accompany them and set out through the lush vegetation that grew along the river, advancing in silence, their eyes fastened uneasily on the waters that were rushing past with ever increasing vehemence.

As they were proceeding, they met some Indians. "What's all that noise?" they asked them.

"You're approaching the abyss!" the Indians said, shaking their heads. "You'll be meeting your end!"

"Why? What's happening?" asked the Greeks.

"You're approaching the terrible rapids where the two rivers merge—the whirlpool where ships are swallowed whole. No man has ever dared cross it."

The men turned back. They boarded the flagship and reported to Nearchos what they had seen and heard.

"Have the trierarchs report to the flagship at once!" ordered Nearchos.

The thirty-three commanders got into their boats and hastened to the flagship.

"We have come to the most dangerous point of the river," Nearchos told them. "Don't let it frighten you. We shall cross it, but we'll have to be extremely careful. Are you ready?"

"We're ready!" answered the stalwart trierarchs.

"Order your rowers to pull slowly, spread your ships out so that they don't collide with one another, and command your pilots to hold the rudder firmly toward the south. Whatever happens, they are not to lose the line! They must pilot the ship evenly toward the south. And be on the alert to rush to the aid of any ship in danger. Do you follow me?"

"We follow you," answered the men.

"I'll go first and show the way. Back to your ships now! Let's go!"

The trierarchs returned to their posts, the trumpets blasted, and the fleet began to move again.

The din was growing more and more frightening as they advanced. The riverbanks had begun to converge toward one another, and the rapids were narrowing, concentrating in ever more violent fury.

Nearchos was standing erect at the bow of his ship, looking ahead. Suddenly, there it was—another river, plunging down from the mountains and spilling with foaming rage into the Hydaspes. The waters of both rivers were clashing and roaring furiously, colliding in a narrow gorge, and spilling out toward the south.

At once the Admiral hoisted his signals and gave the commands: ROW WITH ALL YOUR MIGHT. SPREAD OUT. HOLD THE RUDDER STEADY TOWARD THE SOUTH. FORWARD! And setting the example, he led the way, catapulting his craft toward the terrifying whirlpool.

For an instant the flagship disappeared in the foam. Suddenly it surfaced again, spinning like a top directly in the vortex where the two rivers were colliding.

"They're lost! They're lost!" an anguished cry went up among the sailors who were watching the flagship struggling. "They'll be swallowed by the waters!"

Nearchos, who had taken hold of the rudder himself and wouldn't let it off course, was trying to shout orders to his men. Nothing could be heard but the deafening din and he was signalling with his eyes and his head, motioning exhortations to his rowers to keep pulling with all their might. Indeed, how else would they ever hurdle the whirlpool of those rivers!

"FORWARD!" flashed the signal on the mast of the flagship again.

"She made it!" came shouts from the crews in the other ships. The flagship had won. She had hurdled the terrible crossing and was floating calmly in waters that were growing wide and more tranquil.

Emboldened, the ships shot forward toward the whirlpool. The battle was ferocious. Oars and rudders broke, ships foundered, some were dashed to pieces and sucked in by the whirlpool, drowning crew and all. Alexander himself was imperiled and at one point he stripped and was ready to leap overboard to make a swim for it to shore.

The natives had gathered along both river banks, following with amazement the Greeks who were showing such disregard for the forces of nature. The armies, too, that were marching parallel to the right and left had stopped and were watching it all in agony. The ships were putting up a superhuman fight, and in the end most succeeded in breaking through and were steering toward the flagship that was navigating in calm waters.

"These are not mortal men," shuddered the Indians among themselves. "They're immortal gods!"

Man's daring had won. After an hour of battle, the fleet had broken through and was paddling triumphantly in tranquil waters, most of its crew from the few capsized ships having managed to swim to safety, too.

65

"Give the signal to halt," commanded Alexander. "Rest the fleet, repair the damaged ships, and bury the drowned sailors with military honors." And having so commanded, accompanied by his select soldiers, he went ashore.

He had learned that one of the most powerful and savage of Indian tribes, the Mallians, had amassed sixty thousand foot soldiers, ten thousand cavalry, and seven hundred battle chariots, and were preparing to attack him. Summoning Hephaistion and Crateros, he ordered them to synchronize an attack on the enemy, to seize certain positions, encircle the Mallians and prevent them from escaping.

The collision was savage. The Mallians, fiercely valorous, defended their land with fury, and Alexander barely missed getting killed in one of the battles. As usual, he was fighting in the front line, oblivious of the danger, and seeing the Mallian capital resisting with such tenacity, and his own soldiers dropping dead all around him from the poisoned arrows that the Mallians were shooting at them from behind their wall, Alexander hurled himself at the enemy wall and charged to the top, alone but for three brave Companions—Peucestes, Leonnatos, and Abreos, who charged up the wall after him. Leaping over the top, Alexander hurled himself into the Mallian city, directly into the midst of thousands of enemies who, losing no time, pounced on him, piercing his breast with an arrow. By the time the rest of his army had rushed to his aid, they found Alexander collapsed on the ground in a pool of his own blood. Enraged at sight of him thus, the Greek soldiers went at the enemy then with a vengeance and before long made quick work of their city. But the horrifying news had made the rounds of the camp:

"Alexander was killed!"

A great lamentation went up and soldiers were running about in shock announcing the tragic calamity.

"What is it?" asked the King, hearing the wailing. "What's all the crying about?"

"They think you've been killed, my King."

"Help me into a ship," he commanded at once. "And have the oarsmen row down the river slowly so that the men can see that I'm alive and be reassured."

"But we can't move you, King!" exclaimed the horrified doctors.

"Do as I tell you!" ordered Alexander. "And quickly!"

They propped him up in a large ship, then, and the rowers began to paddle the oars slowly so the army and fleet could see their King. Alexander, half-sitting, half-reclining against the pillows, smiled and waved to them as they rowed past, and everyone, soldiers and sailors, set up a mighty cheer and wept with joy.

In a few weeks Alexander was completely recovered. The trumpets blared the signal again, and the fleet, along with the two armies, resumed the journey.

The lush forests and gardens began to give way to land that was turning into wild, harsh wilderness. Summer came. The heavy rains began. The formidable army pressed on, and whatever tribes lived in these wild parts fled at sight of it as it approached.

Toward the end of July they arrived at the city of Pattala where the Delta of the Indus begins, at the wide mouth where the river spills into the Indian Ocean. Alexander conquered Pattala, fortified it, and enlarged its harbor. This city, he thought, ought to become the center of commerce between India and Persia.

Leaving his army there to rest, he took Nearchos and a few ships and set out for new adventures.

"Where are you off to?" Hephaistion asked him uneasily. "Sit still a while. Rest!"

But how could this untiring soul rest! "Let's go," he said to Nearchos, "let's investigate the mouth of the river and see if it's navigable, and if ships could sail on it. Then later..."

Nearchos smiled, pleased.

"Why are you smiling?"

"Because I know what you're going to do later."

"What?" asked the King jovially. "Rest?"

"Rest! Is it possible for King Alexander to rest? Later we're going to open sail toward the high seas, to explore the Indian Ocean!"

"You guessed it!" laughed Alexander. "A Nearchos goes well with an Alexander. We both burn with the same longings. Let's go!" And turning to Stephan, "come along," he said to our friend. "Let's not be separated."

66

Navigating the Delta of the Indian Ocean is very difficult and perilous. The rapids are so powerful that they sweep along huge chunks of earth and these masses crash down from up high and imperil the passing ships below. Then, too, there are the whirlpools that develop here and there, catching the ships in the vortex and smashing them to bits. Even today no one can journey there without guides and pilots.

Alexander and Nearchos were daring this formidable journey without guides, travelling through these mysterious dangerous lands for the first time, with only their faith and their boldness.

It was mid-August, and the river was swollen from the ceaseless rains that fell during the monsoon season in India. The first day they proceeded without any disagreeable adventures. But the second day a violent south wind lashed down on them almost shattering their ships and sweeping away the sailors. The third day the river began to broaden. During the first two days the heat had been unbearable; but now, suddenly around evening of the third day, a gust of cool wind blew in from the south.

"It smells of the sea!" announced Nearchos, sniffing the air with joy.

"We're approaching the Indian Ocean!" murmured Alexander, pleased.

The next day a violent south wind blew over them again. The waters of the river billowed in giant waves and the rowers strained to pull at their oars. Around noon they were passing a small, sheltered bay.

"Let's moor here until the wind dies down," said Nearchos. "We can't proceed like this."

Pulling with great effort they managed to get close to the shore and entered the placid bay. But no sooner had they moored than the river began to recede suddenly, its waters began to drain away and before long had completely disappeared, leaving the ships scattered about on dry land, some grounded in thick mud.

"What could this be?" muttered the soldiers, terrified. "This place is hexed! We're done for!"

"Take heart, men! We'll heave the ships to deeper water!" shouted Nearchos. "All together now. Let's go!" And just as they set themselves to pushing and straining at the ships, lo! there was the river filling up again, and great roaring waves began crashing down on the ships, slamming into the shore, flooding the fields, inundating everything until nothing but a solitary hilltop could be seen sticking up here and there above the foaming waters.

Petrified, the sailors scrambled to get into the ships that were being scattered helter skelter by the waves, oars and rudders breaking all about them. The peril was grave and Nearchos and his officers were shouting commands, trying to save the fleet.

But the tempest weakened at last, the waves diminished, the ships re-grouped, and they resumed their journey.

"What was all that?" Alexander asked Nearchos who was standing at the bow of his ship mopping the sweat from his face.

"The ebb and flow of the tides. You've seen a similar phenomenon in Euboea, at the Chalcis Straits, only here it's like something out of this world. I've never seen such fury—with the river receding and the sea rising the way it does, the collision is devastating. It will bear careful watching, or we could drown."

In the distance a small island was coming into view.

"Send two light craft out to investigate," ordered Nearchos.

Two light craft were dispatched. They tore through the water like arrows and in an hour they were back.

"It's a beautiful island," reported the captains. "It's called Cilloutas. It has a good harbor and sweet water."

"Let's go," said Alexander, and in a short while the small flotilla was beaching at the little island.

"What do you see out there?" asked Alexander, directing Stephan's attention toward the south.

"A larger island."

"And behind the island?"

"Endless ocean."

"Let's go," said Alexander again. They took the two best ships and set out. The others remained at the harbor to rest the crews and repair the craft that were seriously damaged.

The two ships sailed for the island. It was low-levelled and deserted as they approached, with beautiful sandy beaches. "Do you see anything beyond it?" Alexander asked Stephan.

"Nothing. Only endless ocean."

"We've reached the end of the populated world," said Alexander with a note of satisfaction. "From here on, there's nothing more. Now we can go back."

They returned to the little Cilloutas island and went ashore. "Do you remember, Stephan," said Alexander, "what the Oracle of my father, the god Ammon, prophesied to me in the Lybian desert?"

"How could I not remember that, my King," replied our friend: *"The Greeks will sacrifice to the gods on an island that is found at the end of the world."*

"This is the island," exclaimed Alexander triumphantly. "This is the one! Let's sacrifice, then, to the gods of the Greeks."

They lit fires and sacrificed to the gods; then everyone, officers and sailors together, ate and drank, and after they had eaten, they put out to sea again. And there in the far regions of the open waters, Alexander raised his golden wine-filled cup once more and poured libations to his ancestors.

"I have fulfilled your wishes, O my mighty Ancestors," he shouted. "I have reached the end of the world. And now, my spirit calmed, I turn back!"

The crew breathed a sigh of relief.

"Our mission is completed," said Alexander. "Let us return to Pattala and join the other comrades."

"And now, O King Alexander," said Nearchos, when they had finally arrived at Pattala and army and navy were united, "have we finished now?"

Alexander smiled. "How can we be finished!" said he. "The true man must keep struggling until he dies. He can never say 'Enough!' Don't you know that, my dear Nearchos?"

"I know it," answered the dauntless seafarer, "that's why I'm asking you."

"Very well, then, we haven't finished. Perhaps we're only beginning."

"I like that!" Nearchos exclaimed delighted. "Let's start new adventures. Will you allow me, my King, to ask what plans you have in mind now?"

"Not yet," said Alexander. "I have a new design in mind, but I'll tell you when it finally ripens. And maybe I'll entrust you to execute it again."

"It will be my honor and my pleasure," answered the proud Cretan.

67

All that day and the next Alexander remained in solitude, concentrating on his plan. "These lands are very rich," he was thinking. "I must find a road for them to communicate with Persia. I have opened a road from Greece to Persia; now it remains to be done from Persia to India. It will be difficult to do it by land. There are too many vast deserts and savage tribes. I must find a route by sea, where ships could set out from the Persian Gulf, from the mouth of the Tigris and the Euphrates, and sail in a straight line to the mouth of the Indus River. Then all the vast segments of my Empire will unite and become one."

"But can it be done?" he wondered, pacing the floor of his tent. "Will ships be able to cross these unfamiliar, perilous seas?" A cold sweat broke over him at the thought that his beloved fleet could be destroyed and that so many valiant comrades could be lost.

"And yet it must be done!" he decided. "I must attempt it. I have the utmost faith in Nearchos. But will he be willing, I wonder, to accept such an awesome responsibility?"

He emerged from the tent. Stephan was standing guard outside his door. "Stephan," he said, "call Nearchos."

Nearchos arrived in haste.

"Let's go inside," said Alexander. "I must talk to you," and they went inside and closed the tent flap.

"Do you know what I've been thinking these past two days in solitude?" asked Alexander confronting his valiant friend with his level gaze.

Nearchos smiled. "Of course I know, my King."

"Oh, you're a soothsayer, then?" laughed Alexander.

"No, my King, but if you will permit me to say so, I, too, have the same burning longings."

"Tell me, then, what would you be contemplating if you were in my place—if you were Alexander?"

"I would be contemplating how I could find a route from the Indian Ocean to the Persian Gulf," answered Nearchos without a second's hesitation.

"Why?"

"To unite my Empire. To enable my people to communicate with one another."

Alexander pressed the hand of his noble friend. "If I die," he said with deep emotion, "you are worthy of continuing my work."

"If you die, my King," said Nearchos, and his voice shook, "all of us will lose the greatest part of our worth. We'll all break up in factions, and for all I know, we'll turn on one another and destroy ourselves. You, alone, blow the breath of life into us."

Alexander lowered his head. He had suddenly turned pale. "Maybe Nearchos is right," he thought. "All the world that I've conquered will disintegrate when I die." He tossed his head back, as if to shake off the funereal thoughts. "Let's not talk of death," he said. "I'm only thirty years old. I have no intention of dying early.

"Let's return to the present. You've figured out what I have been contemplating. Yes, we must open a route via the sea. Is it difficult?"

"Let's try!" said Nearchos.

"Is it difficult?" repeated the King.

"Of course it's difficult. But that's precisely why it's worth trying. We can leave the simple things to others."

"True," said Alexander. "Well, then?"

"Are you entrusting this difficult project to me?"

Alexander put his arm around his friend's shoulder. "To whom else can I entrust my navy and my honor?"

The brave Cretan's eyes filled. He had asked for no greater joy in his life than these simple words from his King.

"I'm entrusting this difficult project to you," continued the King, "because there's another, even more difficult one that I am reserving for myself."

"What is that?"

"The march through the formidable Gedrosian Desert. No army has ever crossed it. I will cross it with my army."

"You are King," said Nearchos. "You have the right to keep the greater danger for yourself."

"Take the best ships with you," said Alexander. "Choose whatever men and officers you want to take with you, and load up on all the food, equipment and arms that you will need. I'll send soldiers on ahead to open wells along the beaches so that you'll be able to find water on the way, and I'll instruct them to leave food supplies so that your crews won't go hungry or thirsty. In the meantime, I and the main army will cross the Gedrosian De- 201 sert and we'll all meet at Ecbatana. Agreed?"

"Agreed," answered Nearchos.

"Your hand on it!"

Alexander gripped his friend's hand warmly. And without another word they parted.

68

The next day the trumpets blared the signal for the camp to assemble. Officers, soldiers, sailors all gathered around the King's tent. Alexander emerged, dressed in his full campaign regalia.

"Comrades," he shouted, "we're off! We shall proceed together westward, Crateros with one segment of the army, Nearchos with the navy, and I with the main body of troops in the center, and we will all meet in our beloved capital in Susa.

"Forward! With the constant help of the gods of Greece, forward!"

Cheers rang out, trumpets blared, drums rolled, and the land forces began to march.

Alexander turned to Stephan. "Alka will never be able to endure the terrible hardships that await us in the desert," he said to his friend. "I am ordering you to go with her. Don't hang your head now, and don't sigh. Endure our parting like a man. We'll meet again in the capital. Go now. Until we meet again!"

"Until we meet again," said Stephan, struggling to control his emotion.

Philip, Stephan's father, turned to him now, too. "'Til we meet again, my son," he said to him. "I must remain with the King. He may need my help."

"Farewell, father!" said Stephan. "'Til we meet again!"

They parted. Alexander mounted his favorite elephant and soon disappeared with his army into the western horizon.

Alka took her husband's hand. He was still standing immobile, gazing at his King who was disappearing in the distance. "Come," she said gently, and they walked to the river bank and boarded the ship that belonged to her father Nearchos.

"Who would have told us," she said, "that we would be spending our wedding trip at the end of the world?" But Stephan was inconsolable. It was the first time in all these years that he had been separated from Alexander. He was thinking, too, of all the things he had heard about the Gedrosian Desert—how they wouldn't find water, not even a tree or a bird, and how they'd all die of hunger and thirst. The winds, they said, were violent and scorching and the sand whirled up in great gusts and buried entire caravans. The army would never be able to cross that wilderness full of human bones.

"Don't worry, my lad," Nearchos assured his son-in-law. "Alexander isn't like us ordinary mortals. He's half god and the gods protect him. He fears nothing. He'll overcome the obstacles and in a few months we'll see him safe and sound. All the gods of Greece are with him."

In a few days favorable winds blew in and the admiral hoisted the signal on his mast to embark. The horns resounded, anchors were raised, sails unfurled, and the momentous journey began.

It was the second of October, 325 B.C. The perilous journey, from the mouth of the Indus to the mouth of the Euphrates in the Persian Gulf, the first great journey of exploration in recorded history, was under way. The distances were vast; the sea, treacherous. Astounding daring was needed to undertake so uncertain an expedition with the ships that were available in those days. Even were they to succeed in getting through the violent storms, how were they to escape death from starvation and thirst?

A voyage of such magnitude required a leader who was not only daring and brave, but equally clever and enterprising to carry it off. And to be sure, Nearchos was like the bold and crafty Odysseus. If Alexander proved to be the equal of Achilles, the hero of the *Iliad*, Nearchos showed himself equal to the hero of the *Odyssey*.

His fleet was composed of one hundred and fifty select ships with a stalwart crew of twelve thousand soldiers and sailors, and two thousand officers. They were to sail due west along the coastline. He had instructed the captains before sailing not to stray too far out to sea or the fleet would be in danger of scattering and getting lost. "Inspire your men with courage along the way," he exhorted them. "Don't let them give in to fear. Show them by your own example how to be brave and patient and persevering. Alexander has entrusted us with a difficult mission. We must not disgrace ourselves."

And so the fleet of Nearchos embarked on the celebrated journey. They sailed out of Pattala, came to the mouth of the river, and put out in the Indian Ocean. In the Indian Ocean a violent storm broke over them.

203

69

Tremendous winds lashed at them without let-up during their first days out. On the ninth day of October they came upon a protected bay.

"Let's take shelter in this bay until the winds subside," ordered Nearchos. "We'll name it *Alexander's Harbor*. And pulling the ships ashore they set up camp near the sea, fortifying themselves securely with a hedge that they built with stones.

"Why so many precautions, father?" asked Stephan, curious.

"Because I'm afraid all these beaches and islets that we've been coming across are full of pirates. We'll have to be on our guard night and day."

Thirst was plaguing the crew and Nearchos sent men out to look for water, perhaps some spring or well. Nothing. They came back empty-handed. And as if this were not enough, their food had run out, too. The crews were scattered about the island searching the sand and rocks, looking for bits of food—shellfish, oysters, limpets, sea-urchins—anything to placate their hunger somewhat.

Eventually the winds calmed down, the sea grew tranquil, and the admiral gave the order to set out again. It was the third of November.

70

The Admiral's log has been preserved and from it we can follow all the dramatic adventures of the journey. They sailed only by day. At night they moored wherever they chanced, and waited for daybreak to bring them favorable winds. Savages along the way pelted them with arrows, and Nearchos was forced to send out landing parties to chase them off. And what horror the prisoners who fell into the Greek's hands elicited! They had hairy bodies like apes, and long claw-like nails that they used to tear at things like lions. They ate nothing but raw fish, prompting the Greeks to name them *Psarophages* (Fisheaters).

Day after day they sailed along wild seacoasts, barren and treeless, without a single water source. The crews suffered terribly

from thirst and hunger. But that wasn't all—the seas they were navigating were unfamiliar and mysterious and they didn't know where they were going. There were times when even the bravest hearts faltered with terror.

One day the ocean was thrashing and pitching in foaming rage, and great spouts of water were shooting into the air with a terrifying roar out in the open waters where a herd of gigantic animals had appeared. "Wild beasts!" they all cried, and the oars went flying out of their hands.

"They're whales," said the Indian guides who were accompanying the fleet. "They're terrible monsters. They can smash even the biggest ship to pieces with a flick of their tail."

Nearchos leaped to his feet. "After them, men!" he shouted to the panic-stricken sailors. "Don't be afraid! We'll give the monsters a naval battle. We'll beat them, take heart! Don't forget you're Greeks!" And ordering the ships to draw up in battle formation, one close behind the other, he instructed the men to await his signal and to charge at the beasts the instant he gave the command, yelling the terrible war cry and beating the drums and blaring away at the trumpets. The sailors took courage.

"Forward!" he shouted.

Forward shot the fleet, streaking in an ear-splitting beeline for the whales, trumpets blasting, oars beating, shields clanging. So devastating was the crashing din that the jolted, terrified animals scattered, leaping in gigantic, plunging dives through the water until the last one disappeared.

The Greeks were very pleased with this victory.

But their joy was short-lived. Hunger was mowing them down, the beaches were deserted and barren, and help was nowhere in sight. Day after day, starving and thirsty and exhausted, they rowed on, not knowing where they were going. "Courage, boys!" Nearchos exhorted them. "Don't be afraid. Man's spirit can overcome everything!" And the stalwart seafarers would take heart, but as the weeks went by, many began dying of exhaustion and hunger.

At last one day jubilant cries echoed back from the lead ships. "Trees! rivers! towns!" came the word. And indeed, unfolding before them was Carmania, a rich, fertile land with civilized people.

They anchored and went ashore. The friendly inhabitants gave them wheat and lambs and grapes and dates. They filled their wineskins and barrels with water and many sailors wept with joy. They remained in this hospitable country for several days. Then, rested and revived in spirit, they set out again.

Eighty days from the date they had embarked, the fleet finally streamed into the Persian Gulf, back in familiar territory. They had come full circle. The purpose of their journey was fulfilled.

Nearchos looked at his son-in-law. He was profoundly moved. "We achieved our goal," he said. "We suffered terribly, but we won."

"You should be proud, father," said Stephan. "But I don't see the light of joy in your face."

"I'm very troubled, my son."

"About what, father?"

"About what has become of Alexander."

Stephan lowered his head. All through the trip he, too, had been thinking of Alexander. He knew how treacherous the Gedrosian Desert was. It had devoured many armies. Two mighty royal personages had undertaken to cross it before—Cyrus the Great, and the legendary Queen Semiramis. But out of all the thousands that had made up these armies, the former survived with only seven soldiers and the latter with only twenty. The rest all died in the desert of hunger and thirst.

Lush green vegetation awaited them ashore—trees, water, plants everywhere. But no huts. Not a human being was in sight. In the distance a lone hill spired against the horizon.

"Let's go up that hill and have a look around," said Stephan. "Maybe we'll spot a town," and taking some soldiers he set out. They walked briskly, without talking, and soon arrived at the hill and began the ascent. Suddenly they stopped. A glint of armor had flashed through the thickets. They raised their spears.

"Who's there?" shouted Stephan.

"A Greek!" came a voice, "A soldier of Alexander's!"

Jubilant shouts. Stephan and his company pounced on the soldier. They embraced him, firing questions at him—"Where was Alexander? Had he survived the desert? Were many Companions lost?"

The soldier sighed and began to relate the indescribable hardships they had endured in the desert—hunger, thirst, sickness. Their horses were dead, thousands of soldiers were dead, many had gone mad. Alexander had survived and had reached Susa with the remaining army, but he was sick with worry over the fate of the fleet and had been sending out scouting parties all over the beaches to see if the fleet had arrived.

"...and that's how I happen to be here," the soldier sighed at last. "And you? Who are you? How did you get here?"

Then Stephan, too, began to relate the adventures of the fleet.

"Has it survived?" cried the soldier. "Has the fleet survived? Have the ships arrived? Where are they? Quick, let me see them!"

"Come," said Stephan. And in a short while Nearchos, tears streaming from his eyes, was embracing the jubilant soldier and declaring this the happiest day of his life. King Alexander was alive!

At once then he ordered the ships be pulled ashore and repaired, and after seeing that fortifications were put up, and guards stationed, he took Stephan and five officers and, mounting the fastest horses, sped off for Susa.

They galloped day and night in their haste to get to Alexander with the good news that his fleet had survived. They knew how anxious he was.

And indeed, the fate of his fleet was constantly on Alexander's mind, keeping him awake with worry. "Had it survived? Had it been wrecked by some storm at sea?" Tormented with apprehension, he kept an unbroken chain of scouts coming and going to check all the seacoasts, while he sat in his Palace, his eyes riveted toward the south, waiting and wondering when that herald of good news would ever arrive.

At last one day two soldiers came and fell prostrate at his feet. "My King, seven men from the fleet are approaching!"

"Who are they?"

"We don't recognize them, they're emaciated and pale. They're galloping this way on horseback. Look, they're here!"

And, indeed, out in the courtyard Nearchos and his comrades were already dismounting.

In an agony of suspense Alexander rushed out to greet them. He clasped Nearchos in his embrace. These seven, he thought with anguish, are all that are left. "Nearchos! is the fleet destroyed? Speak!" His voice trembled.

Nearchos laughed. "I brought it through intact, My King. The entrances to the Tigris and the Euphrates are jammed with ships!"

And now Alexander could no longer hold back the tears. "In all my life," he said, "I have never felt a greater joy."

Alexander set about at once arranging for magnificent festivities to celebrate the safe return of the fleet. That same evening, as he was presiding over a splendid banquet in honor of the commanders, the Indian sage Calanos, who had been given to him by Poros, appeared before him.

"Farewell, King Alexander," he said.

"Are you leaving?" asked Alexander. "Where are you going? To your country?"

"Yes, to my country," smiled Calanos pointing with his finger to the earth.

"Why do you want to die?"

"Because my life is becoming worse than death. I'm old, and for days now I have been plagued with illness. Farewell."

Alexander, who did not believe the Indian sage would indeed go through with his plan, laughed. "Have a pleasant journey, my faithful comrade!" he called to him in jest. "Good journeying!" and he went on talking and drinking with his friends.

But Calanos went out to the courtyard and gathered some sticks of wood. He piled them in a heap, poured oil over them to speed the flame and then began plaiting a wreath of flowers which he placed on his head. And now as he was starting to climb onto the pile of wood, chanting religious hymns, Alexander and his friends sprang up from the banquet and came out to watch this unheard-of spectacle. Calanos had already climbed to the top of the pyre and turning for an instant, saw Alexander. "'Til we meet again, Alexander, in Babylonia!" he said prophetically with a friendly wave. Then, setting fire to the wood, he lay atop the pile and in a short while the flames had burned him to ashes.

"Sound the battle trumpets!" ordered Alexander then. "This is how heroes die!"

71

"Have you heard the news? Have you heard the news?" officers and soldiers were asking each other as the rumor buzzed through the vast city of Susa setting them all agog.

"Is it really true?" they wondered aloud.

"I don't like it," said Philip the physician to his son. "Greek blood will be contaminated. It isn't right!"

"What is it?" asked Alka, hearing her father talking so angrily.

"What is it?" cried Philip. "Listen to this! Alexander wants to marry off all his friends and officers to Persian women. He's planning to marry, too, and take Statira, the daughter of Darius for his wife, and that same day he wants to marry off ten thousand of his choice officers and soldiers to Persian women. To create, he says, a new race, the Hellenopersian race, that will rule over the East and the West!"

Stephan was listening to his father and smiling. "My father," he was thinking, "hasn't been able to understand yet that with the coming of Alexander a new cosmogony has begun. We've departed from our small province; we've spread out across the entire East. New men must be born now to govern the new country."

Philip was still railing against this new "madness" of Alexander's. Stephan laughed.

"I can imagine, father," he said, "how thankful you must be that I hurried and married Alka. Now you won't have to put up with some Persian daughter-in-law."

Philip laughed, too, and embraced Alka tenderly.

"My dearest Alka, " he said, "from now on I will cherish you doubly."

Meanwhile, Alexander had summoned his officers. "Greece must unite with Asia," he told them. "The first part of our mission is completed; we conquered Asia. Now, before we set out on the next campaign, we must clearly show Greece and Persia that our purpose is to unite the two countries. We have decided, therefore, that in a few days I and all my most beloved generals, along with ten thousand select officers and soldiers, will marry on the same day, taking Persian women as our wives.

"I will marry Darius's daughter, Statira. Hephaistion will marry her younger sister."

He spoke, then turned to his generals—Crateros, Ptolemy, Perdiccas, Clearhos, and the others: "For you," he smiled, "I have chosen brides from the wealthiest princely families of Persia. New years are beginning, my beloved collaborators. May our offspring, the Hellenopersians, continue our great mission!"

The marriage rites of Alexander and ninety of his generals took place together in the vast royal gardens of Susa. The celebrations and banquets lasted five days and nights. Actors and poets and jugglers provided uninterrupted entertainment for the guests who were invited to the grand symposium. Alexander presented each groom with a golden wine cup and each bride with splendid clothes and jewels. On the last day of the banquet Alexander raised his gold cup and drank to the health of the newlyweds. And from the lungs of the thousands of invited guests a tremendous roar broke out:

"Long live Alexander the King of Macedonia, Commander-in-Chief of the Greeks, Monarch of Asia, Lord of Babylonia, Pharoah of Egypt!"

Alexander felt himself truly happy in that moment. For eight years, ever since he had left Macedonia, how he had struggled, how he had suffered, how many times he had endangered his life to achieve the glory that he exulted in today! "I have completed the first part of my mission," he thought to himself. "Now it is time to start putting the second part into motion—I must conquer Africa and return to Greece via the Pillars of Heracles."

He had assigned a general to train thirty thousand *Epigones*, that is, young Persians, and to teach them all the secrets of Macedonian warfare. He had admitted into his intimate circle of friends many Persian and barbarian princes and had entrusted them with important satrapies, even armies and ships.

Now when the Macedonians saw that he was creating a new army for the new campaign, they began to grow uneasy. "He wants to get rid of us and make up a new army of Persians," they grumbled. "We sowed, and now are we to stand aside and watch the very Persians that we defeated come in and do the reaping?" So they gathered before the Palace and set up a great clamor.

Alexander came out. "You rebelled against me before, at the Indus River," he shouted, "and you demanded to go back to Greece. Go! The road is open. Go! and leave me abandoned alone at the ends of the earth!" And he turned quickly and went back into the Palace, unable to hold back his anger and grievous pain.

Stricken with remorse at his words, the Macedonians threw down their arms and called for Alexander to come out. "Forgive us!" they cried. "Come out and forgive us!" and setting up a siege around the Palace they threatened to remain there without sleep or food or drink until he forgave them.

Relenting then, Alexander came out and the soldiers clamored about him in tears and fell at his feet and when he opened his mouth to speak he, too, broke into sobs and the whole army surged forth then in one body to kiss him. And gathering up their arms from the ground they flung themselves, tearful and laughing, into a fierce dance.

And that evening Alexander gave a great banquet of reconciliation to which he invited nine thousand Macedonians, Greeks, Persians and barbarians. "Let us be united," he said when he raised his wine cup. "May Greece and Asia unite for our new campaign!"

72

Alexander was at the pinnacle of his happiness and glory. And then the great calamity struck. It was a summer morning in Ecbatana where he had transferred his Court. Two reputed wrestlers were competing at the stadium that day and Alexander had gone to watch the match when Philip the Physician broke in on him. His face was deathly pale.

"O King," he said, "Hephaistion is ill!"

Alexander sprang to his feet. "Is it serious?" he asked, his heart sinking.

"Very," answered Philip in a choked voice. "He has a high fever and he's lost consciousness."

In an agony of dread, Alexander rushed to Hephaistion's palace. He flung open the doors, strode through the gardens, raced up the stairs, and burst into Hephaistion's room. Hephaistion lay in his bed, dead.

Alexander's mind reeled. He fell upon his dead friend, embraced him, and wouldn't let him go. All day and night he clung to him, not bearing to leave his side. He refused to sleep or eat. All through the following day he wept over the beloved body and cut his hair and scattered it over the corpse.

"All horses' manes and tails are to be shorn," he ordered. "No subject is to sing again, no one is to dance or play music, no one is to laugh. Hephaistion is dead!"

He summoned his great architect Dinocrates who had drawn the plans for Alexandria in Egypt, and ordered him to erect a magnificent five-storied monument for his friend in Babylonia. Then, with a brilliant entourage made up of his best cavalry, he transported Hephaistion in a golden chariot to Babylonia to bury him.

As he was arriving at the gates of the city, the Persian priests came out in trepidation to speak to him. "O Lord of Asia," they said, "do not cross the threshold of Babylonia. A great calamity will befall you!"

But Alexander waved them aside. "There is no greater calamity than this," he said with a bitter smile, pointing to his dead friend.

He buried Hephaistion and offered a sacrifice to him as though he were a demigod, and all that winter he remained in Babylonia, plunged in mourning.

With the approach of spring he began to recover, and summoning Nearchos, "I want you to build me a new fleet," he told him. "I'm going to build cities along the seacoasts from the Indus River to the Euphrates. After that we'll set out by sea to cross the Persian Gulf to find out where it ends. Perhaps in the Red Sea! And from there, we'll begin our new march."

"At your command, my King," answered Nearchos, and he left, pleased to fulfill the royal wishes.

Alexander turned now to the mouth of the Euphrates where he gave orders for an immense irrigation project. "If we don't plan for the irrigation of the land here," he thought, "Mesopotamia will soon become a desert."

After that he applied himself to organizing his army. He reviewed the *Epigones*, and was pleased to see with what discipline and quick perception they responded to the commands of the officers. "With Greek leaders," he thought, "the Persians will become formidable warfaring people." There were no longer separate Macedonian and Greek battalions now, nor separate Persian ones. He had integrated all the nationalities and no longer distinguished between them.

New, great plans were beginning to torment him again. One day his famous architect Dinocrates approached him. "O King," he said, "once when I was passing through the Chalcidice Peninsula I saw Mount Athos towering serenely and majestically over the plain. And now a plan has generated in my mind and I think it is worthy of you."

"Speak, Dinocrates," answered Alexander. "I am pleased that a great architect is my contemporary and is capable of understanding me."

"I would like," said Dinocrates, "to carve out all this Mount Athos into a statue of you."

Alexander felt his spirit stir. Never had his mind envisioned such a bold monument.

"In your left hand," continued Dinocrates, "you will be holding a city, and out of your right, a river will be flowing down into the plain."

Alexander clasped Dinocrates' hand. "You are worthy of being my collaborator," he said. "It shall be done."

But for the moment Alexander had his mind on the new campaign. His new fleet was to be ready soon. His new army, too, was impatient to perform its share of great exploits and he felt that he should not be wasting time. Africa could turn out to be very

213

big—he'd have to set out without delay if he was to be in time to conquer it before he died. He had conquered the East. Now the West was waiting.

He summoned his commanders, not the Greeks and Macedonians this time, but the Persians and some Indians whom he had taken into his service, and some barbarian princes who were allies. "Very soon," he announced, "we will be embarking on the new march toward the West. Prepare yourselves!"

But then something terrible happened, something that no one expected, nor could have imagined!

73

On June 8 they began the sacrifices that were always offered to the gods before a campaign began.

Alexander had a fever. He could hardly stand on his feet, but he summoned all his strength and appeared before the army to attend to the sacrifices.

On June 9 the fever increased. Philip sat vigil at the King's bedside, and toward evening he gave orders to have him moved to the royal gardens of the Palace on the opposite banks of the Euphrates where the air was cooler and he might be more comforable.

On June 10 the fever dropped somewhat and the King sat up in bed and summoned his friends to talk with them again about his grand plans. "I can't die," he reassured them. "I'm only thirty-two years old, and I haven't finished my obligation yet."

That night the fever shot up again, but Alexander summoned Nearchos to confer with him and to give him his final orders. "Everything must be ready in three days," he told him. "We're setting out!"

The fever persisted, but Alexander had no intention of resting. In vain his physician Philip begged him to rest, to sleep a little, to keep from exhausting himself.

"But I don't have time, my dear doctor," Alexander kept saying. "Don't you understand? I don't have time. I must hurry!"

All that night he was restless. He couldn't sleep; he was rambling incoherently. Around midnight the hall door opened and Stephan came in. He saw his father bending over the sickbed, putting snow that he had ordered from the mountains on the King's forehead. "Father," he said in a tremulous whisper, "how is he?"

The doctor shook his head. "I'm afraid," he answered softly.

Stephan leaned against the doorpost to keep from falling.

"Go now," said Philip. "Go, and don't say a word to anyone!"

Dawn broke. Alexander, his head turned face down into the pillows, was breathing with difficulty. For a brief lucid moment he opened his eyes and spoke: "Summon my generals."

His faithful devoted generals were all assembled in the antechamber, waiting. Philip went to the door. "The King wants you," he announced in a choked voice.

"How is he, doctor?" asked Perdiccas. But Philip didn't answer. He turned and went back to his patient. The generals followed and stood around the bed. Alexander opened his eyes, looked at them, but didn't recognize them.

"Leave now," said Philip quietly. "Leave, he can't talk."

The generals filed out, their heads bowed in gloom.

By now word had spread among the soldiers that Alexander was dead and that his death was being hidden from them. The Palace gardens outside were teeming with old battle comrades who were rushing to the Palace in tears, cramming the courtyards. They knocked on the doors.

"Don't let anyone in," the physician ordered, and the doors remained closed.

"Open! Open!" shouted the soldiers. "We want to see our King!"

A threnodial cry was sweeping through the gardens and courtyards. Alexander half raised his head. "What is it?" he asked the doctor softly.

"The army has gathered, my King," answered Philip. "They want to see you."

"Let them come," whispered Alexander.

"You mustn't, my King," implored Philip. "You'll tire yourself."

"Let them come!" whispered Alexander again. "Let them come!"

The doors opened. The valiant warriors jammed the corridors. Quietly, on the tips of their toes, their heads bowed in silence, they came up the stairs, and one by one began to file past the sick man's bed.

215

Alexander had propped himself up on his pillow. The blood was drained from his face. His hair lay flattened against his perspiring forehead, and his eyes looked enormous, fathomless, each wreathed in a black shadow. His lips were dry and white as a sheet.

He tried to talk but couldn't, and he laid his hand on the edge of the bed and nodded as each soldier walked past him and bent down mutely to kiss it. Out in the corridor as the soldiers filed out, they broke into sobs.

It was the thirteenth day of June. Toward nightfall Alexander closed his eyes and never opened them again.

GLOSSARY

1.   Callisthenes was believed to be the nephew of Aristotle, the famed Greek philosopher. He was a student of Aristotle's, as was Alexander, and entered Alexander's Court on the recommendation of the renowned teacher as Royal Historian. This gave him the opportunity to follow Alexander on his campaign and write a history based on first-hand observations which provided ancient scholars with a valuable eye-witness account of Alexander's life. All that has survived of his history are some quotations in the works of other writers.

2.   Ptolemy eventually became a brilliant commander in Alexander's army. He, too, wrote a biography of Alexander, fragments of which survive in the works of other historians. After Alexander died in 323 B.C., his generals divided his empire and Egypt fell to Ptolemy. Under Ptolemy's reign, Alexandria, the center of Egypt, became one of the most renowned cities in the civilized world. From him came the succeeding generations of Ptolemies who ruled Egypt until Augustus Caesar's conquest in 30 B.C. when Cleopatra, the last among the ruling Ptolemy dynasty, ended her life.

3.   Pericles (495-429 B.C.) was an Athenian statesman under whose reign Athens reached a pinnacle of greatness that has never been surpassed. Historians refer to this period of Greek civilization as the Golden Age of Pericles.

4.   The Marathon warriors (called *Marathonomachoi*) derive their name from the village of Marathon in the Attic plain some

twenty miles northeast of Athens where one of the most decisive battles in Greek history was fought. Here in the month of September, 490 B.C., a small army of Greek soldiers defeated the Persian army that had descended on Marathon to march against Athens. Anxious to reassure his countrymen without delay, the Greek general Miltiades dispatched a speedy runner to Athens to bring them the news, and the runner, fired with eagerness to announce their victory, ran the twenty-mile distance with such speed that upon his arrival he gasped out the message and fell dead from exhaustion.

5. Salamis is the tiny crescent-shaped island off the coast of Attica in whose straits one of the decisive battles of the world, the Battle of Salamis, was fought. It was here on September 29, 480 B.C., that the Greek fleet destroyed the Persian navy, and Salamis henceforth became a symbol of victory for the Greeks who, with this battle, turned the tide of Persian conquest.

6. Olympian *Dia* is the Olympian god Zeus.

7. The Muses were nine ancient goddesses, believed to be the daughters of Zeus and Mnemosyne (memory). In very ancient times they were without individual attributes and were known only as the goddesses who protected and inspired poets. Their leader was Apollo who provided the rhythm for their dances with his lyre. Around the fourth century B.C. they came to be referred to by individual names and attributes: Calliope—epic poetry; Clio—history; Erato—love poetry; Euterpe—lyric poetry; Melpomene—tragedy; Polyhymnia—sacred poetry; Terpsichore—choral dance; Thalia—comedy; and Urania—astronomy.

8. *Margites* is the hero of a mock-heroic poem believed to be traced to Homer.

9. The island of Samothrace in the northeast Aegean was the site of a religious movement founded by Orpheus, a Thracian prince and prophet of Dionysos. The religion attracted followers from all over the Greek world who came to be initiated into the Orphic mysteries, a kind of rites of passage to the Orphic nether world of eternal life.

218

10. Dionysos (son of Zeus and a Theban princess called Semele) was the god of plants, primarily the grapevine and ivy. Eventually he became known as the god of wine.

11. The Maenads were the maidservants of Dionysos who followed him in ritual processions. They are often portrayed in a state of euphoric ecstacy, half-crazed by the intoxicating ivy that they chewed.

12. Pangaion is a mountain in Thrace, famous for its gold and silver mines.

13. These three plays by Aeschylos are based on the ancient story of Prometheus. Prometheus was a Titan and a cousin of Zeus who, legend has it, was entrusted by Zeus with the task of making men out of mud and water. Having done so, Prometheus took pity on them and, stealing fire from heaven, gave it to men to improve their lot. Angered, Zeus had Prometheus chained to a rock in the Caucasus and sent an eagle to eat at his liver which he decreed was to grow and be eaten in a never-ending cycle. This would have continued eternally had not Heracles rescued Prometheus by killing the eagle with an arrow.

14. Dancing, which was more serious in ancient Greece than in modern society, had its origin in religion. It was not considered an amusement but rather an expression of deep feeling (joy, sadness, anger). A dance was often performed in honor of a god for a particular occasion, often to express triumph after a successful battle. The dances were varied, ranging from the wild Pyrrhic dance, which took its name from the fire that was at its center, to the sedate *Syrta* dances, which have survived antiquity and continue to be danced at weddings and festivals by modern Greeks today.

15. The Greek word for satyr is *satyros*. *Sa*, in Greek denotes ownership, and *Tyros* is the name for Tyre. Therefore, "Tyre is yours" (*Sa* = yours, *Tyros* = Tyre).

16 and 17. *Miden aghan* (nothing in excess) and *pan metron ariston* are ancient maxims that continue to live in the modern Greek language. They point to the Aristotelian principle of excel-

lence which comes from the proper balance between extremes—
the ancient Greek ideal that men should act in accordance with
the proper mean.

18. Some historians speculate that the Egyptian priest,
wishing to show courtesy toward Alexander, addressed him in
Greek with "O paidion" (O son), but not being fluent in Greek
grammar, may have said "O paidios" (O son of Zeus: pai = son,
Dios = Zeus); thus, Alexander could have assumed that the priest
was addressing him as the son of the god Ammon, the Egyptian
Zeus.

19. Triremes were the ancient galleys equipped with three
banks of oars. Trierarchs were the commanders of the triremes.

20. Gymnosophists were a sect of naked ascetics highly
respected in ancient India for their wisdom. They renounced all
worldly goods, including clothing, as revealed in their name which
comes from the Greek words gymno (naked) and sophistes (wise
man).

ABOUT THE AUTHOR

Nikos Kazantzakis, one of the great European writers of the Twentieth Century, is best known in the United States as the author of the popular novel, *Zorba the Greek.*

His numerous works include novels, dramas, poetry, travel journals, translations and essays. The most monumental of these is *The Odyssey—A Modern Sequel*, an epic poem of 33,333 lines which picks up the adventures of Odysseus where Homer left off and brings them into the modern age.

He was born in Crete in 1883, studied law at the University of Athens where he took a Doctor of law degree, and continued his education in philosophy, literature and art in Paris, Germany and Itlay. He traveled extensively throughout his lifetime and during brief intervals in his native Greece served as Greek Minister of Education and as President of the Greek Society of Men of Letters. In 1947-1948 he was Director of UNESCO's Department of Translations of the Classics.

His work earned him the highest international acclaim, including nomination for the Nobel Prize in 1951. He died in Germany in 1957.

ABOUT THE TRANSLATOR

Theodora Vasils has translated several works by Nikos Kazantzakis. Among them, *Serpent and Lily* (University of California Press, 1980), *Journeying* (Little, Brown and Company, 1975) and *Symposium* (Thomas Y. Crowell Company, 1975); the latter two, co-translated with Themi Vasils.

Among her other translated works are short stories published in various literary journals, and a book of poetry, *In Another Light*, by Koralia Theotokas (Ikaros Publishing Company, Athens).

Her work, for which she has received an honorary Doctor of Letters degree from Rosary College, is cited in the *Encyclopaedia Britannica*, Greece 323 (15th edition, 1977 printing).

ABOUT THE ARTIST

Virgil Burnett's illustrations have accompanied a wide variety of texts including his own recently published novel, *Towers at the Edge of the World* (St. Martin's Press). His style, characterized by a meticulous regard for detail and a poet's imagination, is particularly suited to the archaic atmosphere of the bygone events that are his subjects. A native of Kansas, whose work is exhibited both in Europe and North America, he is presently a professor of Fine Arts at the University of Waterloo in Ontario, Canada.

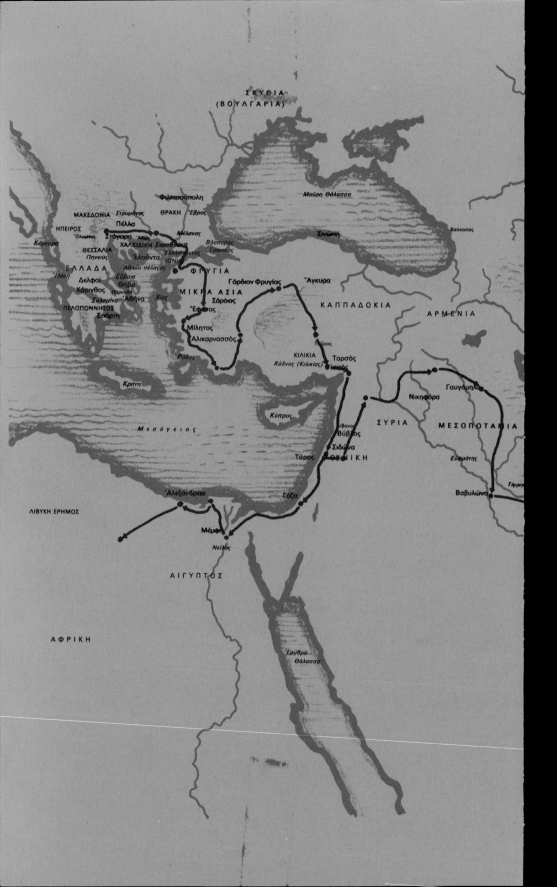